AP 3'91	DATE DUE	
AP 25'91	NO 5'91	AG 28'92
MY 25'91	NO 22'91	DE 1'92
JE 8'91	DE 14'91	
JE 22'91	DE 30'91	MR 20'93
JY 6'91	JA 17'92	FE 28'94
JY 22'91	FE 3'92	MR 25'94
AG 1'91	FE 17'92	AP 20'94
AG 19'91	MR 9'92	JY 4'94
SE 23'91	MR 24'92	JE 8'95
OC 1'91	AP 6'92	AG 12'95
OC 21'91	JY 8'92	FE 12'96
	AG 4'92	

GAYLORD 234   PRINTED IN U.S.A.

DEMCO

A FIRST CLASS MURDER

A
*F*IRST
*C*LASS
*M*URDER

Elliott Roosevelt

St. Martin's Press
New York

Design by Glen M. Edelstein

Library of Congress Cataloging-in-Publication Data

Roosevelt, Elliott, 1910–1990
    A first class murder / Elliott Roosevelt.
      p.   cm.
    "A Thomas Dunne book."
    ISBN 0-312-05527-7
    1. Roosevelt, Eleanor, 1884–1962—Fiction.   I.
Title.
    PS3535.0549F5   1991
    813'.54—dc20   90-48994
                                        CIP

First Edition: April 1991

10 9 8 7 6 5 4 3 2 1

To my wonderful children (all eight of them), and, as always, to my wife, Patty

A FIRST CLASS MURDER

1

"I don't feel at all comfortable about this," said Mrs. Roosevelt. "You know, Tommy, it doesn't seem right. But—" She vouchsafed a tiny smile at Malvina Thompson, her secretary. "I suppose we may as well enjoy it, since the matter is settled and there isn't much we can do about it."

Tommy was more than content. She was, in fact, thrilled—as, for that matter, was Mrs. Roosevelt, secretly.

They were aboard the *Normandie*, the huge, luxurious transatlantic liner, pride of the French Line, pride, actually, of France. And they had been installed in one of the four *appartements de grand luxe* that opened on the sun deck, high above the stern of the great ship. They had four bedrooms and four baths, a sitting room with grand piano, and a dining room—plus a private promenade that overlooked the first-class promenade. The rooms were like no ship's cabins Mrs. Roosevelt had ever seen. They were huge, spacious, and elegantly furnished with that special French touch that no one could quite define but everyone recognized and enjoyed.

Her installation in this suite was a gesture by the captain and by the French Line—actually, a gesture by the government of France, to honor the wife of the President of the United States.

Her presence aboard the *Normandie* was a gesture of her own. She had come to France on an American ship and had intended to go back on one—in a comfortable but not luxurious stateroom for which she was paying her own fare. During her brief stay in Paris, Ambassador Bullitt had called on her to say that the French government would be most pleased if she would return home on the *Normandie*. She had resisted, saying she was not visiting France in an official capacity but only as a private citizen, and that she should not be treated as a government representative. Only after Ambassador Bullitt had explained that the French would be offended if she refused to travel on their flagship did she agree, most reluctantly, to change to the *Normandie*—and then only on the condition that she would pay her own fare and that of her secretary.

"We shall eat well," said Tommy Thompson. She was looking at the luncheon menu, a card of fifty-two lines, beginning with green and black olives and celery and ending with American coffee, French coffee, and Sanka. "Look. For lunch you can have one of six soups, eggs four different ways, beef half a dozen ways, lamb three or four ways, ham . . . five ways, turkey, lobster—"

"The French," said Mrs. Roosevelt, "can serve the same slice of beef a dozen ways—and the only difference is a teaspoonful of one sauce or another."

"They offer six kinds of tea," said Tommy.

"And wines," said Mrs. Roosevelt, glancing at the menu. "But I'm not sure we have brought along the right clothes for this kind of voyage. I wasn't expecting it. Dinner will be white-tie. You can count on that."

"God . . ." breathed Tommy. "A little girl from the Bronx—God, how will I handle myself?"

"There is a rule, Tommy," said Mrs. Roosevelt. "And it covers everything. Be *yourself.* Avoid being conspicuous, but be yourself, above all. Stay observant. Watch what others do—" Mrs. Roosevelt smiled broadly. "And you will see mistakes gross enough to make any of yours invisible."

Miss Thompson walked to the wide French doors that overlooked the deck set aside as promenade for the suite. She could see the harbor behind the ship, and the tugs dropping away as the huge bulk of the *Normandie* got under way. The gray-green water behind boiled into white froth as the ship's propellers began to turn. The basso-profundo note of its steam whistles blasted across the water to the receding French coast and was returned by yapping little replies from boats and shore.

Normandie would pay a brief call at Southampton to pick up passengers from Britain, then would head out into the North Atlantic for its four-day passage to New York. The First Lady—Tommy reflected—might pretend reluctance to return to the States on the world's most luxurious passenger liner, but if Tommy knew her friend and employer, Mrs. Roosevelt was every bit as pleased and thrilled as she was.

The year was 1938. The day was September 29. It seemed odd to Mrs. Roosevelt, who was no stranger to travel, that only two weeks ago she had sat with the President in the sitting hall during his cocktail hour and discussed the idea of a short trip to France.

Their daughter Anna had been there, on the last day of a week's visit. William O. Douglas, Kennedy's successor as chairman of the Securities and Exchange Commission had been there also. The President was able to have a few friends in for poker occasionally, and Bill was one of his favorite poker-playing buddies. Though he was no longer able to take part, the President enjoyed Bill's stories of his mountain climbing and wilderness hikes.

She had been notified through the French embassy that she had been awarded the *Médaille de Grand Honneur* of the *Société Humaniste de France*. The ambassador had urged her to travel to Paris to accept the award. The society, he had said, would pay her travel expenses.

"It is possible," the President had said, "that the country will survive a brief Eleanorian vacation. Indeed, there is a faction in the Republican press that would welcome a protracted Eleanorian vacation."

"That same faction," she had suggested, "will have a few acid things to say about my traveling to Paris at the expense of the society."

"No doubt. On the other hand, I suspect a famous newspaper columnist has been able to put aside a nickel or two in her savings account."

"Enough to take Tommy along and get the column out each day," she had said.

"Oh, Dad could write 'My Day,'" Anna had said. "He's got the country in such good shape he needs a new project to occupy his time."

The President had laughed as only he knew how—a jolly, genuinely amused laugh, head tipped back, mouth open, no restraint. "And when Bill Hearst asks who paid for the trip, we'll tell him—"

"Tell him it's none of his business," Bill Douglas had said in his usual blunt way.

The President had resumed the ceremonial mixing of the day's shaker of martinis. "Exactly. And while you are there, you may have a word to pass along to Monsieur Daladier. Official-unofficial. Very convenient."

"What word, Franklin?"

"I will have something by the time you are ready to leave. Secretary Hull and I will have to work it out."

But by the time she left for New York to board the ship for France, he and Secretary Hull had not prepared a message for Premier Daladier. The French premier, plus Prime Minister Chamberlain and the Italian dictator, Mussolini, were in constant contact, trying to find some resolution to the problem of Hitler's demands on Czechoslovakia. American policy was severely restrained by isolationism, though the President wanted to act. He had responded warmly to the suggestion he act as mediator between Hitler and the Czech government—until Hull pointed out what a storm that would raise in Congress. The President understood full well that the American people were not ready to support any kind of intervention in the affairs of central Europe; and however important he thought it was to help Britain and France resist Hitler, the country didn't think it was so important and was not behind him.

In her stateroom aboard the ship on which she traveled to France she had found two letters, one from Bill Douglas, one from Anna. Anna wrote:

> I hope you enjoy every minute of your voyage to France. Let it constitute a vacation you well deserve. With you comes all our love—I mean the love of all your children and of Father as well.

5

Bill Douglas wrote:

It will be impossible, I suspect, for the Boss to send along with you any firm word for Daladier. I know, though, that you fully understand the threat of this fellow Hitler and will convey, in any subtle way you can, without making it appear a matter of policy, that the *intelligent* element of the American public stands foursquare behind the French and British in their effort to stall the Nazi plan to conquer all of Europe, if not all the world.

Let me suggest that there is a fellow in England you ought to talk to if there is any possible way to arrange it. Winston Churchill, almost alone of all Englishmen, understands the threat and the necessity of standing up to Hitler now. You will remember he is the son of Lord Randolph Churchill, younger son of the Duke of Marlborough, and Jennie Jerome of New York. Damn impressive fellow, Eleanor.

Also, watch out for people who talk to Lindbergh. He is in Germany looking at their air force, and he seems to have fallen for the line that it is *invincible*. He is preaching that all over. Defeatism. He is wrong, but the fact that he managed to drive an airplane all the way across the Atlantic all by himself made him a hero and seems to make him an authority on aviation—though only God knows why. Why can't our little tin heroes rest on their laurels and forswear grandiose posing?

In fact, Mrs. Roosevelt had already noted, looking over the passenger list, Colonel Lindbergh, as he was called, was a passenger on the *Normandie*. Doubtless she would have her chance to see his posing, hear his preaching. She would reserve judgment.

Two weeks later, when *Normandie* sailed from Le Havre, Premier Daladier, Prime Minister Chamberlain, Duce Mussolini, and Führer Hitler were meeting at Munich. Hitler had promised his army would enter the Sudetenland—the allegedly German part of Czechoslovakia—on Saturday, no matter what the conference decided. Europe was tense. War seemed likely. Mrs. Roosevelt was gripped by two emotions—a sense of relief to be at sea and on her way back to America before another European war broke out, and a sense that she was sailing away from great events and would be isolated at sea while decisions were taken that could shake the world.

The call at Southampton was a short break in the voyage. By seven, the *Normandie* was at sea again, steaming west along the English Channel, putting Europe behind, heading out into the open Atlantic. At dusk the ship's lights were switched on, and Mrs. Roosevelt reflected that *Normandie* must have looked like a glittering little city illuminated for Christmas.

Other vessels saluted as *Normandie* glided by. She was capable of thirty-two knots, and other ships, freighters and passenger liners, were smoothly overtaken and passed. People crowded the decks of other liners to watch her, glad of the opportunity to see the famous *Normandie*. Men waved their hats, women their handkerchiefs, and captains hailed the great ship with blasts of their horns. *Normandie* returned each greeting with a bellow of her great whistles—which were tuned to so low a frequency that their note was barely audible aboard but carried authoritatively for miles across the water.

It was impossible to escape the excitement of sailing on this ship. Mrs. Roosevelt decided not to try.

"Look at this," said Tommy. The ship's daily newspaper had been delivered, and on this first day it contained a list of some of the famous people who were on board.

Mrs. Roosevelt was standing before her trunk, staring at the clothes she had brought. It stood on its end and when open made a small wardrobe, with dresses and suits hang-

7

ing on the left side and drawers on the right packed with her smaller clothes, cosmetics, and jewelry. She decided the dress she had brought for the awards ceremony in Paris—a rose-colored silk—was suitable for white-tie dining on *Normandie*.

"You head the list," said Tommy, handing over the newspaper.

Mrs. Roosevelt glanced over the list. A few of the other names:

—Colonel Charles A. Lindbergh. His name, like hers, was followed by no identifying information. Everyone knew who he was.

—Boris Vasilievich Troyanoskii, Ambassador Extraordinary and Plenipotentiary from the Union of Soviet Socialist Republics.

—Henry Luce, publisher of *Time* and *Life*.

—Jack Benny, star of stage, screen, and radio; and Mrs. Benny, also known as Mary Livingstone.

—Wilhelm von Heinroth, industrialist, and Frau Margot Heinroth.

—Josephine Baker, singer and *danseuse*.

—John F. Kennedy, son of Joseph P. Kennedy, United States Ambassador to the Court of St. James.

All of these were of course traveling first-class. *Normandie* carried almost nine hundred first-class passengers and more than a thousand in tourist and third class. If there were celebrities in the tourist and third-class cabins, the ship's newspaper had not yet discovered them.

"Kennedy. . . ?" Tommy asked.

"As I recall, he's a student at Harvard. He should be on his way home for the academic year," said Mrs. Roosevelt. "Indeed, it seems to me he should have returned two or three weeks ago."

8

"He's made quite a splash in London society, I've read," said Tommy. "I'm surprised he's coming back to the States at all. If *I'd* had such an opportunity when I was his age—"

She was interrupted by a rap on the door.

Tommy hurried to answer—and found two people there. One was a uniformed ship's boy, bearing a large basket of flowers. The other was a dark-haired young woman, wearing a sleek, stylish black dress and a black hat with a broad brim that swept down across her forehead.

"Moira . . ." said Mrs. Roosevelt, unable to conceal her surprise.

The young woman walked past the delivery boy and into the apartment. "You remember me," she said quietly.

"Indeed I do," said Mrs. Roosevelt. "Did you think I wouldn't?"

"It has been three years," said the young woman.

"And I've thought of you often," said Mrs. Roosevelt. "Please sit down. Tommy—"

Tommy Thompson was showing the ship's boy where to place the basket of flowers. She had pulled the card from the spray already.

"Tommy, I'd like to introduce Miss Moira Lasky," said Mrs. Roosevelt. "You remember the problem we had in 1935, when our Dutchess County neighbor Alfred Hannah was accused of a crime and was then murdered—and Adriana van der Meer wanted to marry Alfred's son—and all of that . . . You do remember?"

Tommy Thompson regarded Mrs. Roosevelt with a quizzical expression. "I'm afraid I don't," she said with a weak smile.

"Ah, well . . . Anyway, it is good to see you again, Moira. I . . . The suite is *awash* in champagne. It seems to come from everywhere. I'm not sure we can wash our faces, for fear champagne will run from the faucets. Would you like a glass?"

"In fact, I would," said Moira.

"Tommy—"

Now Tommy smiled genuinely, glad of the opportunity to pour a glass of the vintage champagne for herself as well. "The flowers," she said, "are from Boris V. Troyanoskii, the Russian ambassador."

"Yes," said Mrs. Roosevelt. "I understand he is on his way to Washington to meet with Mr. Hull and with the President. Something about czarists and their property. Anyway . . . Moira. How nice to see you! Isn't this a lovely ship?"

"It is in fact," said Moira Lasky. "And, if you don't mind, Mrs. Roosevelt, I'd appreciate a private word with you."

"Of course," said Mrs. Roosevelt. "Tommy won't mind. Tommy wants to begin dressing for dinner."

Tommy had poured three glasses of champagne, and she put two on the small table between Mrs. Roosevelt and Moira Lasky, then left the room.

Moira watched the secretary go. "I'm sorry. I hope that wasn't rude," she said. She sipped champagne, then took out her cigarettes and an amber holder and lit a smoke. "I mean—"

"Not rude at all," said Mrs. Roosevelt. "Tommy makes life possible for me, but a part of that is that she must sometimes be . . . Well, I don't want to use the word 'dismissed.'"

Moira smiled. "Status . . ." she mused. She drew a deep breath. "Uh, it is in fact my own that I would like to mention to you."

"Moira," said Mrs. Roosevelt. "I don't need to know."

"You are very gracious," said Moira. "But I want you to know. I am still what I was. If the ship's officers knew, I would be confined to my cabin until we dock in New York. I . . . I spend a great deal of my time crossing and re-crossing the Atlantic, and the officers of the ships I use don't know who I am. If it became known—"

"It would destroy a lucrative business," said Mrs. Roosevelt a little crisply.

Moira sipped champagne and nodded. "Yes," she said quietly. "Definitely."

"I had hoped," said Mrs. Roosevelt, "that in the past three years you would have . . . changed your style of life."

"I might have," said Moira. "But, to tell you the truth, I am too damn honest. Half a dozen times I could have married. But— Well . . . You know."

"I'm afraid I don't understand."

Moira smiled at Mrs. Roosevelt. "I'd have to *tell* the man—wouldn't I?" She nodded. "Well . . . Maybe some wouldn't. I would. So— So I'm not married and not likely to be."

"You said it was the Depression that made you choose what you chose," said Mrs. Roosevelt. "You're a graduate of Wellesley—"

"Which makes it possible for me to work these great liners," Moira interrupted. "I have the style. I have a degree of *class*. I travel first-class, and I make a lot of money, Mrs. Roosevelt. But—"

"But if the ship's officers knew what you do—"

"They don't like professional gamblers on board," said Moira. "Or professional . . . girls. I could be blacklisted on the French Line, which would pass the word to Cunard." She paused to pull smoke from her cigarette. "I'm sorry, Mrs. Roosevelt, but that's why I came to see you—to ask you to protect my secret."

Mrs. Roosevelt shook her head sadly. "I am most disappointed to know that you still pursue this style of life,

Moira," she said. "Apart from being a young woman with a fine education and, as you yourself have said, a great deal of style, you showed us in 1935 that you have courage, too, and shrewd intelligence. But—" She shrugged. "It's not for me to try to reform you, particularly by exposing you to the ship's officers. Your secret is safe with me."

Moira smiled. "I've already made a connection for this voyage," she said. "I met him in Paris. A nice man. You'll see, probably."

"An American?" asked Mrs. Roosevelt.

"A German," said Moira. "Ernst Richter Remer. He's a dealer in wines, champagnes, and brandy. He's on his way to the States to sell whole shiploads to American importers."

"A follower of Herr Hitler?" asked Mrs. Roosevelt.

Moira grinned. "A totally apolitical man," she said. "He doesn't know Nazis from Communists, Tories from Labourites, Democrats from Republicans. I do hope you'll let me introduce him. He's a man worth knowing."

"Maybe you should tell him about yourself and establish a more conventional relationship, Moira," said Mrs. Roosevelt innocently.

Moira laughed. "I doubt Frau Remer would appreciate that suggestion," she said.

"Oh, Moira!"

Moira laughed again. "My very best to the President, if I don't have another opportunity to talk with you," she said. "On the other hand, we may see you at dinner. Of course . . . *you* will be at the captain's table."

She was indeed seated at the captain's table, escorted there in fact by Captain Paul Colbert himself, who came to her apartment to escort her to dinner. Tommy Thompson was escorted to another table by one of the ship's officers.

The *grande salle à manger,* Captain Colbert quietly explained to Mrs. Roosevelt, was almost one hundred meters long and was the largest room afloat. It could be entered by elevators that carried first-class passengers down from their cabins, or by descending the grand staircase. The captain led Mrs. Roosevelt forward, through the first-class smoking room and grand salon, then down to the entrance and to the head of the staircase.

There was no announcement, but many people already at their tables fell silent as the handsome, uniformed captain led the wife of the President of the United States down the stairs and toward the table in the center of the dining room. A little polite applause greeted them. The captain nodding affably, Mrs. Roosevelt smiling and nodding, they made their way to the table just beneath a huge bronze statue of Peace; and there they joined the others invited to dine at the captain's table.

"Mr. Luce I believe you know," said Captain Colbert. "And probably Colonel Lindbergh. Perhaps also Mr. and Mrs. Jack Benny. Also, I am sure, Mr. John Kennedy. But allow me to present Ambassador Troyanoskii, Herr and Frau von Heinroth, and Mademoiselle Josephine Baker. And finally, my first officer, Jacques Brillant."

The gentlemen had risen. The ladies remained seated but bowed and smiled warmly. Mrs. Roosevelt spoke to each of them. She sat down.

Captain Colbert presided at the head of the table. Mrs. Roosevelt sat to his right, Ambassador Troyanoskii to his left. Charles Lindbergh sat to Mrs. Roosevelt's right, then Jack Benny, John Kennedy, and Frau Margot von Heinroth. Wilhelm von Heinroth was on the left of Troyanoskii, followed by Henry Luce, Mary Livingstone Benny, and Josephine Baker. First Officer Brillant occupied the chair at the foot of the table.

With the guests seated at the captain's table, serving began. Scores of waiters streamed from the doors, bearing trays.

Mrs. Roosevelt glanced around, hoping perhaps to spot Tommy. She didn't, but the moment offered her a chance to see more of the dining room. The walls were tall glass panels, with brilliant lights set behind, filling the huge room with bright yet warm illumination. White tie was the order of dress for men; the women wore silks, jewels, and flowers.

Charles Lindbergh nodded at Mrs. Roosevelt and spoke quietly to her—so quietly as almost not to be heard at all. "It is an honor to be seated by you," he said simply.

"It is I who am honored, Colonel Lindbergh," she said.

He smiled and said nothing further. She reflected that he was an urbane young man, for a once-awkward country boy who had earned his living flying the mail. The recognition that had followed his great exploit had not spoiled the boyish modesty that had so impressed the world; yet, he had learned all the elements of persuasive speaking, good manners, and poise. He had married well. The tragedy of the kidnap-murder of his infant son was perhaps the source of the solemnity in his eyes.

"We are most honored to make your acquaintance, Mrs. Roosevelt," said Ambassador Troyanoskii from the other side of the table. He reached out and moved a small vase of roses, to place them out of the line of vision between himself and her. "I am on my way to America to meet the honored President, and it is most good to see you here and now."

"Thank you, Mr. Ambassador," she said. "It is a pleasure to meet you."

Troyanoskii was a compact, muscular man in his fifties. His head was smoothly shaved, and his wide mouth curled into a caricature of a smile, hinting of evil and cruelty. At the same time, in odd contrast, his brown eyes looked guileless and merry, and in his gestures and tone of voice he seemed almost to plead for approval and trust. He wore an immense diamond in a gold ring on his left pinkie, and his evening clothes were well tailored. There was an odd contrast, Mrs. Roosevelt decided, between his status as the representative of the proletarian régime in Moscow and traveling first-class on *Normandie,* comfortably aristocratic in this splendid setting.

Young John Kennedy leaned forward and grinned at Mrs. Roosevelt. He did not attempt to speak across Jack Benny and Charles Lindbergh. He was twenty-one years old, all teeth and red hair, and he was perhaps the most amiable of Joe's extended brood.

Jack Benny spoke past Lindbergh. "Do you *remember,*" he asked in his signature drawl, "what *Mark Twain* said when he was introduced to President Ulysses S. Grant?"

Mrs. Roosevelt smiled at the famous comedian and said she did not remember.

"What he said was . . . 'Are *you* embarrassed?'" Benny turned up his hands and lifted his shoulders. "Well, I am. And pleased and honored, but I feel like I'm supposed to have something to say."

"Believe me, Mr. Benny," she said, "with years of experience you reach a point where you have something to say on every occasion."

Jack Benny laughed heartily.

"It's a great honor for us all, Mrs. Roosevelt," said Josephine Baker from the far end of the opposite side of the table.

"And for me to meet you, Miss Baker."

Mrs. Roosevelt was genuinely glad to meet the lithe American expatriate, star of *Revue Négre* and *Folies*

Bergére, in both of which—and in other shows as well—
she had captivated Paris with the caramel color of her
skin, her infectious exuberance, and her sensuous style of
singing and dancing. She had introduced the Charleston to
Paris, dancing it naked; and her *Folies* costume—sixteen
bananas slung around her hips—had been a must-see
spectacle of Paris in the late twenties. She was as big a
star as any who performed in France. She was also, as
Mrs. Roosevelt knew, one of the most generous contrib-
utors of time and money to France's League Against
Racism and Anti-Semitism.

Mrs. Roosevelt could not help wondering how the German, Wilhelm von Heinroth, accepted being seated at a
table with a Negro woman. She had already noticed some
sidelong glances from von Heinroth to the end of the table;
and it was not possible to tell if they were manifestations
of resentment or admiration or maybe only curiosity. She
decided to reserve judgment. Not all Germans, after all,
had adopted the racist attitudes of their chancellor, Herr
Hitler.

As if he had read her mind, von Heinroth spoke—"It is a
genuine pleasure to meet the famous wife of the American
President, of whom we have heard much favorable." Then
he glanced around. "As it is a pleasure to meet all this
distinguished company. I shall travel on the ship again,
Captain, if I may be assured of the like."

"We can never promise so distinguished a company as
this," said Captain Colbert with practiced suavity.

Except for Mary Livingstone and Frau Margot von
Heinroth, who had joined with smiles in their husbands'
words of greeting, this left Henry Luce. He knew it. He
nodded at Mrs. Roosevelt. "I hope we'll have a chance to
talk during the voyage," he said.

"I am sure we will, Mr. Luce," she said.

So far as she was concerned, Henry Luce was anything but a journalist. He did not report news; he *manufactured* it. He did not report the truth, either; he concocted stories and labeled them truth. If he wanted to talk with her during this voyage, he would have to pursue her.

A string orchestra began to play in an alcove at one end of the dining room. Its music was carried electrically throughout the room. It began its concert by playing an abbreviated version of the "Marseillaise," but no one stood, no one saluted.

"We should all, I believe, profit from hearing your appraisal of the events now transpiring at Munich," said Ambassador Troyanoskii to Mrs. Roosevelt.

"I'm afraid I am out of touch with them," she said. "Since realities seem to change by the hour . . ."

"It is distressing," said Troyanoskii, "that my government is not represented at the conference. We have, after all, a considerable interest in the fate of Czechoslovakia."

"Your country was, of course, intentionally excluded," said Luce.

"That is true," said Troyanoskii. "But I tell you, Mr. Luce, there will be no settlement of boundaries and national interests in that part of Europe that ignores the concerns of the Soviet Union."

"It is a two-nation question," said von Heinroth. "Czech atrocities against the German-speaking population of the Sudetenland cannot be allowed to continue. No nation could tolerate such things. Our government has no choice but to—"

"Invade Czechoslovakia, Herr von Heinroth?" asked Luce. "Isn't that what your chancellor has threatened to do?"

"German troops will enter the Sudetenland on Saturday," said von Heinroth firmly.

"Regardless of what the Munich conference decides?" asked Mrs. Roosevelt.

Von Heinroth nodded curtly. "The Führer has given his word on it."

"Saturday," said Luce. "The Czechs will fight, you know. They will fight. Their border is secured by heavy fortifications, and their army amounts to thirty-five well-trained and well-equipped divisions. If the German army crosses the Czech frontier on Saturday, it will mean a European war."

"There will be no war," said Lindbergh. "There must not be war. If there is—" He shook his head. "Ladies and gentlemen, I have *seen* the Luftwaffe. Marshal Göring understands air war like no other leader in the world. He has built an invincible air force. Thousands of bombers, capable of striking Paris and London, even maybe capable of bombing New York."

"New York?" said Jack Benny. "Surely—"

"You have heard of the Condor, Mr. Benny?" asked Lindbergh. "It flew from Berlin to New York carrying passengers. Why can it not fly from Germany to New York carrying bombs?"

"A frightful prospect," murmured Josephine Baker.

Lindbergh nodded. "Terrifying. While the leaders of the other European nations and—you must forgive me, Mrs. Roosevelt—the United States have sat on their hands, hoarding money, ignoring the new technology, the Germans have built an air force stronger than all the others in the world *combined*. The Czech border defenses mean nothing, Mr. Luce. The Luftwaffe will overfly them, bomb Prague, and land German troops behind the Czech lines."

Luce smiled condescendingly. "I have to doubt it, Colonel Lindbergh. When Hitler invades Czechoslovakia, the Poles will invade Germany."

Troyanoskii laughed. "The *Poles,* Mr. Luce? Will invade Germany? And will they perhaps invade the Soviet Union as well?"

"The Poles have *spirit,* Mr. Troyanoskii," said Luce, satisfied—if his tone and expression said anything—that he had just settled the question.

But Troyanoskii laughed at him. "How was it that Bismarck put it, Mr. Luce—that the great issues of the day will be settled by blood and iron? I don't recall that 'spirit' has ever weighed very heavily in the equation."

Luce, who was not accustomed to being contradicted, much less laughed at, turned angry red and reached for his glass of champagne.

"In London yesterday," said young Kennedy, "people really were afraid there would be war. Within the week, I mean. But when Prime Minister Chamberlain announced he was going to Munich for another meeting with Herr Hitler, everyone relaxed. He made the announcement on the floor of the House of Commons. The House rose and cheered him. Except for a few members. Winston Churchill got up and walked out."

"That man . . ." said von Heinroth. "He *wants* war."

"Well, he's not going to get it," said Troyanoskii. "The Czechs will be compelled to surrender. The Poles will manifest what Mr. Luce calls their 'spirit' by grumbling and doing nothing. And the German army will march into Czechoslovakia with Mr. Chamberlain's blessing. And Monsieur Daladier's. If the Soviet Union had been included in the negotiations, our weight, combined with that of the Czechs and Poles, might have brought a different result. Unfortunately, Mr. Chamberlain and others fear the Soviet Union more than they do Hitler. So . . ." He raised his glass. "Your health, ladies and gentlemen."

2

Before they rose from the captain's table, Ambassador Troyanoskii invited everyone there to come to his suite for—as he put it— "an hour of conviviality." He occupied another of the four *appartements de grand luxe* and was, for the voyage, Mrs. Roosevelt's next-door neighbor.

"I believe I'll accept his hospitality," young Kennedy said to Mrs. Roosevelt as they left the dining room. "Won't you?"

"It would be, I suppose, the diplomatic thing to do," she said.

They were strolling through the ship's grand salon, on the way to the sun deck and her apartment. She had suggested going outside and walking in the fresh sea air, but he had told her a sharp wind was blowing and suggested she should not go out without a wrap.

"I've been asked to tell you something about Ambassador Troyanoskii," he said.

"And what would that be, Mr. Kennedy?"

"Uh . . . Please. Jack."

"Very well."

"Troyanoskii," he said gravely, "was a member of the Cheka, the secret police the Soviets established immediately after the Revolution. In fact, he probably still is. They call it the NKVD now, and it's very likely he's an NKVD agent."

"How do you know? Who asked you to tell me?"

"My father," said Kennedy. "When he learned that you would be on the *Normandie,* he told me to be sure you were told. He sent word to the President, in the diplomatic pouch. Troyanoskii is going to the States ostensibly as an ambassador, and probably he's carrying some sort of message for the President. But that's very likely just a cover; and he is probably traveling on some kind of NKVD business."

"But still, Jack— How does your father know this?"

"British Intelligence. MI6. Sir Vernon Kell himself spoke to my father and told him. Warned him, I suppose is a better word."

"Are we to believe Ambassador Troyanoskii has blood on his hands?" she asked.

Kennedy shook his head. "He was not so described. Only as a manipulator. A survivor, too. Obviously, the Ambassador is hardly a typical Bolshevik."

"How do you come to that conclusion, Jack?"

Kennedy returned the smile of a young woman who had met his glance as he and Mrs. Roosevelt walked through the grill room. The smile remained as he addressed the question. "Troyanoskii speaks English. He knows wine and food. He dresses like an aristocrat. He didn't come from the Russian working class his government pretends to represent. No—" He shook his head for emphasis. "Ambassador Troyanoskii is no proletarian."

"Did British Intelligence have nothing to say of von Heinroth?"

"No. Nothing. Only of Troyanoskii, and my father wanted me to tell you about it."

Charles Lindbergh, Henry Luce, and the von Heinroths apparently elected not to join the Ambassador in his apartment. Otherwise, the people from the captain's table were there, including Captain Colbert and First Officer Brillant.

Ambassador Troyanoskii had arranged a lavish buffet for his after-dinner party; and, to Mrs. Roosevelt's surprise, he and his guests were eating and drinking heavily, in spite of having just eaten ample meals at the dining tables. In the dining room of the suite, a buffet was laid with hors d'oeuvres, platters of beef and ham, a dozen kinds of cheese, plus plates of fruits, nuts, olives, and assorted raw vegetables. In a corner of the sitting room, a steward attended a table set up as a bar, offering red and white wines, champagne, brandy, whisky, and vodka.

"Ah! Mrs. Roosevelt! We are doubly honored!" exclaimed the Ambassador. "First at dinner. Now at our poor little party! Allow me to offer . . . what? Wine?"

"A glass of wine," she said.

"Ah. And Mr. Kennedy. Will you choose for yourself? Do you like vodka?"

"I've little experience with it, Mr. Ambassador," said Kennedy.

"Let me recommend it. No time like now to become its acquaintance. May I— Ah, I should like to introduce both of you to someone very charming. Nina!"

A slight, dark-haired girl broke away from a conversation she was having and obeyed his summons.

"Mrs. Roosevelt, Mr. Kennedy, let me present Nina Nikolaievna Rozanov," said the Ambassador. "She is a ballerina, on her way to the United States to perform. What a wonderful coincidence that she should prove to be aboard *Normandie*. Her family and mine have been friends for decades."

The ballerina was no more than five-feet-two and could not have weighed more than eighty pounds. Her solemn blue eyes settled curiously, first on Mrs. Roosevelt, then on Jack Kennedy; and Mrs. Roosevelt could not remember having seen before such depths in anyone's eyes, such a suggestion of sadness and worldly knowledge on the face of one so young.

"It is . . . pleasure to meet you," she said.

"The pleasure is ours," said Mrs. Roosevelt.

"Indeed it is," said Jack Kennedy, who was unable to conceal how much this beautiful little girl impressed him.

Unlike the other women in the suite, she was not dressed in a long silk dress. She was, to the contrary, quite simply dressed, in a black skirt and a dark green, short-sleeved sweater. But she wore around her neck a chain of heavy gold, from which hung a magnificent diamond, all out of character with her simplicity.

"I would introduce you to Messieurs Ignatieff and Goldinin, my staff, but they speak no English and would make dull conversation if they could," said the Ambassador with a chuckle. "Nina is far more interesting."

"The Ambassador recommends vodka, Miss Rozanov," said Jack Kennedy. "Will you show me how to enjoy it?"

The tiny ballerina looked up into his face, her eyes full of solemn wonder. "You *drink* it," she said. It was impossible to tell if she had made a small joke or was as serious as she looked. But she plainly understood the motive behind his invitation. She nodded and led him toward the table where the bottles waited.

"Do you know who she is?" Kennedy asked Nina Rozanov. "I mean, Mrs. Roosevelt. Do you know who she is?"

Nina shook her head. "Not really. The wife of the President of the United States, hmm?"

"Yes. And do you know who I am?"

"No."

Jack laughed. "Well, it makes no difference. Show me how to drink vodka."

Ambassador Troyanoskii watched Kennedy lead the ballerina away. "Handsome young people," he said to Mrs. Roosevelt.

"Young . . ." she mused. She herself was to be fifty-four years old that year and was more conscious of age than she had ever been before. "And handsome, to be sure."

"Mr. Benny," said the Ambassador, extending an arm toward Jack Benny as if to sweep him in. "And Mrs. Benny. How good of you to come. Will you excuse me for a moment? I will return, while perhaps you and Mrs. Roosevelt have a few moments to talk, as you didn't have at dinner."

Jack Benny stared after the Ambassador, who hurried across the room to say something—something harsh, from the sound of it—to his two staff men.

"I listen to your radio show as often as I can," said Mrs. Roosevelt.

"Well . . . do you eat Jell-O, then?" asked Benny, mock-serious.

"In fact, I do," she said. "Probably because of the commercials on your show. Now, the President . . . no. I can't get him to eat it."

"The President has good taste," said Mary Livingstone.

"Next year," said Benny, "they're coming out with a new flavor—borscht. Then maybe— Then maybe I'll eat it myself."

Mrs. Roosevelt laughed. "Maybe they'll make sauerkraut, too," she suggested. "Sauerkraut Jell-O."

"Yuck!" squawked Mary Livingstone.

Captain Colbert approached, bringing Josephine Baker.

"You must forgive Mary and me, Miss Baker," said Jack Benny. "We've never had the pleasure of seeing your show."

La Baker rolled her big brown eyes. "I've never seen yours either, Mr. Benny," she said. She spoke English with the accent of her origin—St. Louis. "Nor for that matter yours, Mrs. Roosevelt," she added with a sly smile.

"I hope you stay home long enough to see all our shows," said Mrs. Roosevelt.

"Mais non," said Captain Colbert. "She is a national treasure of France and must not stay away more than a few days. Indeed, I am trying to persuade her to return on *Normandie.*"

"And I will, too," said Josephine Baker. "But not on the next crossing. I'll be in the States a month. Just a month. Of course, the dogs . . ." She shook her head.

"I have explained to Mademoiselle Baker that her dogs, which are in the ship's kennel, cannot accompany her as she travels in the States. They will remain in quarantine in New York. Or— They *would* have."

"Yes, would have," said Josephine Baker. "I'm not going back on the return crossing, but my dogs are. Home to Paris. I'm not leaving them in any New York quarantine."

"Lovely dogs," said Captain Colbert.

"At that, their welcome in the States may be warmer

than mine," said Josephine Baker with a hint of bitterness.

"A problem?" asked Mary Livingstone.

"Well . . . You know the States. Not many hotels will accept a Negro. And a fine congressman from Texas has suggested I am an immoral person and ought not to be permitted to enter the holy precincts of the United States of America. I may be immoral, but he's so ignorant he doesn't know I'm an American citizen."

"Mr. and Mrs. Benjamin Kubelsky have been refused rooms in hotels, too," said Mary Livingstone. "Not to mention the problem with the country club in Los Angeles."

"We formed our own," said Benny. "George and Eddy and . . . well, a lot of us. Now the people who wouldn't let us in *their* country club want to join ours, because we serve better *food*."

"Do you let them?" asked Josephine Baker.

"Sure," said Benny with a shrug. "Why not? They can't help it that they weren't born Jews."

"I hope you know that my husband and I are wholly committed to ending all this kind of thing," said Mrs. Roosevelt.

Mary Livingstone smiled at her. "We know you are," she said. "The President can't help it that he's a Democrat."

Jack Benny waved his hand. "Let's change the subject," he said. "I mean, we had Hitler for dinner . . ."

"Plus the elegant and charming Mr. Luce," said Josephine Baker. "And the pessimistic views of the boy hero of aviation."

"Personally," said Benny, "I feel like I'm in paradise—in such distinguished company on so distinguished a ship. You know . . . I'm from Wau*kegan,* and Mary's from *Cleve*land, and—"

"And I can remember eating from a garbage can," said Josephine Baker. "The world has been good to me, and I'm very lucky to be here tonight. Forgive the negative note, Captain, Mrs. Roosevelt. Let's talk of more optimistic things. Like, how about those Cubs? If they win today, it'll be ten in a row."

"I'm amazed," said Mrs. Roosevelt, "to hear of Dizzy Dean pitching for the Chicago Cubs."

"Not only that but got a big win for them," said Josephine Baker.

"The Cubs paid two hundred thousand dollars for him!" said Benny.

"Jack . . . It's only money," said Mary Livingstone.

Jack Benny took her straight line and turned up his eyes in one of his signature injured-look pauses. *Well!* he said finally.

"American baseball . . ." said Captain Colbert. "I will never understand it."

"Neither do we, really," said Mrs. Roosevelt. She had used one of her few bits of baseball knowledge in remarking that Dizzy Dean had been traded to the Cubs.

The Captain nodded to Troyanoskii, who had just returned to their group. *"Monsieur l' Ambassadeur,"* he said. "Is everything in order?"

"Is anything ever otherwise aboard *Normandie*?" asked Troyanoskii. With a toothy grin he bowed to the Captain. "You oppress the workers with élan that Louis XIV would have envied."

Captain Colbert laughed. "A few things remain, Monsieur," he said, "that capitalism does better than socialism."

"To achieve socialism, we must make a few sacrifices," said Troyanoskii, his grin broadening. "Ah— Ah, Nina! A vodka, if you please."

The little ballerina stood across the sitting room, still talking with Jack Kennedy. With a dutiful nod she acknowledged Troyanoskii's command and stepped away from Kennedy to go to the table where the bottles were arrayed. Kennedy followed her.

"A charming girl," said Mrs. Roosevelt, inclining her head toward Nina Rozanov. "Is she a first-rank ballerina?"

Troyanoskii shrugged and turned down the corners of his mouth—while still managing to convey an expression of amused irony. "Not really," he said. "Not in the great tradition. But she is good. She has a secure career, if not with the Ballet Russe de Monte Carlo, then with some provincial troupe. If not as a *première danseuse,* at least as a dancer in the chorus."

"Are you sponsoring her?" asked Josephine Baker.

The Ambassador's grin broadened again. "You are perceptive, Mademoiselle," he said.

Nina stepped up and with a shy smile handed Troyanoskii a tumbler of vodka, poured over ice cubes.

"Ahh . . ." he said. "I show you how to drink vodka. Then maybe you will all want to try it. *Prosit!*"

He tipped back his head and drank half the glass in a few noisy gulps.

"It is Stolichnaya," he explained. "I brought it with me from my country, where we know how to appreciate fine vodka. Would anyone else like to try it?"

"As a matter of fact, I will," said Jack Kennedy.

"And so will I," said Jack Benny.

"Well, then. Come. We will fill your glasses."

Ambassador Troyanoskii led the two men toward the table of bottles. Mrs. Roosevelt, Mary Livingstone, and Josephine Baker remained where they were, amused.

"Stolichnaya!" grunted the Ambassador as Jack Kennedy and Jack Benny took cautious sips and he himself emptied his glass. He poured another glass over his ice and drank some more.

"Stolichnaya," chuckled Josephine Baker. "I knew a Russian named Stolichnaya once. Or was that what they called a Russian dance some of them used to do? Paris is full of them, you know—Russians who can't stand their new government."

"With reason," said Mrs. Roosevelt.

"Yes," said Mary Livingstone. "A wicked government."

"I— Oh!" exclaimed Mrs. Roosevelt. "Uh . . . please excuse me."

She had been surprised to see Moira Lasky walking through the broad doorway between the sitting room and the dining room. Moira was dressed in black, in a silk dinner dress that clung to the lines of her body like oil poured over her shoulders and allowed to run down. The sleeves covered her arms to just above her elbows, where they split and trailed almost to the floor. She carried a small plate heaped with hors d'oeuvres, and in her other hand a glass of wine.

"Mrs. Roosevelt." she said. "Allow me to present Herr Ernst Richter Remer."

Remer was a man in his forties, if Mrs. Roosevelt judged right. He wore his black hair slicked down and determinedly combed, so that not a strand did not lie hard against his scalp, exactly where he wanted it. He wore, too, a black pencil mustache, matching his heavy black eyebrows. His evening clothes were expertly tailored and conspicuously expensive. Not every man wore white-tie with style, but Ernst Richter Remer did—with style and confidence.

With quick grace, he put his plate and glass aside on a table and bowed, then offered his hand. "Mrs. Roosevelt!" he said. "A signal honor! Moira told me she was acquainted with you. I did not expect to have the privilege of meeting you."

Mrs. Roosevelt allowed Remer to kiss her hand. Then she said, "Do enjoy your food and wine, Herr Remer. It is pleasant to meet you, too, but I should be more comfortable if you would go ahead with your refreshment."

"Thank you, gracious lady," he said.

He spoke English. The accent was unusual, not easy to identify.

"I am surprised to see you here, Moira," said Mrs. Roosevelt quietly.

"Invited," said Moira under her breath, suppressing a grin. "That is, *he* was, and he insisted I come with him." Remer was having a little difficulty retrieving his plate and glass in such a way as to let him eat and drink without sitting down—so they could speak for a moment out of his hearing. "Really."

"I see."

Moira raised her eyebrows and allowed herself the grin she had denied herself before. "I'm not here to see if I can improve pickings, if that's what worries you."

Mrs. Roosevelt shook her head quickly. "Not at all. I hadn't thought—" Then she stopped and smiled. "Before this voyage is over, you will dine at the captain's table, Moira. If I know you. And it will be *you* who is invited, not Herr Remer."

Moira smiled at Remer, who now had plate and glass in hand again. "Ernst has some kind of business venture to discuss with Ambassador Troyanoskii," she said.

"He is a broker in wines and champagnes, I believe you said."

"And brandies," said Moira.

"Well, the Ambassador is a connoisseur of such things."

"Why, that's Jack Kennedy," said Moira, nodding toward the little group with glasses of vodka in their hands. "And Jack Benny!"

"You know young Jack?" asked Mrs. Roosevelt.

"Personally," said Moira. "Not professionally." She grinned. "I know his father, too."

"Uh . . . The Ambassador seems to—"

She had been about to say that the Ambassador looked ill. He *was* ill, quite obviously. He was gasping loudly, and his body shook as if with a convulsion.

"Mr. Ambassador!" cried Jack Kennedy.

Troyanoskii jerked his head from side to side. His eyes rolled up, and he continued to gasp. He dropped his glass and staggered back against the table, knocking over bottles.

His two staff men trotted across the room and grabbed him by both arms. That seemed to agitate him. He flailed with both arms, knocking them aside. Captain Colbert rushed to his side.

"A heart attack, for God's sake!" cried Moira.

Troyanoskii stumbled forward, then fell. His face was bright red. He rolled on his back on the floor, where he seemed to relax, as if the seizure, whatever it was, was over.

"Le médecin!" the Captain barked to First Officer Brillant, who had hurried to his side. *"Vite!"*

The Ambassador looked barely conscious. He eyes remained open, but his pupils had dilated, and he stared without seeing. His breath was shallow.

One of his two staff members—Ignatieff or Goldinin; no one but the Ambassador himself had yet determined which was which—knelt beside him and seized his arm.

"Tovarishch Posol!" he whispered shrilly.

Troyanoskii stiffened and began to jerk, in another paroxysm. His red face twisted into a grotesque grin. His eyes

31

bulged. His subordinate drew back in horror—it was as if his touch had triggered the second attack.

Captain Colbert turned to the crowd that had gathered around the prostrate man. "Ladies and gentlemen," he said. "It would be well, I think, to leave him alone. May I suggest you leave the apartment? We will send word of the Ambassador's condition as soon as the doctor has examined him."

Nearly everyone began a reluctant progress to the door, looking back to stare with curiosity and concern.

"Uh . . . Captain," said Kennedy. "It is possible the Ambassador has been poisoned. And if so—"

"My God!" interjected Jack Benny. "We were drinking the same stuff! The vodka!"

Mary Livingstone had overheard. She rushed to her husband's side. "Jack! Are you all right? Do you feel—?"

Benny nodded reassuringly at her, but he sat down abruptly.

Mrs. Roosevelt stepped to the side of Jack Kennedy. "Jack—"

He smiled weakly. "So far, so good," he said.

Troyanoskii had once more ceased to jerk. Once again his breath seemed almost to have stopped.

"Could he be epileptic?" asked Captain Colbert.

Mrs. Roosevelt glanced at the terrified Ignatieff and Goldinin. "We can't even ask," she said. "But— Miss Rozanov. The ballerina. She speaks Russian and English."

"Miss Rozanov!" called the Captain.

Nina Rozanov was among the crowd leaving the suite. She turned and came back.

"Can you ask the members of the Ambassador's staff if he is an epileptic?"

She nodded and spoke quietly to the two Russians. They shook their heads.

"They say no. But—" She stepped apart from the Ambassador and his two hovering staff men. "They wouldn't tell you if they knew. And don't be sure what languages they speak. They may well speak English, French, German . . ."

"Why do you say that?" asked the Captain.

"They are almost certainly NKVD agents."

"Isn't it dangerous for you to tell us this?" asked Mrs. Roosevelt.

The girl shrugged. "I live in Paris. I will never return to Russia. Not until there is a complete change of government. My family are White Russians, refugees from the Bolshevik *coup d'état*."

"Could he have been poisoned?" asked Kennedy.

She nodded. "Yes. By *them*."

Troyanoskii went into another paroxysm, this one weaker than the first two. He jerked. The distortion of his face became more pronounced. The doctor hurried in just in time to see him relax.

The doctor knelt beside the Ambassador. When he lifted his arm to take his pulse, Troyanoskii began to twitch again. The doctor held his wrist firmly and searched for a pulse.

"*Faible*," he said. "*Mais rapide*."

"He may have been poisoned," said Jack Kennedy tensely. "And so may we have been, Mr. Benny and I. We were drinking from the same bottle."

"*Empoisonné?*" the Captain translated.

"*Oui*," said the doctor. "*Strychnine. Une grande dose. Capitaine . . . L' homme est mort*."

"If there is nothing more you can do for Ambassador Troyanoskii then I think you had better examine Mr. Kennedy and Mr. Benny," said Mrs. Roosevelt.

The Captain translated, and the doctor turned first to

Jack Kennedy, because he was standing closer. After a moment he shook his head. *"Pas de strychnine,"* he said. Then he examined Jack Benny and made the same pronouncement.

He knelt again beside Troyanoskii. The doctor shook his head.

"Murder," said Mrs. Roosevelt quietly.

3

Monsieur Edouard Ouzoulias was introduced to Mrs. Roosevelt and the others as *"agent de la police de sûreté de la Compagnie Générale Transatlantique."* He was, as Jack Kennedy shortly put it to Mrs. Roosevelt, "The French line's house detective."

A tall, emaciated man with a sharp chin and a long, Gallic nose—who pronounced his name "Oh-zo-LEE-ahs"—he smoked a pipe, which he somehow managed to transfer back and forth from his hand to the pocket of his tweed jacket without setting the jacket on fire, though a wisp of smoke sometimes issued from the pocket. He affected—or perhaps it was real—an imperturbable calm. Immediately on arriving in the apartment, he examined the bottles on the bar and selected and poured for himself a glass of fine red Bordeaux. Only when he had taken a sip

35

of the wine—and a moment to appreciate it—did he squat beside the body of Ambassador Boris Troyanoskii.

"Streek-nine, hmm?" he said to the doctor.

The ship's chief physician, whose name was Dr. Jules Grasse, nodded. *"Oui. Deux milligrams, ou trois, peut être. Peut être plus."*

"Assez," said Ouzoulias. Two or three milligrams, or more, would be enough.

"Dans un verre du vodka," said Dr. Grasse.

"Ah, vodka," Ouzoulias muttered, wrinkling his nose with fine Gallic scorn. *"Ou est le verre? Et la bouteille?"*

Captain Colbert answered his questions in English, so Mrs. Roosevelt and the others could understand. (He did not know that Mrs. Roosevelt and Jack Kennedy had been following the conversation with no difficulty at all.) "The glass," he said, "is there." He pointed. "The bottle is in the bucket of ice. Ambassador Troyanoskii liked his vodka ice-cold."

"It is so drunk," said Ouzoulias disdainfully.

"The doctor has found poison in the glass but none in the bottle."

"Ah, so. Suggesting that—"

"That the strychnine was added to the drink after it was poured from the bottle."

"Suggesting, then of course, that *I* put it there," said Nina Rozanov.

"Ahh?" murmured Ouzoulias.

"I carried the vodka from the bar to the Ambassador," she said. "If there was no poison in the bottle—"

"But poison in the glass," Ouzoulias interrupted, "then it would seem you had to have put it there."

"I was with her," said Jack Kennedy. "I didn't see her do it."

"Who poured the vodka from the bottle to the glass?" asked Ouzoulias.

"I did that, too," said Nina.

"I watched her," said Jack. "She poured from the bottle that has no poison in it."

"There is no need, Monsieur, for you to interject constantly your defense of the young lady. There are—how many?—ways in which the poison could have been received by the unfortunate Ambassador Troyanoskii. One, that the poison was in the bottle of vodka—and perhaps another bottle has been substituted. Two, that the poison was added to the glass after it was poured. Three, that it was already in the glass. Four, that someone standing near the Ambassador dropped it in as he held it in his hand. Five, that it was not in the vodka at all but in something the Ambassador ingested before or after. (Did anyone see him pop into his mouth a pill or mint?) Six, that the Ambassador used strychnine as a means of committing suicide—though, of course, it does seem an oddly painful way to do it. And . . . Seven— Oh, there may be seven, and eight, and nine. Or more. Possibilities. Let us not reach conclusions too readily."

"I think that is an admirable idea," said Mrs. Roosevelt.

"Yes," said Ouzoulias. "We must reach no conclusion before its time. And now, *Monsieur le Docteur . . .*"

He asked the doctor two questions. Captain Colbert translated the questions and answers.

QUESTION: "You found traces of strychnine in the glass, even though it had been dropped and was empty?"

ANSWER: "Yes. I sent to the infirmary for the chemical that tests for the presence of strychnine. Even though the glass was empty, traces of the poison clung to the glass, and the test was most positive."

QUESTION: "Did you perform the test on the carpet, where the glass spilled?"

ANSWER: Yes. It tested very positive for strychnine."

Agent Ouzoulias nodded, turning down the corners of

his mouth so much as to wrinkle his chin. "So . . . If the unhappy Ambassador Troyanoskii ingested two milligrams, maybe three or more, of strychnine, still the glass contained at least that much more. He did not drink it all. An interesting point, no?"

"Suggesting what?" asked Mrs. Roosevelt.

Ouzoulias shrugged. "I have no idea. But a fact we should note, no? Anyway, we know now that the poison did not come from a mint or hors d'ouevres."

"A fact we should note," agreed Mrs. Roosevelt.

Ouzoulias replenished his glass of red Bordeaux. He glanced at the people around him. "All of you were present when the Ambassador collapsed, hmm?"

"As were a dozen other people," said Mrs. Roosevelt.

"But who was closest to him?" asked Ouzoulias.

"Mr. Kennedy and I," said Jack Benny.

Ouzoulias reached into his pocket with his left hand and took out the pipe. He sucked hard on it and got smoke—it had not gone out during its minutes in his pocket. "Did the Ambassador say anything?" he asked. "Complain he was ill?"

Jack Benny shook his head. "No, nothing."

"And who was standing around him when he drank the vodka?"

"Well . . ." said Benny hesitantly, frowning. "Mrs. Roosevelt. My wife and I—"

"Your wife is—?"

"I'm Mrs. Benny," said Mary Livingstone.

"Ah. And you saw him drink the vodka?"

"Yes."

"Who else?"

"I was there," said Jack Kennedy. "And Miss Rozanov. Also, Josephine Baker."

"*La Baker?*" asked Ouzoulias. He pronounced the name "Back-air." He smiled. "And where is she?"

"We asked most of the people to leave," said Captain Colbert.

"Ah," grunted Ouzoulias as he drew on his pipe and coaxed his tobacco into flame. "Now . . . When Monsieur Troyanoskii drank the vodka, did he say anything about it?"

"He expressed himself as most satisfied with it," said Mrs. Roosevelt. "But, of course, it was ice-cold, which would have impaired his sense of taste."

"Ahh. A shrewd and pertinent observation," said Ouzoulias. "Now. Was there not a steward attending the bar?"

"Yes," said the Captain. "One of the ship's stewards."

"And where is he?"

"Brillant," said the Captain to the First Officer. "Do you know?"

"Waiting outside," said Brillant. "I ordered all the ship's personnel to wait outside."

"Bring in the man who was attending the bar, please," said Ouzoulias.

The First Officer nodded and walked out of the suite. In a moment he returned, leading a uniformed steward.

"His name is Philippe LeClerc," said Brillant. "Fortunately, he speaks a bit of English."

Philippe LeClerc was distinguished only for his hair, which was almost white, and abundant, though slicked down with a dressing. Otherwise, he was an ordinary-looking young man, of average height and build, with blue eyes and a slightly flushed face. He stared for a moment at the body of the Russian ambassador, which remained uncovered on the floor, its sightless eyes staring at the ceiling.

"You were attending the bar, is this correct?" asked Ouzoulias.

"*Oui, Monsieur.*"

"You are aware that a man drank poison from a glass of vodka served at this bar?"

"Oui, Monsieur," said LeClerc apprehensively.

"Do you have any idea how the poison got in the man's drink?"

"Non, Monsieur."

"Who poured the Ambassador's vodka?"

LeClerc nodded at Nina Rozanov. *"Mademoiselle,"* he said.

"Why? Why did *you* not pour it? Was that not your duty, since you were attending the bar?"

LeClerc frowned uncertainly. *"Mademoiselle . . ."* She take . . . bottle . . . from ice. And—" He tipped his hand, suggesting the motion of pouring.

"Where did she get the glass?" asked Ouzoulias.

LeClerc frowned again. "Glass?"

"Le verre."

"Ah. I give glass to her. Many . . . glass . . . on table. I give glass."

"Who put in the ice?"

"I put in."

"Where did the vodka come from?" asked First Officer Brillant. "Stolichnaya is not a brand carried in the ship's stores."

"Monsieur l'Ambassadeur has bring it . . . from his . . . from . . . *sa chambre à coucher."*

"From his bedroom," said Ouzoulias, translating.

"Who opened the bottle?" asked Mrs. Roosevelt.

"It was open already," said LeClerc. "Maybe . . . two, three drinks already drinked."

"Ah," said Ouzoulias. He glanced around. "Further questions? If not . . ." He dismissed the steward with a wave.

Philippe LeClerc left the suite, looking relieved that an ordeal was over.

Edouard Ouzoulias suggested that the ladies join him on the sofa that faced the piano and that the gentlemen draw up chairs. When they were seated and he was satisfied with the heavy cloud of harsh smoke his pipe was producing, he rubbed his hands together and said—

"*Eh bien*. Perhaps it will not be necessary to ask you to remain longer, unless of course you wish to do so. You in particular, Mrs. Roosevelt. It is of course inconceivable that you could have anything to do with this unfortunate event, so—"

"Actually, I should like to rémain," said Mrs. Roosevelt. "I've had a bit of experience in the investigation of crimes, odd though it may seem. Including murder, in fact. I am far from squeamish about the ugly facts of it."

Only now was the doctor covering the body of Ambassador Troyanoskii.

"We should not wish to inconvenience you, Mrs. Roosevelt," said Captain Colbert.

"I have, in fact," she said, "been complimented for contributing a few minor insights into the investigation of more than one murder."

"In that case," said Agent Ouzoulias, "we shall welcome your assistance. Now, if I may— I know, of course, who you are. May I inquire of each person present who you are and how you come to be aboard *Normandie* for this voyage."

His eyes seemed to stop first on Jack Kennedy, so Kennedy gave the first explanation— "Well . . ." he said. "My name is John Kennedy. I'm from Boston. My father is United States Ambassador to the Court of St. James. My family lives in London, therefore; but I'm still working on my degree at Harvard University. I'm on my way home to go to school."

"I can vouch for all that," said Mrs. Roosevelt.

"Monsieur, uh, Benny?"

Jack Benny glanced at Mrs. Roosevelt with a little smile. "My name is Benjamin Kubelsky. I am known as Jack Benny—"

"Mr. Benny is one of America's best-known entertainers," Mrs. Roosevelt interrupted.

Benny nodded. "In show business, my wife is known as Mary Livingstone. We're on our way back from London, where we did a stage show."

"And . . . Mademoiselle Rozanov?"

The ballerina shrugged. "My father was Count Nicholas Alexandrovich Rozanov," she said. "My mother was the Countess Andrea Leovna Rozanov. They were murdered by the Bolsheviks. I managed to survive and—"

"You escaped?" Ouzoulias interrupted.

"My uncle brought me out of Russia," she said. "I have lived with him and his . . . his mistress ever since. In Paris. My uncle is a ballet master and committed me to the ballet. We are of the White Russian community in Paris."

"And what, may I ask, was your relationship with Ambassador Troyanoskii?"

"An intimate relationship, Monsieur, if you must know," she said defiantly. "Boris Vasilievich was a friend of our family in the old days, and he befriended and sponsored me in Paris."

"Your voyage to the United States?" asked Ouzoulias.

"Arranged by Boris Vasilievich," she said.

"You have a tourist-class passage," said First Officer Brillant.

Nina Rozanov shrugged. "I didn't expect to spend much time in it," she said quietly.

"I believe it might be advantageous," said Mrs. Roosevelt, "if you told us all you know about Ambassador

Troyanoskii—his background, his position with the Soviet government, and so forth."

The ballerina glanced at the covered body lying on the floor only a few feet from her. She sighed. "He is—was—about forty-five years old. He was a native of St. Petersburg—Leningrad—where his family were quite prosperous, though not aristocrats. His father was a lawyer. His paternal grandfather was a broker in timber and lumber. He was educated by private tutors, then at university in St. Petersburg and Berlin.

"He was twenty-one years old in 1914, when war broke out between Russia and Germany," she went on. "Through his family's influence, he evaded military service. He continued his studies, with tutors, at the family's country estate. Then—" She hesitated, sighed again. "When the Bolsheviks effected their *putsch,* he was readily assimilated into their ranks. One or two of his late tutors were Marxists and had taught him the cant. He survived, though he was the son of a rich man. Boris Vasilievich was a professional survivor."

"You suggested," said Mrs. Roosevelt gently, "that he was of the secret police."

Nina nodded. "I think so. I don't know it for sure, but I think so. He was, I think, of the Cheka, later of the NKVD."

"And his two servants?" asked Ouzoulias, nodding toward Ignatieff and Goldinin, who stood well apart, regarding the discussion near the sofa with apprehension and suspicion.

"Chekists, almost certainly," said Nina.

"You were traveling with him to the United States, then," said Ouzoulias. "Why?"

Nina lifted her chin. "As for me," she said, "I was not going back. Boris Vasilievich had arranged for me to dance in New York, and I did not expect ever to return to Paris, much less to Russia. I want nothing further to do with my bleak homeland, or with its cheerless people who are always contending over who will prevail there in the end. The Bolsheviks are . . . brutal murderers, the scum of the earth. And they will continue to govern Russia, because the Whites who want to overthrow them offer nothing much better."

"A pessimistic view," said Kennedy.

"A realistic view," she replied.

"I see," said Ouzoulias. "Ah, Mademoiselle. You wear a beautiful diamond. It must be worth a fortune."

"All that remains to me of my mother," the ballerina said bitterly. "I am taking it with me to America."

"The Ambassador was supposedly on his way to America for a meeting with the President," said Mrs. Roosevelt. "Do you have any reason to think his purpose was anything else?"

"Boris Vasilievich did not confide government business to me," said Nina. "He knew what I think of his government."

"Very well," said Ouzoulias. "I believe that is all we need ask for now. Everyone is entirely at liberty to do whatever you wish."

Mrs. Roosevelt remained behind with the French detective when all the others, including the Captain and First Officer, had left the *appartement de grand luxe*. Unless she read him wrongly, Edouard Ouzoulias had with his eyes suggested that, as the others took one final glance at the covered body on the floor and hurried to the door.

"The speculations of the little dancer are correct," said Ouzoulias when they were alone. "I was warned before we sailed that Monsieur the Soviet Ambassador was not as he seemed. I am anxious that my company not be embarrassed—also that my government and yours should not be. It is possible, Mrs. Roosevelt, that you have been witness to a political assassination."

"I guessed as much," she said.

"You do not, I assume, function as . . . How shall we say? An unofficial representative of the government of the United States?"

"No."

"Nonetheless, you will understand, I am sure, what an embarrassment it could be if this assassination was carried out by a citizen of the United States."

"But *which*, Monsieur Ouzoulias?" she asked. "Not young Mr. Kennedy, surely. Or Mr. Benny."

"Of this you feel certain?"

"I could not be more certain," she said.

"I am pleased to have the assurance," he said skeptically.

"It is inconceivable," she said. "Simply inconceivable."

Ouzoulias nodded. "You recommend I strike them from my list of suspects?"

"I cannot do that," she said. "I will not interfere—"

"Of course. You are very gracious. I will regard you, however, as confidential and unofficial representative of the government of the United States."

"I am not," she said firmly.

"Of course," he said with Gallic smoothness. "You will not, however, object if I inform you from time to time of the course of the investigation?"

"Not at all. I hope you will." She paused to smile. "I have an insatiable curiosity about these matters. And, in all modesty, I have been able to contribute a few ideas to detectives charged with the heavy responsibility of investigating murders. My husband calls me a would-be Sherlock Holmes."

"I see. I shall be most disappointed, my dear lady, if the mystery remains unsolved when we dock in New York. No? You as well?"

"I as well, Monsieur Ouzoulias. The game is afoot. Let us bring it to a quick conclusion."

4

Tommy Thompson did not know that Ambassador Troyanoskii was dead, much less that he had been murdered. Word had circulated aboard the *Normandie* that the Ambassador had suffered some kind of attack and had required medical attention; but so far it was not known that he had died of poisoning and that someone aboard the ship was a murderer. When Mrs. Roosevelt returned to her apartment, Tommy was exhilarated—full of happy stories about her dinner companions.

". . . from San Francisco. They had no idea who I might be and talked about you and the President . . . Well! They look forward to January 1941, when *'that woman'* will be out of the White House! Also, they are returning from a summer in Europe that included a stay in Italy, and they can't wait to tell all their friends at home what wonderful things Signor Mussolini has done—how Italy is so *clean* now, so orderly, and—"

"And the trains run on time," said Mrs. Roosevelt dryly.

"Yes. That, too."

"Did they suggest a leader like Mussolini is just what our own country needs?"

Tommy sighed. "Not in so many words. But . . . Yes, you could tell they had some such thought."

"When they find out who you are, they are going to be angry," said Mrs. Roosevelt.

Tommy shrugged. "I shouldn't be surprised."

"Tommy— We've got to get off a radiogram. Ambassador Troyanoskii is dead. Not only that, he was murdered. The message will have to go in cipher. Do you have the book handy?"

Tommy's jaw had dropped, in shock. But she said nothing and hurried into her bedroom to pick up her shorthand pad and the little book that contained the simple code they could use to send confidential messages back to the White House.

The code was nothing unbreakable, just one Mrs. Roosevelt used to send the President news or comments they didn't care to have pondered over by any curious cable clerk. During her visit to Paris she had sent back one message through the embassy, in diplomatic code, a far more formidable cipher.

Her message to the President:

SOVIET AMBASSADOR BORIS TROYANOSKII MURDERED ABOARD NORMANDIE THIS EVENING STOP HE WAS POISONED IN MY PRESENCE AND THAT OF YOUNG JACK KENNEDY, JACK BENNY, JOSEPHINE BAKER, AND OTHERS STOP NO AMERICAN PRESENTLY SUSPECTED STOP SUSPECT FRENCH LINE AND SOVIET GOVERNMENT WILL TRY TO KEEP MATTER SECRET STOP

THAT WILL BE IMPOSSIBLE STOP TOO MANY WITNESSES STOP WILL INFORM YOU IF MATTER INVOLVES ANY POSSIBLE INVOLVEMENT OF AMERICANS OR EMBARRASSMENT TO UNITED STATES STOP

Tommy took the message down and then set to work with the cipher book, encoding the words into a garble. While Tommy worked at that, Mrs. Roosevelt changed her clothes, taking off the silk gown she had worn to dinner and substituting a brown tweed skirt and jacket, with a yellow linen blouse.

When the message was encrypted, Tommy telephoned for a steward to pick it up and carry it to the radio room. Then she sat down with Mrs. Roosevelt, and they began to work on a newspaper column. "My Day" had to be written every day, and from aboard ship it would be radioed to New York. This column would tell about the great ship, omitting any mention of the murder.

The telephone rang. Tommy answered and told Mrs. Roosevelt that Jack Kennedy was calling.

"They've arrested Nina Rozanov," he said excitedly. "They're charging her with the murder of Ambassador Troyanoskii."

"How do you know?"

"She called me, since she thought I was sympathetic to her. It's odd. They've *chained* her in her cabin, but she has a telephone there."

"Oh, dear," said Mrs. Roosevelt quietly. "On what evidence, did she say?"

Kennedy sighed. "If you want my opinion, it's probably on none at all. They want to settle the case and forget it— in whatever way they have to do it."

"That's not my judgment of Monsieur Ouzoulias, Jack," said Mrs. Roosevelt. "I imagine they have *some* evidence."

"I was with her all the time," he said. "She put nothing in the man's drink. She couldn't have done it without my seeing her."

"Still—"

"Can I come to your apartment? Can we ask Ouzoulias to come? I can't believe the girl is guilty. I—"

"Yes. Why don't you? I'll telephone Monsieur Ouzoulias and see if he won't agree to join us."

It was almost midnight when Agent Ouzoulias arrived in Mrs. Roosevelt's suite. Tommy Thompson had gone to her bedroom and closed the door. Jack Kennedy, still dressed in white tie, sat unhappily in a chair near the piano. Mrs. Roosevelt was sipping tea.

"I'm grateful to you," she said to Ouzoulias, "for coming here so late. But we did agree to keep in touch about the murder, and I understand you have solved the mystery."

"Not necessarily," said Ouzoulias, frowning over the set of bottles the ship had provided for Mrs. Roosevelt's suite. He selected a brandy and poured himself a generous splash. "Not necessarily at all."

"But Miss Rozanov says you have placed her under arrest," said Kennedy.

"Not for the murder, actually," said the detective insouciantly as he sat down. "Indeed, Mr. Kennedy, I take note of your testimony that Mademoiselle Rozanov could not have put the strychnine in the Ambassador's vodka. How it came to be there remains unsolved. Perhaps she used some clever method that escaped your attention. She is a suspect. She must be. But I did not arrest her for killing the Ambassador. No. Rather for theft."

"Theft?" asked Mrs. Roosevelt, surprised and curious.

"Yes, Madame. Of jewelry, worth perhaps hundreds of thousands of francs. Part of a very large quantity of jewelry Ambassador Troyanoskii had in his suite."

As Kennedy shook his head, openmouthed, Mrs. Roosevelt protested with lifted hands—"But how did you find out?"

"As soon as I was called and told the Ambassador had collapsed, probably from poison, I sent my staff to search Mademoiselle Rozanov's cabin. It was—" He lifted his shoulders in an expressive Gallic shrug. "—a routine precaution. You see, we already knew Mademoiselle Rozanov was the Ambassador's mistress."

"When you speak of stolen jewelry, I hope you do not refer to the diamond Miss Rozanov was wearing this evening. She was wearing it in the Ambassador's presence, and he raised no objection."

"Ah. I am glad you make that point. But we found many other items in her cabin."

"And you believe they were stolen from the Ambassador?" Kennedy asked. "How do you reach that conclusion?"

"We have also thoroughly searched the Ambassador's apartment," said Ouzoulias. "In which we have found ten times the quantity of jewelry. In a small trunk. It looks like something from mythology, perhaps the Arabian Nights."

"I am curious to know," said Mrs. Roosevelt, "why you believe the jewelry you found in Miss Rozanov's cabin came from Ambassador Troyanoskii's trunk."

Ouzoulias rolled his brandy snifter back and forth between his hands, warming the brandy and inhaling the vapor. "Aboard a ship like *Normandie*," he said, "one of our chief problems is theft. Our passengers carry much valuable property. Why they do this, I have always wondered; but they do—money, jewelry, furs, expensive cameras . . . all kinds of eminently theftable properties. We must be alert all the time for thiefs. The most shrewd and bold burglars in the world will try to sneak aboard a ship like this. And, if they come aboard, they will attempt the most amazing thefts."

"I see," said Mrs. Roosevelt.

"Also," said Ouzoulias, warming to his topic, "we must search among our passengers constantly for the . . . the prostitutes, who would ply their trade among our lonely male passengers and perhaps steal from them or blackmail them. Also, the dishonest players of cards—the professional gamblers. All these. *Normandie* is paradise for them."

"But the jewels—"

"Ah, yes. Forgive my extended explanation. In consequence of what I have explained, I must tell you of the jewels I have much experience. In my office I have albums of photographs of stolen pieces—stolen, you understand, not from *Normandie,* but from other ships, from hotels, from homes . . . I am looking in them when I find a piece of suspicious jewelry aboard. I have been compelled to become something of a connoisseur of the fine jewelry."

"And?" said Kennedy impatiently.

"The jewels we found in Miss Rozanov's cabin are much similar in kind to the collection in the Ambassador's trunk."

"How so?" asked Mrs. Roosevelt.

"Of an age," said Ouzoulias. "The late nineteenth-century sort of jewelry, no longer in fashion. Heavy. Dark yellow gold. What is more, some of the pieces have been broken to make them more compact, so that more can fit into the trunk. Tiaras. Broken, as with a hammer, to retain the value of the gold and gems, absent the value of the items as works of art. It was as if he expected to remove all the gems from their settings and melt down the metal. Among the items in Mademoiselle Rozanov's luggage were the broken pieces of a gold-and-ruby tiara."

"Which doesn't prove they came from Troyanoskii's trunk," said Kennedy.

"It does not prove it," Ouzoulias agreed. "It *suggests* it."

"I find this information most significant," said Mrs. Roosevelt. "Ostensibly, Ambassador Troyanoskii was on his way to the United States to meet with the President. There is reason to believe, however, that his purpose was otherwise. Now—"

"I see two possibilities immediately," said Ouzoulias. "Forgive me for interrupting. First possibility, perhaps *Monsieur l'Ambassadeur* was in the process of defecting from the Soviet Union—in which case, he was perhaps murdered for that reason. Second possibility, perhaps the jewelry, to be marketed in America, was to provide a fund for Soviet spy operations."

"Miss Rozanov," said Kennedy, "told us she intended never to return to Russia. If she was Troyanoskii's mistress, maybe *he* didn't intend to go back either."

"Ah. Mademoiselle Rozanov," said Ouzoulias. "Another element that directs suspicion against her is that in Paris she lived most modestly, almost in poverty, as did her uncle the ballet master. Her tourist-class ticket for this voyage—like those of the two Russian servants, Goldinin and Ignatieff—was purchased by Troyanoskii. If this jewelry was not stolen from Troyanoskii, perhaps since they came aboard *Normandie,* then why did Mademoiselle live in almost-poverty in Paris?"

"Maybe it is all that is left of what her uncle managed to bring out of—"

"No," Ouzoulias interrupted Kennedy. "He arrived in Paris in 1919 with nothing. He has lived nineteen years like a man who has nothing."

"France has kept these people under close surveillance, I gather," said Mrs. Roosevelt.

"Troyanoskii, yes," said Ouzoulias. "He is a Chekist. He is—was—almost certainly a murderer, in Russia. My government has kept an eye on him, you may be certain. And on anyone associated with him. When Mademoiselle became his mistress— Well . . ."

"A powerful motive for murdering him," said Mrs. Roosevelt. "That he killed someone in the Soviet Union."

"But only three Russians were in his apartment this evening," said Ouzoulias. "Ignatieff, Goldinin, and Mademoiselle Rozanov. There are other Russians among the passengers and some among the crew. But none of them have first-class passage. None of them were on this deck."

"Oh, can you be so sure of that?" asked Jack Kennedy. "Really? There were—what?—forty people in and out of that suite when I was there. Are you absolutely certain all of them were first-class passengers? Does no one ever slip by?"

Ouzoulias shrugged. Like many Frenchmen, he could make a variety of comments with a shrug. This time it was a concession. "Of course," he said. ("Uv gairss" was how it sounded.)

"I do not see the case as proved, Monsieur Ouzoulias," said Mrs. Roosevelt. "I mean, the case of theft."

"Well . . . allow me to make a telephone call," said the detective.

He stepped to the telephone, which was on a nearby table, and dialed a number. He spoke rapid French to someone on the line—much of it being *"Eh bien," "C'est dommage," "Bien," "Vraiment?"* and so on. Mrs. Roosevelt exchanged glances with Jack Kennedy while this went on.

"So . . ." said Ouzoulias at last. "Too bad. I have on my staff a man who knows how to take the fingerprints. Earlier he found Mademoiselle Rozanov's on the jewel trunk.

Now— Well, now he has found the Ambassador's on three of the pieces of jewelry found in Mademoiselle's luggage."

"Which *still* doesn't prove—" Jack Kennedy began.

"Correct," Ouzoulias interrupted. "But it does add a weight of evidence to the case, would you not agree? She cannot be allowed to leave the ship in New York. She will be returned to France to be tried for the theft. If evidence is found that she poisoned the Ambassador—" He shrugged again. "I may tell you I hope we do not find it. The girl is a person of sympathy to me."

"Do we understand that you are keeping her in *chains*, Monsieur Ouzoulias?" asked Mrs. Roosevelt. "If so, I protest—"

"Oh, ho!" laughed the detective. "Not in chain, Madame. No! We have no prison cells aboard *Normandie*. If we did, I would be unhappy to put so charming a girl in such. She is in her cabin, with telephone, access to steward service for her food and drink. We have place on her ankles some very light restraints, to prevent her wandering about the ship. Indeed—" His face darkened. "On a voyage eight months ago, a young woman caught stealing was confined to her cabin. She managed to effect an exit and threw herself overboard, into the sea. It is in Mademoiselle Rozanov's own advantage to be restrained lightly. You wish to visit her? You will find her circumstances not uncomfortable."

A tourist-class cabin on the *Normandie* was much like a small hotel room. It was paneled with dark wood, carpeted in royal blue, furnished with a bed, dresser, dressing table, night table, two armchairs, and a small sofa. A door opened on a bathroom equipped with commode, basin, and shower stall. Everything was clean and brightly lighted.

Nina Rozanov opened the door to admit Mrs. Roosevelt and Jack Kennedy. She was dressed as she had been earlier, in black skirt and green sweater. As she quietly welcomed them and took the three steps back to her sofa, the "restraints" Ouzoulias had spoken of were painfully evident. She was hobbled by steel shackles that looked like oversized handcuffs locked around her ankles and joined by about a foot of steel chain.

"I am . . . humiliated," she said softly.

"And we are outraged," said Mrs. Roosevelt. "We will make the point to Captain Colbert in the morning."

Nina sat on her sofa. Mrs. Roosevelt and Kennedy sat facing her.

"You are not accused of murdering Ambassador Troyanoskii," said Mrs. Roosevelt. "Only of stealing jewelry from him."

Nina smiled sadly. "A preliminary," she said. "They accuse me of stealing so they can hold me prisoner. When I am returned to France . . . in chains . . . they will charge me with murder."

"My child," said Mrs. Roosevelt. "Where did you get the jewelry they found in your luggage?"

Nina glanced back and forth between Jack Kennedy and Mrs. Roosevelt. "It is mine," she said quietly but firmly. "It belonged to my mother."

"How was it brought out of Russia? You were only a child when you were helped to escape. Did you carry the jewelry with you? If not, how—"

"There is a community of White Russians in Paris," said Nina. "We work together. Not all of them are . . . ballet masters, like my uncle. Some of them are hard, effective men and women."

"Did they steal it for you?" asked Mrs. Roosevelt.

"I don't know. But when I saw it, I knew it. I have studied photographs of it, made for the insurance company."

Mrs. Roosevelt sighed. "They found Ambassador Troyanoskii's fingerprints on it."

"I suppose so," said Nina. "You might find his fingerprints on anything that is mine. You might find his fingerprints on *me,* if human flesh took fingerprints."

"Are you saying he examined your jewelry?"

"He treated me as his, everything that was mine was his," said Nina bitterly. "He found satisfaction in that."

"And you accepted it?"

"Yes. He was an influential man, a very wealthy man. Besides, he had ways of imposing his will on people."

"On the French government?" asked Jack Kennedy.

The ballerina nodded. "If the Bolsheviks want me . . . If they want me guillotined, I will be guillotined. There are newspapers in Paris that will demand my death."

"The Popular Front . . ." muttered Kennedy to Mrs. Roosevelt.

"Many in France believe they need the Soviet Union to help fight Hitler," said Nina. "But Stalin will betray France. He has much more in common with Hitler than with democratic politicians in France and England."

"Ambassador Troyanoskii served Stalin, did he not?" asked Mrs. Roosevelt.

Nina drew a deep breath. "He would have cut Stalin's throat, if he had seen the opportunity," she said. "Just as Stalin would have cut his, for little reason or for no reason at all."

"Then who killed him?" asked Jack Kennedy.

To stretch her weary muscles, Nina Rozanov thrust her feet forward, unconsciously displaying her leg irons. "Not I," she muttered. "You saw. As you told Ouzoulias, you would have seen me put poison in his vodka, if I had done it. Anyway—if I had wanted to kill him, would I have killed him that way—in a way that put suspicion on me? Am I a fool? I have had a thousand opportunities to kill him secretly, if that was what I wanted." She sighed heavily.

"I think that's a powerful argument," said Kennedy.

"As do I," said Mrs. Roosevelt.

Kennedy stared thoughtfully at Nina for a long moment. Then he asked, "Where did the Ambassador get all the jewelry he was carrying?"

"Loot," said Nina.

"From what?"

She lifted her chin indignantly. "From the families he . . . From people destroyed by the Bolsheviks. Chekist loot."

"And what was he going to do with it? Why was he carrying it with him on this voyage?"

"He had money in number accounts in Swiss banks, I am sure," said Nina. "He had money in South American banks. The jewelry— Well, I imagine he wanted to sell it in the United States and set up accounts there. Boris Vasilievich meant to survive Stalin."

"Are you sure the jewelry was from—" Mrs. Roosevelt started to ask.

"*Yes*. If you had known this man—"

"Did he kill for it?" asked Kennedy.

Nina Rozanov leaned back on the sofa. She closed the book she had been reading when Mrs. Roosevelt and Kennedy came in—John P. Marquand, *The Late George Apley*. She sighed and shook her head. "Has Stalin killed?" she asked. "Could we identify one person shot by Stalin, strangled by Stalin? Or Hitler? Who has he murdered, specifically? The Bolsheviks have killed millions. The Nazis have killed thousands. And in Stalin's rooms in the Kremlin you will find beautiful things that were owned by fine people. In Hitler's rooms? I don't know. In Boris Vasilievich's? Yes. But I can't say he ever killed anyone. In fact, I doubt he ever did. It was not his way."

"In the morning," said Mrs. Roosevelt, "I will speak very

firmly to Captain Colbert about the chains on your legs. I venture to say they will be removed."

Jack Kennedy grinned. "*I* venture to say that if Mrs. Roosevelt wants them taken off, they will *be* taken off. My father says she has ways of making her will effective."

"I shall be grateful," said Nina, looking down at her shackles. "I can't say they are painful. But . . ."

"We entirely understand," said Mrs. Roosevelt. "Entirely. It is brutal. I will do whatever I can. And, until then, good-night, Miss Rozanov. Do not despair. If you are innocent, you have nothing to fear."

5

Jack Kennedy walked with Mrs. Roosevelt to her *appartement de grand luxe* on the sun deck. They were thoughtful and silent most of the way, and when he left her he decided to walk outside in the fresh air on his way to his first-class stateroom on the upper deck.

Though the sky was overcast and the night cold, he enjoyed the walk. He was captured by a sense of the power of the great ship, carrying all these people in all their fine accommodations across the broad Atlantic. It was like a great city, never dark, never silent. He was not alone on the decks. People wandered about in the after-midnight hours, laughing, smoking, some of them conspicuously drunk. On the upper decks all the men were dressed in white tie, the women in silks. Stewards roamed the decks, pushing carts, offering hot coffee but also still serving champagne and cocktails.

In the corridor outside his stateroom he encountered a
tipsy young woman who greeted him with a great smile,
blinking and struggling to keep her balance. She invited
him to go with her to the bar for a nightcap, but he side-
stepped her with a grin and told her he would rather have
a drink with her tomorrow afternoon.

His stateroom was handsomely appointed—paneled in
oak and olive wood, with Oriental rugs laid on hardwood
floors, a marble-topped coffee table, a sofa upholstered in
leather, leather chairs as well, and a double bed now laid
back and ready for him to retire.

He searched in his luggage for a small tool, found it, and
put it in the right-hand pocket of his coat. For a moment
he considered changing out of white tie; then he decided he
would be less conspicuous walking about the ship at this
hour if he remained in evening dress.

He left his stateroom. Tourist-class cabins were only one
deck below, and he walked down the stairs and into the
corridor off which opened Nina Rozanov's cabin. At the
door, he knocked.

"Oui est là?"

"Kennedy."

"Attendez un instant."

She opened the door. Since he had been there before she
had changed into a nightgown, and he could see that she
had gone to bed. Only one light burned in the cabin—the
lamp beside her bed. She stepped aside to let him in, then
hobbled across the cabin to the bed—her ankles still
shackled—and sat down.

"I've brought you something," said Jack Kennedy.

"What?"

"This," he said, reaching into his pocket and taking out
the little tool he had brought from his stateroom. "It will
open any simple lock. A very handy thing to have if you're
a college man and—"

"I dare not," she said. "They come tomorrow, they find me without my chains, they will do something worse to me."

He smiled and shook his head. "Put them on again in the morning, before anyone comes in," he said. "Tonight . . . be comfortable. Let me show you how it works, and you can have it and use it whenever you want."

The ballerina frowned, but she lifted her legs onto the bed and presented her chained ankles to Kennedy. He pushed the little hooked tool into the keyhole of the shackle on her left ankle. For a moment he wiggled the pick inside the lock. Then it caught, he turned it, and the lock opened.

"See? A very simple lock, nothing much. You do the other one."

Nina took the pick and used it to open the other lock. She removed the leg irons and put them aside on her night table. "You are a gallant young man," she said. "You take a risk doing this."

He grinned and shrugged.

"Mr. Kennedy," she said. "You and Mrs. Roosevelt are kind people. But you cannot save me from whatever it is the French and the Soviet governments want to do to me."

"By the time we arrive in New York," he said, "they will have learned who really killed Ambassador Troyanoskii. And why. You will be free."

"This I can hope," she said solemnly. "Only hope."

"Well . . . Hope's a fine thing," he said. "It's what makes life possible."

Nina Rozanov smiled warmly at him. "Mr. Kennedy—"

She was interrupted by a rap on her cabin door.

She grabbed the pair of shackles and quickly closed them around her ankles again. "They must not find you here," she whispered. "Go in the bathroom!"

Kennedy nodded and went inside the bathroom, closing the door. He could hear what was said in Nina's cabin—

"Monsieur. . . ?"

"You don't know me. Never mind who I am. It doesn't make any difference. I've seen you before, but probably you didn't notice me. I've got to know something and know it damn quick, sister. Who killed Troyanoskii? And why?"

Kennedy kept his ear close to the bathroom door. The man's voice was American-accented. It was demanding, if not threatening.

"I don't know," said Nina fearfully. "*I* didn't."

"Yeah? Well, that makes two of us. But somebody did, for damn sure, and whoever it was messed up a good deal for both of us. I believe you, sister; I don't think you did do it; I can't think of why you would. Say, you ain't dumb, are you? You know how to appreciate a good proposition?"

"I—"

"Hey, lemme do somethin' for you, to show my good faith. Look here, I got somethin' for you. Take it, I got a spare. That'll open any handcuffs ever made. Try it, see if it won't."

"Mister—"

"Never mind the name. Listen, I got a proposition for you. The two Russian boobs. What's their names?—Ivanovsky and Gobolovsky?"

"Ignatieff and Goldinin."

"Yeah. If they got the stuff, the deal may still be good. Why not? You can talk to them. I can't. I want to watch my chance and get one of them together with you. Then you can translate for me. If things work out, you can have a piece of the dough. Okay?"

"Okay . . ." she said hesitantly.

"Good enough. And you keep that pick in your handbag or somewhere, and sometime when nobody is lookin' and nobody thinks you can do it, you get rid of the leg irons and take a powder. Hey, that's payment in advance, for helpin' me. And I'll do more for you. Like I said, a piece of the dough. Deal?"

"Uhh . . . Yes. It is a deal."

"Good. Just take it easy, be patient. We'll work somethin' out."

Kennedy heard the stateroom door bang shut. He opened the bathroom door. Nina was sitting on the bed, once more removing her leg irons, this time with the pick her visitor had given her. She smiled shyly at Kennedy, as though amused that two men had had the same idea, to give her a way to remove her shackles.

"Who was he?" Kennedy asked.

"I don't know. I never saw him before," she said.

"A member of the ship's crew, you think?"

"He was dressed as you are," she said. "In white tie. A man in his forties, I would guess."

"An American," said Kennedy.

"Yes," she said. "He speaks with a funny accent—something like yours."

"Actually," Kennedy laughed, "hardly any Americans speak as I do. Only the Boston Irish, and of those only the ones with Harvard educations."

For a second time the little dancer laid aside her ugly, heavy leg irons and sat rubbing her ankles. "I am grateful to you, Mr. Kennedy," she said.

"We have a serious problem, Miss Rozanov," he said. "I very much hope it can be resolved."

Jack Kennedy assumed Mrs. Roosevelt would be in bed by now, and asleep, so he did not return to her apartment to tell her what had happened. His judgment was wrong. The First Lady was not in bed. She was in her sitting room, awake and active.

She had received a radiogram from the President and had decrypted it herself. It read—

APPRECIATE YOUR ADVISING OF SHIPBOARD MURDER STOP SO FAR NO WORD FROM FRENCH OR SOVIET GOVERNMENTS STOP PLEASE EXERCISE UTMOST DISCRETION STOP INTERNATIONAL INCIDENT LIKELY STOP WE DO NOT WANT TO BE INVOLVED STOP PRIME MINISTER CHAMBERLAIN AND PREMIER DALADIER SURRENDERED CZECHOSLOVAKIA TO HITLER LATE TONIGHT STOP CANNOT BUT REGARD THE RESULT AS UNMITIGATED DISASTER STOP NOTE HOWEVER THAT PUBLICLY I AM COMPELLED TO COMMEND THE TWO WHO SURRENDERED AS HAVING PRESERVED THE PEACE STOP YOU MUST NOT DISCLOSE OUR TRUE FEELINGS STOP HOPE YOU ARE ENJOYING VOYAGE STOP EAT DRINK AND BE MERRY AND LET THE FRENCH AND SOVIETS SOLVE THEIR OWN MURDER MYSTERY STOP

Since Tommy was in bed, Mrs. Roosevelt drafted a "My Day" column on a notebook pad, rather than dictating it. This was one of those nights she occasionally experienced, when the excitement of the previous day's events wearied her, yet left her too tense, too full of thought, to sleep. As she wrote the column, only half her attention was focused on it. Half her thought went to the poisoning of Ambassador Troyanoskii.

She would never forget—who could?—the death throes of the Russian. The doctor had looked up from him while he was still breathing, still jerking, and said, *"L' homme est mort."* She could not help but wonder if Troyanoskii had not heard and understood those terrible words.

It was the French way. She knew the French, and she liked them. The teacher who had most influenced her when she was a girl—Mademoiselle Marie Souvestre—had of course been French. Yet, there was about them a certain heartless practicality, in their system of law, in their social relationships, and apparently in their medicine. Would an American doctor, an English doctor, look up from a patient who could perhaps still hear and understand and say—"This man is dead?"

By the same token—and this troubled her deeply—the little ballerina lay in her bed tonight in shackles. It didn't bother Agent Ouzoulias, and probably not Captain Colbert—it was simply the practical thing to do. That was characteristic of the French, as she knew them—to proclaim, with total sincerity, their devotion to the rights of man and yet to imprison people for a year before trial, or to fasten leg irons around the ankles of a beautiful little girl who was only suspected of a crime that was far from proved.

Well, it could be worse. Nina Rozanov would receive better, fairer treatment at the hands of the French than she would if she were in the custody of the Germans or, heaven forbid, the Russians.

Could it be that Troyanoskii was a Chekist. . . ?

Someone was at the door. *At three A.M.?* She opened the door.

Agent Ouzoulias stood in the passageway. "Seeing that you remain awake, Madame . . . May I come in?"

"Of course. I was about to order a pot of coffee. Would you care for some?"

"I should be honored to have coffee with you, Madame," he said. "And you will forgive me perhaps if I help myself to a bit of this excellent cognac?"

"Certainly. Do pour for yourself, and feel free to replenish your glass whenever you wish."

"Thank you."

Ouzoulias poured himself a generous amount of the brandy, held the glass in his right hand, and fumbled in his pocket with his left. He pulled out his pipe, which again was still burning. He remained standing, savoring the smoke from his pipe and brandy from his snifter, alternating.

He was not what she would have expected in a French detective. His sallow cheeks collapsed inward as he sucked on his pipe. His hands were long and thin, and his fingers were nervous, ever in motion. His lips curled almost erotically around the stem of his pipe and in turn around the rim of the brandy snifter. His eyes were unmemorable, calm and uncommunicative, as if he practiced to hide his thoughts and feelings.

"Was Mademoiselle Rozanov comfortable?" he asked blandly.

"Well, hardly," said Mrs. Roosevelt indignantly. "She—"

And someone else rapped on the door. Josephine Baker was there, wearing the silly, faintly apologetic grin that was a recognized element of her personality.

"Saw your lights on." La Baker was a wee bit tipsy. "Uh . . ."

"Come in, Miss Baker. Monsieur Ouzoulias is here, too."

"I know. I saw him coming along. That's how I knew you were still up. He and I have met. He asks tough questions!"

"I must ask the question of everyone present when the ambassador drank poison," said Ouzoulias.

"I was about to call the steward and order a pot of coffee," said Mrs. Roosevelt. "Would you join us in some?"

"Sure. Glad to." Josephine Baker headed straight for the bar table and poured herself half a snifter of brandy. "Wanta know why I left the States?" she asked. "Wasn't 'cause they called me 'Nigger.' Not really. It was 'cause you couldn't get a *drink*."

"If you had lived in the States through Prohibition," said

Mrs. Roosevelt, "you would know anyone could get a drink who really wanted it."

Baker nodded. "Yeah . . . No, really it was because— What would I be if I hadn't left America? I'm a *refugee*."

Mrs. Roosevelt had picked up the telephone and was ordering the coffee—with a small platter of pastries. She nodded at Josephine Baker. "I understand," she said.

"Yes, I think you do—as well as anybody could who never experienced . . . Say! I really think you do."

"A lot of Negro people have achieved immense success in the United States," said Mrs. Roosevelt.

"Sure . . . Entertainment. You ever hear what the woman did to my hands?"

Mrs. Roosevelt shook her head. "No, I guess not."

Josephine Baker nodded. "St. Louis. I was—what?— twelve years old? My momma got me a job in a white lady's house—doing cleaning, you know. Hard work. Not much money. But it was a *job*. This was . . . 1918, I think it was. I did somethin' dumb. Broke some dishes. The lady grabbed me by the arms and shoved my hands down in a pot of boiling water." She nodded sadly. "In boiling water . . ."

"Oh, dear!" gasped Mrs. Roosevelt.

"The doctor called the cops," said Josephine Baker. "The lady was fined fifty dollars."

Mrs. Roosevelt shook her head.

"Well . . ." mused Josephine Baker. A playful little smile returned to her face. "Long time ago. And since then, I—"

"You've become about as big a star as France has ever had," said Mrs. Roosevelt.

"This is true," said Ouzoulias. "You are a beloved figure."

Baker shrugged. "Not big in America, though. I came

home, you know, and tried to do the Ziegfeld Follies. Flopped. Americans don't like me."

"Well, don't quote the wife of the President of the United States as saying this, but America isn't everything. You're a beloved figure in France. Anyone is lucky who has a nation that loves her."

"Thanks. I . . . I didn't stop by just for a drink. When I saw Monsieur Ouzoulias at your door, I decided to come and see if you would be interested in something I know about Troyanoskii."

"We are indeed interested," said Mrs. Roosevelt.

"Okay. You know, in Paris all kinds of men chase after me. All kinds. Businessmen. Artists. Politicians." She paused and grinned. "Kings, princes, and dukes—or men that *say* they're kings, princes, or dukes. Anyway, all kinds. And they talk to me, tell me things. Troyanoskii came to my show several times. He sent flowers back. Champagne. He wanted me to meet him for a late supper at some club. Uh . . . We both know what he had in mind. Anyway, I wouldn't go out with him, not alone. But when he asked me one night to join his table at Maxim's, with him and others, I did. I got to know him. He got to know me well enough to understand he wasn't going to get anywhere with me. That annoyed him, pricked his ego. Before we wound up at the captain's table this evening, I hadn't seen him for about a year." She laughed. "I bet he liked seeing *me* there!"

Josephine Baker rose and poured herself another splash of brandy. It was a measured amount, just a little.

"He was quite the playboy in Paris," she said. "Made a strange man for the Russian government to be sending to the States as an ambassador, don't you think?"

"It occurred to me," said Mrs. Roosevelt.

"I don't think he's been in Russia in five years," Baker

went on. "He had some kind of official position in Paris, though. They say he was a Chekist, secret police. I bet he was."

"Do you have any evidence of that?"

Baker shook her head. "No. I will tell you something, though. I know a man in Paris who calls himself the Count Sergei Ilyich Something-or-Other. Wispy little old man with a very funny accent and a very big ego. Claims he was a big shot under the Czar. Anyway . . . He wanted an emerald. Now, that's not so odd, is it? *I* want an emerald, don't you? He wanted a *certain* emerald, claimed it had been in his family since the time of Christ or some such time. He asked Troyanoskii to help him get it. And Troyanoskii got it for him. It wasn't a matter of money. It was a matter of prying it loose from somewhere. And Troyanoskii did it."

"The man you refer to is Sergei Kandinsky," said Ouzoulias. "He is not a count. He is a fraud. If he wanted the emerald, he wanted it as evidence to try to prove his claim to nobility—either that or he bought it from Troyanoskii and sold it for a profit. But are you sure he bought it through Troyanoskii?"

Baker shrugged. "All I know is what he told me."

"He also told you he is a count," said Ouzoulias dryly.

Baker shrugged and insisted, "All I know is what he told me."

"Do you know anything of Miss Rozanov?" Ouzoulias asked Baker.

She shook her head, then grinned. "The only Russians *I* know are the *rich* Russians," she said.

"There seem to be jewels everywhere in this mystery," said Mrs. Roosevelt.

"*Les bijoux*," laughed Josephine Baker. "Everyone loves them. I have been known to appear on stage wearing jewels and nothing but jewels."

"Surely a few feathers," said Mrs. Roosevelt with a smile.

Baker shrugged, still laughing. "Well . . . Usually."

A steward arrived with a small cart bearing a silver pot of coffee, cups and saucers, cream and sugar, silver spoons and forks, plates, and a platter of warm pastries.

"Sea voyages are good for the appetite," said Mrs. Roosevelt as she poured coffee for the three of them. "Tell me, Monsieur Ouzoulias, how long have you been chief security officer on the *Normandie*?"

"Since the maiden voyage," said Ouzoulias as he accepted his cup of coffee. "Before that, five years aboard *Ile de France*. Before that, I was a detective with the Paris police. We keep very close relationship with *Sûreté,* as you may imagine."

"So you know who everyone is who comes aboard?"

"Well . . . Not everyone. But we do try to protect our passengers from criminals and parasites."

"Gamblers . . ." said Mrs. Roosevelt.

Ouzoulias nodded. "Jewel thiefs."

"Naked dancers?" asked Josephine Baker playfully.

"Mais non, Mademoiselle," Ouzoulias chuckled.

"I believe you mentioned prostitutes earlier," said Mrs. Roosevelt as she sipped coffee.

Ouzoulias tipped his head and regarded her quizzically—a rare display of reaction to anything said to him. "If . . . if, Madame," he said hesitantly, cautiously, "you are concerned about the young woman from New York who visited you this afternoon, you need not be. We know who she is and why she is aboard. She travels on our ships from time to time, though this is her first voyage aboard *Normandie*. She creates no problems and is welcome."

"Her, uh, *companion* brought her aboard, I believe," said Mrs. Roosevelt.

"Yes. This time," said Ouzoulias gravely. "It is not usually so. But she is a young woman of discretion, and we permit her to travel on our ships—even knowing what she is."

"What do you know about her companion?" asked Mrs. Roosevelt.

"Herr Ernst Richter Remer," said Ouzoulias. "He is new to us. A German businessman, a dealer in wines and spirits. He was in Paris for about two months before this voyage. He placed orders for a considerable quantity of *le beaujolais nouveau,* to be delivered in New York when it is ready to travel."

"I suppose," said Mrs. Roosevelt, "it would be impossible even to identify everyone who was in Ambassador Troyanoskii's apartment last night, much less to find an explanation for each person's presence. I had understood, though, that all of us were there by invitation; and I would be curious to know why Herr Remer was invited. Do you have any explanation?"

"None," sighed Ouzoulias. "I have been in radio contact with Paris several times during the night. This is a question I asked, too. We have no record of any prior contact between Troyanoskii and Remer."

"Between Ambassador Troyanoskii and Moira Lasky?"

"No."

"Have you learned anything further about Goldinin and Ignatieff?"

Ouzoulias shook his head. "Vladimir Goldinin and Grigorii Ignatieff joined Troyanoskii's staff in Paris only a few months ago—for what purpose we have no idea. They do not have diplomatic passports. It is of course difficult to talk to them. They are, I think, a pair of very frightened men—though they may be frightened because they were supposed to be Troyanoskii's bodyguards and let him get killed. It could be they are afraid to return to Russia."

"It could be, it could be," laughed Josephine Baker gaily. "Speculation, Monsieur."

"Yes," Ouzoulias admitted. "We know nothing about those two."

"A person who could translate their Russian into French or English lies in leg irons in a cabin below," said Mrs. Roosevelt.

"Ah . . . Mademoiselle Rozanov. You saw for yourself, she is in no great discomfort."

"I disagree with you about that, Monsieur Ouzoulias. I—"

"You've got someone in *chains*?" asked Baker.

"Mademoiselle Rozanov, the little ballerina," said Mrs. Roosevelt indignantly. "She is suspected of . . ." She sighed angrily. "Of *theft*."

Josephine Baker frowned at Ouzoulias. "Shame . . ." she muttered.

"I want you to take the shackles off that poor child's legs, Monsieur Ouzoulias," said Mrs. Roosevelt firmly. "I realize it is a . . . French custom and—"

"But they are nothing, those little—"

"I don't believe you'd think them nothing if they were locked on *you*, Monsieur."

"But what if she elects to wander away? There are more than three thousand people aboard this ship, passengers and crew. She could hide. If she has accomplices— And what if she becomes despondent and wishes to throw herself overboard?"

"I have four bedrooms in this apartment," said Mrs. Roosevelt. "We are using two. I want you to bring her here in the morning. I will accept responsibility for her."

"Will you assure me that either you or Miss Thompson

will be with her at all times—except times when she is locked inside your stateroom?"

"I so assure you, Monsieur Ouzoulias."

"Very well, Madame. In the morning, then, it will be as you wish. I hope she does not give you cause to regret your trust."

6

Although breakfast was served by stewards to the passengers in all the first-class staterooms, Henry Luce invited Mrs. Roosevelt to join him for breakfast in the Grill Room at nine. He telephoned at eight. She was not anxious to see him, but she could not decline without being ungracious, so she consented. At nine she sat down opposite him at a small table by a big window, with a view of the ship's wake and a gray sea and sky. Most people in the room were selecting their own breakfasts from a buffet, but Luce sent a steward to bring food.

"The European powers settled the Czech problem last night," said Luce when the steward had hurried away. "A surrender, I guess you'd have to call it."

Mrs. Roosevelt was careful to show no reaction. She did not mention the President's radiogram, which had informed her of what had happened.

"It's all very well, all very easy, for some people—like some professional liberals in America—to scream for war; they don't have to fight it. The British and French would have had to fight it, and the Czechs, and it took a lot of courage for Chamberlain and Daladier to swallow what they had to swallow to avoid war. Churchill is furious, of course. He was hooted down on the floor of the House of Commons this morning. He's another one; I mean another irresponsible critic. Little old fat politician, he wouldn't have to fight, or bear the responsibility."

"He represents a point of view," said Mrs. Roosevelt noncommittally.

"We'll use Chamberlain for the *Time* cover subject next week," said Luce. "He's the man of the hour."

"Here's Colonel Lindbergh," said Mrs. Roosevelt, looking up and greeting with a smile the tall, boyish man approaching their table with a plate of fruit. "Would you care to join us, Colonel?" she asked.

"Honored," he said.

He sat down. Luce poured him a cup of coffee.

"I've been listening to the radio in my stateroom," said Lindbergh. "I'm grateful to hear that good sense prevailed at Munich."

"We were just talking about it," said Mrs. Roosevelt.

"It's a frightful government that they've set up in Germany," said Lindbergh. "A menace to humanity, really. But the men in charge of it are young and decisive, and they understand the relationship between technology and power as no other government in the world does."

"You said last night you are convinced the Germans would have won, should war have broken out," said Mrs. Roosevelt.

"Yes," said Lindbergh. "I have no doubt of it. They *showed* me their bombers! No one believes how many they have. Hundreds of them. Twin-engine bombers, capable of carrying bombs to any city in Europe, including London. Dive bombers. Fighters. The British used to insist on maintaining a navy more powerful than the navies any *two* nations could bring against it. Well, that's what the Luftwaffe is—more powerful than any other *two* air forces."

"The Czechs would have fought for their country," said Luce. "That is, they would have if Britain and France had backed them. But the British and French—"

"Would have lost," said Lindbergh.

"I hear you had a most unhappy experience last night," said Luce to Mrs. Roosevelt.

"Yes, most distressing," she said.

"I'm afraid I don't know what you're talking about," said Lindbergh.

"Ambassador Troyanoskii was murdered last night," said Luce. "During the party he invited us all to attend. Poisoned. In the presence of his guests."

Lindbergh frowned but obviously was not disturbed, except as one would be to learn that a man who sat opposite him at last evening's dinner had been murdered—and that aboard a great liner on which he expected to have a luxurious, relaxing passage. The matter simply was not personally distressing to him.

Nor was it, much, to Henry Luce. He was not deficient in humanity, any more than Lindbergh was; but the life of Boris Troyanoskii was not of personal interest to him.

Luce was forty years old that year. He aspired to an iron-man look, and—depending on one's attitude toward him, or position relative to him—one found his immense bushy eyebrows formidable or ludicrous. Afflicted young by male-pattern baldness, he took his bullet head as something of an asset to his image. He was a chain smoker. He favored double-breasted suits of heavy tweed, with vests; and this morning was wearing one.

"Clare's new play opened Wednesday, you know," he said. "You wouldn't believe this, but she wrote it in a month. I sent her on home to be there for the opening. Should have been there myself. I'd sort of planned to go to Munich, but then I thought— What happens to *me* if the whole world blows up and I'm in Munich, of all places? Better to be at home. I was lucky to get passage on the *Normandie*. Beautiful ship, isn't it?"

Mrs. Roosevelt nodded, but she turned the conversation toward a subject more interesting to her. "Tell me, Mr. Luce, as a publisher and journalist, do you have any information about Ambassador Troyanoskii?"

Luce shook his head. "Never heard of him before he was introduced to me at the captain's table last night. I can send a radiogram to New York to see what the bureaus know."

"That would be very kind of you," she said.

"May I ask what your interest is?"

She shrugged. "Oh, I have a certain curiosity about things like this," she said.

"Yes. Now that I recall, you were reported as having made a major contribution to the solution of the mystery surrounding the death of Congressman Winstead Colmer, back in 1935. Right?"

"Well," she said, "since the murder occurred in the Oval Office itself, I could hardly help but be interested."

"Solution of mysteries. An unsuspected Eleanor Roosevelt talent," he laughed. "I'll get whatever information I can for you."

She smiled happily at him. "I'll be delighted," she said.

Jack Kennedy had thought he would wait for Mrs. Roosevelt on the private promenade that went with her *appartement de grand luxe*. He discovered not only that wind whipped unmercifully across the unsheltered decks of a ship moving at more than thirty knots but that oily soot from her stacks settled on the promenade. He knocked on the door, was admitted by Tommy Thompson, and found Nina Rozanov at the piano in the sitting room.

"Monsieur Ouzoulias brought me here," she explained. "No chains, you see. The very kind Mrs. Roosevelt has invited me to finish the voyage as her guest in this suite. She has four bedrooms. I am to occupy one."

Nina's toes barely reached the pedals of the piano, but she played competently—to Jack's ear—something soft and rhythmic and unfamiliar to him.

She was wearing a stylish dark-gray dress, cinched at the waist with a broad red leather belt. She had applied red lipstick, a light rouge, and even, he suspected, a bit of eye shadow and mascara. It was difficult to identify her with the pitiful girl who had sat in leg irons in her cabin last night.

For himself, he was conscious of what he had chosen to wear for this day at sea—a light gray pinstriped double-breasted flannel suit, and he had carried into the suite the gray tweed cap he had worn on deck.

"We are going to see some weather, I'm afraid," he said.

Nina glanced through the broad windows of the sitting room. The Atlantic had developed heavy seas during the night. *Normandie* was a great ship, but she rolled just the same. On his way here from his stateroom, Kennedy had noticed a few people who were suffering from *mal de mer*.

He had winced when Tommy Thompson told him Mrs. Roosevelt was having breakfast with Henry Luce. Jack had watched his father smoke cigars and drink with Luce, and entertain him with rough, profane talk. His father wanted Luce on his side and thought he knew how to get him. Joseph Kennedy judged Henry Luce a small man who could easily be won over by flattery and "manly" talk.

Jack thought it would be wrong to underestimate either the man's power or his deviousness. In his judgment, Luce and his magazines were dishonest and unfair and Luce abused his power and was potentially a menace to every man in public life, no matter what political stripe.

Nina stopped playing and sat with her hands on the keys. "Have you told Mrs. Roosevelt about the man who came to my cabin last night?" she asked.

Jack shook his head. "I haven't seen her since then," he said.

"Have you told Monsieur Ouzoulias?" she asked.

"I haven't see him either."

"Shall we tell him? He is returning."

"I think it's best to cooperate. I see nothing wrong with Ouzoulias."

"Then it is best *I* tell him," she said. "Not you. Let us withhold the information that you were listening from my bathroom."

Jack grinned. "I'm for that," he said. "For whatever reason."

She began to play again—once more a captivating little melody he did not recognize.

Jack poured coffee for them, from the pot standing on a side table in the sitting room. Shortly Agent Ouzoulias arrived.

"Madame has breakfast with Monsieur Luce," he said. "She will join us before long, I think. Tell me, Mr. Kennedy, what you think of the settlement arrived at overnight at Munich."

"We may pay a great price for the peace we have achieved," said Jack.

"Ah. That is also my thought," said Ouzoulias.

"Monsieur . . ." said Nina to the detective. "I have something I wish to tell you."

"I am very much interested, I am sure, in anything you wish to tell me," said Ouzoulias. "As soon as I pour myself a cup of coffee."

Jack Kennedy was a little amused with the Frenchman's suit. He had observed before that bourgeois Frenchmen tended to wear styles ten years out of date in Britain and America. Ouzoulias's dark-blue suit was woven in a diamond pattern. It was single-breasted in what had once been called the "cloverleaf" style—three-button, with rounded little lapels that ended at the top button, only an inch or so below the level of the breast pocket.

"So, Mademoiselle . . ." said Ouzoulias as he sat down.

Nina remained seated at the piano. "A man came to my cabin last night," she said. "He asked me to translate for him—into English—the Russian of Ignatieff and Goldinin. He thinks they may have something he wants, something Boris Vasilievich was carrying. He spoke of the death of Boris Vasilievich as ruining some business proposition."

"How did you respond to his request that you translate for him?"

"I said I would do it. After all, Monsieur, when he came to me I was in chains. He said he could help me escape."

"Ah. And why do you tell me now?"

"I have decided," said Nina calmly, "that I would do better to extend you my cooperation and to accept the assistance of Mrs. Roosevelt—better, that is, than to defy you and rely on this man's promises."

"Who *was* the man?" asked Ouzoulias.

She shook her head. "I don't know. I would tell you if I did."

"Uh, she explained to *me*," said Jack, "that the man was, uh, previously unknown to her."

"You will know this man if you see him again?"

Nina nodded.

"Of course, there are almost two thousand passengers aboard, and more than a thousand crew," said Ouzoulias. "How likely is it you will see him? If you are confined to this apartment, or to your cabin, you are unlikely to—unless he comes to see you. Perhaps we can encourage him to come looking for you."

"I will know him if I see him, Monsieur," said Nina quietly but firmly.

"Hmm-mm," grunted Ouzoulias, clearing his throat. "Now, Mademoiselle, you said last night your family were of aristocratic origin and were murdered by the Bolsheviks."

"That is true," she said. "We were of St. Petersburg—"

"Leningrad."

"*St. Petersburg*, Monsieur. And the barbarians from Moscow came to destroy us. Bolsheviks. Murderers. Rapists. Looters."

"You were . . . two years old?"

"When my parents were taken—never to be seen again—I was four years old. In 1919."

"And the necklace—which, incidentally, I will return to you—was your mother's," said Ouzoulias. "Have you seen the jewels Ambassador Troyanoskii was carrying?"

She nodded. "I have seen them."

"Their origin, Mademoiselle, in your judgment?"

"Loot, Monsieur," she said simply.

"Yes," said Ouzoulias. "I think so, too. But to return to your family . . . I believe you said the Ambassador was a friend of the family. Yet, he was a Bolshevik. Is there an inconsistency here?"

Nina shrugged. "He was not a Bolshevik until the Bolsheviks came to power, as I explained last night."

"Your father was Count Nicholas Alexandrovich

Rozanov," said Ouzoulias. He smiled. "You will forgive me; I have made some inquiries by radio overnight. Your uncle is Count Mikhail Alexandrovich Rozanov. Both of them were generals in the Czar's army. Your father was executed because he became a general in the White army and was captured eventually by the Red army. Your mother was killed for the same reason, and you would have been if the Bolsheviks had caught you. You are yourself, incidentally, *Countess* Nina Nikolaievna Rozanov."

"Yes," she said. Her chin rose, and her face hardened with indignation and pride. "In a world with justice, I am Countess Nina Nikolaievna Rozanov."

"You told us your uncle is a ballet master," said Ouzoulias.

"And so he is," she said. A faint sneer curled her lips slightly. "He is far more competent a ballet master than he ever was a general. But—" She shrugged. "Under the old system, a count was expected to . . ." She shrugged again.

"Your uncle Mikhail did not join your father with the White army," said Ouzoulias. "Instead—"

"Instead, he went into hiding," said Nina. "And thank God he did, too—else I would be dead."

"He took you with him?"

"Yes."

"Your mother—"

"Was happy to have me removed from St. Petersburg."

"Well . . . We—"

He stopped because Mrs. Roosevelt had just entered the suite. Jack and the detective stood. She made a small gesture to ask them to sit down again.

"Oh. Miss Rozanov. I am glad to see you here. And sitting at the piano. Do you play?"

"She plays beautifully," said Jack.

"I shall want to hear you play," said Mrs. Roosevelt to Nina. Then she looked at Ouzoulias. "The ship has begun to roll," she said.

"We offer medicine for the *mal de mer,* if you need it," said Ouzoulias.

"In fact, I don't," she said. "I made my first Atlantic crossing thirty-nine years ago, when I was but fifteen years old; and because my aunt, who was taking me to England to enroll me in school, kept to her bed the entire crossing, I supposed I was obliged to do something similar. Two years later, traveling without her, I experienced a rough crossing and found that I rather enjoyed walking on the deck when the ship was rolling and pitching. I've never really suffered seasickness. But there are those aboard who do."

"You have arrived at an interesting point in the conversation we are having with Mademoiselle Rozanov," said Ouzoulias. "I was about to ask her how she explains the jewelry we found in her cabin."

"Everything you found," said Nina, "is mine. And I *demand* its return."

"Ah, so. You demand. But from where did you obtain it?"

"Boris Vasilievich," she said, "identified certain items as rightfully mine. He gave them to me."

"Rightfully. . . ?"

"They were my family's," she said.

"And how did they come into his hands, dear?" asked Mrs. Roosevelt.

"The Bolsheviks . . ." Nina said quietly, "murdered thousands of people . . . of *my* class. Millions of others. Millions of peasants. And all they owned . . . became their loot. In France, England, the United States . . . thousands of fools *glamorize* those murderers—accept their treacherous philosophy as a legitimate way of analyzing the world." She sneered, shook her head. "*Stalin. Lenin.* You want to choose between them and Hitler? Choose Hitler. Any time!"

"But how did Ambassador Troyanoskii get your family's jewels?" Mrs. Roosevelt persisted.

"My family was murdered," said Nina. "Everything we owned became theirs, their loot. What other explanation is needed?"

"But those jewels that were found in your cabin. . . ?"

"Boris Vasilievich let me search through his loot and helped me to identify what was mine," said Nina. "Need I explain how I motivated him to do that?"

"Or, of course, you stole these things and killed him when he discovered what you had done," said Ouzoulias.

"Hardly necessary, Monsieur," she said.

"It does not look good for you, Mademoiselle, that the Ambassador is dead and that we find jewels from his apartment in your luggage," said Ouzoulias.

Nina Rozanov struck a defiant chord on the piano. "So," she said. "*Prove* I killed him. Where did *I* get the strychnine? I believe you can't buy it just anywhere. *Prove* I put it in his vodka. I understand you have had little success proving how it got there. *Prove* your case against me, Monsieur. If you can."

Interrogation of Ignatieff and Goldinin, with Nina acting as translator, was of little value. Both insisted they were only employees of the Ambassador, who knew nothing of the jewels he had been carrying and had no idea why anyone would want to kill him.

Vladimir Goldinin was a thickset Russian, apparently of peasant stock, with half a dozen stainless-steel teeth. He wore an ill-fitting shiny black suit. He said he had been sent from Moscow to join the Ambassador's staff and travel with him to the United States. No, he did not speak English, any more than he spoke French.

Grigorii Ignatieff was younger, an oddly jaunty fellow who might have been judged to be relieved by the death of Troyanoskii—as if it freed him of a burden. He and Goldinin, he said, would return to Europe by the first available ship. They had no reason to stay in America, now that the Ambassador was dead. Did he speak any language but Russian? No. Why had his government sent with the Ambassador two assistants who spoke no English? Ignatieff smiled and shrugged.

"Odd that he should leave his shirt cuff unbuttoned," said Jack Kennedy to Mrs. Roosevelt.

Ignatieff's left hand went instantly to his left cuff. He caught himself, and his eyes flashed angrily at Kennedy— for a moment. Then he smiled grudgingly. "Very clever, Mr. Kennedy," he said.

7

"You told me," said Nina to Ouzoulias, "that you would return my mother's diamond necklace. I would be grateful if you would do it now, Monsieur."

"Of course," said Ouzoulias smoothly. "There is no reason why I should not. It is in the . . . How do you say in English? In *la caisse*."

"In the safe," said Mrs. Roosevelt with a little smile.

"Yes. In the office of the purser." (He pronounced the word "poor-SAIR.")

"Can we go and get it?" asked Nina.

"Yes. Right now, if you wish," said Ouzoulias

"I would like to accompany you, if you don't mind," said Mrs. Roosevelt. "I would like to see these jewels."

"So would I, if it's all right," said Jack Kennedy.

"Very well," said Ouzoulias. "Let us walk inside, so as to avoid the weather."

*   *   *

The ship's safe, in the purser's office, was a small bank vault. It was not located in the purser's outer office, where he received passengers and transacted their business, but in a more spartan rear room where half a dozen clerks labored over the ship's accounts. The safe was at the back, behind the six desks. When the purser led Agent Ouzoulias and his party into this workroom, the door to the vault stood open.

"It is kept open during working hours," Jean Picard, the purser, explained. "We have frequent occasion to enter it. The purser's office is never closed, of course, but the workroom is closed at night, and then the vault is closed."

"The jewels are in those," said Ouzoulias, pointing at two square steel boxes sitting on the floor of the vault.

The vault was not large enough for Ouzoulias, Mrs. Roosevelt, Nina, and Jack to enter at the same time, so Ouzoulias stepped inside with the purser to retrieve the two strongboxes. One of the clerks cleared his desk and stepped aside, to make room for the boxes to be opened.

"Ah!" cried Ouzoulias as he lifted one of the boxes. His face reddened, and he rushed out of the vault, dropping the box on the desk. He snatched a key from his jacket pocket and thrust it into the padlock. He threw back the lid. *"Vide!"* The box was empty.

"Also this one," said the purser somberly. He could tell by the weight, as Ouzoulias had when he lifted the first box.

They unlocked and opened the second box. It, too, was completely empty.

Jean Picard rushed into his vault. With a key from his vest pocket he opened a drawer, then another, then another. Mrs. Roosevelt could see that the drawers were filled with cash—French francs, English pounds, American dollars, German marks, scores of thousands of each. He seemed relieved to find the drawers still full of money. He did not begin to count. With his hands he began to feel the doors of safety-deposit boxes that lined one wall of the vault. He could not open them; the passengers who used them had the second key to each; but he ran his fingers over their doors, as if somehow he could sense whether or not any of them had been opened. He was shaken.

One of the clerks examined the door of the vault. He spoke to Picard in quiet, rapid French.

"How could this happen?" the shaken purser asked Ouzoulias. "It is a . . . sophisticated lock."

Edouard Ouzoulias was as shaken as Jean Picard—betraying the first real emotion Mrs. Roosevelt had seen him show. He ran his hands around the insides of his two steel boxes, as though he could not believe his eyes and would somehow discover the missing jewels if he felt for them.

"Now we know," said Mrs. Roosevelt, "why Ambassador Troyanoskii was murdered. We know for certain."

Ouzoulias nodded.

"We may perhaps even assume," she said, "that the murderer knew that jewels would be removed to this vault—having ascertained in advance that he could open it."

Ouzoulias stared at the door of the vault, almost scornful of it, as if it had betrayed him. "It is not uncommon, this kind of vault," he said. "Manufactured in America, actually. Someone could . . . learn the means of opening it."

"Practice on it, even," said Jack Kennedy.

"Yes," admitted Ouzoulias. "No lock is absolutely safe against the most skilled and practiced of burglars."

"Then you are saying we have on board *Normandie* a skilled and practiced burglar," said Jean Picard. "If so, nothing is safe, not any passenger's stateroom. It is essential that you identify this man, Edouard. We must notify the captain."

"Yes . . ." Ouzoulias agreed. He glanced at Mrs. Roosevelt, Nina, and Jack. "It is important, too, that word of what has happened not be circulated through the ship. Will you—"

"I am sure we will cooperate," said Mrs. Roosevelt.

Nina and Jack nodded emphatically.

"One thing is rather obvious," said Mrs. Roosevelt.

"You have in mind?"

Mrs. Roosevelt smiled at Nina. "Well, obviously Miss Rozanov did not open the vault last night. She was in her cabin with her legs chained together."

Mrs. Roosevelt did not see the meaningful glances exchanged between Nina and Jack.

Ouzoulias nodded. "I suppose so," he conceded.

"She is, then, no longer a suspect?" asked Mrs. Roosevelt. "Is she free of the necessity of being confined to my suite?"

"Yes. You may consider yourself free of criminal charges, Miss Rozanov," said Ouzoulias.

"Even so, I hope you will continue as my guest in my suite," said Mrs. Roosevelt. "It is a bit more comfortable than your cabin, isn't it?"

"You are most kind," said Nina.

For two or three minutes they all stood, staring into the empty boxes, Ouzoulias remembering and the others imagining the rich fortune in jewels and precious metals the boxes had contained.

They were interrupted. *"Ah, Monsieur . . . Monsieur . . ."* murmured one of the clerks. *"Un passagèr."*

Picard went to his outer office and in a brief moment returned. "A passenger wants to enter his box. I tremble! If—"

A man, wearing a crisp little smile, came into the work-room. It was Ernst Richter Remer, the German wine broker who was Moira Lasky's companion on this voyage. He was dressed in sea-voyaging clothes—heavy gray tweeds, complete with tweed cap—and when he spotted Mrs. Roosevelt and the others, he smiled and bowed.

"Ah, Mrs. Roosevelt," he said. "An honor repeated. Very good to see you, Ma'am." He nodded at the others and followed Picard into the vault.

They tried not to watch too conspicuously, but they did watch, with concentration. Picard used his key, then Remer used his, and in a moment Remer was in his box, while the purser looked discreetly away. After a long moment, Remer closed his box and the door and turned his key.

"Guten Morgen," he said with another warm smile as he left the workroom.

Picard emerged from the vault, his face fallen. "What a relief!" he whispered hoarsely. "At least that box was not opened last night. At least one . . ."

Mrs. Roosevelt was sympathetic. "Perhaps all," she said.

They met Captain Colbert in his quarters just aft of the bridge. Since both Mrs. Roosevelt and Jack Kennedy expressed interest in the bridge, the Captain led them out into the functional room from which *Normandie* was controlled.

A young, blue-uniformed sailor with his cap set well forward on his head stood at the wheel. He was the helmsman, controlling the rudder by turning the wheel. Immediately in front of him a big compass floated in its gimbals. An indicator showed him the position of the ship's immense rudder. His magnetic course and the magnetic deviation were scrawled on a chalkboard.

Captain Colbert explained—"Magnetic north and true north are not the same. What is more, they vary as we cross the Atlantic. Here, magnetic declination, as it is called, is about eleven degrees west. By the time we are approaching New York, it will be sixteen degrees." He smiled. "If we followed the compass and did not adjust, we would miss New York by several hundred miles."

The ship was plunging through seas that struck at an angle and tended to throw it off course. The helmsman made constant adjustments.

Engine telegraphs stood ready to signal the engine room—one for each of the ship's huge propellers. All were set on Full Ahead. Clocks indicated Paris time and ship-board time. A wind indicator showed the velocity and direction of the wind. A barometer indicated air pressure.

The bridge officer stood at a window, his hands clasped behind him, staring out at the gray and rolling Atlantic. Another officer sat at a chart table, using plotting tools and a slide rule to calculate the ship's position and to make adjustments in its estimated time of arrival in New York.

"It is essential that we know our exact position at all times," said Captain Colbert. "If—which God forbid—we should experience an emergency, we could radio exactly where we are. Also, of course, other ships need to know where we are, since we are coming through the sea lane very fast, compared to them."

"How far from us is the nearest ship?" asked Jack.

Captain Colbert stepped to the chart table and glanced at the marks on the chart. "About twelve kilometers," he said. "We are overtaking a Dutch motor ship and will pass about two kilometers to the south of him. He knows we are coming. We are talking with him."

"What weather is ahead?" asked Jack.

"Worse," said the captain. "Then clearing tomorrow."

They stood at the windows and for a long moment stared out thoughtfully at the seas rising around the *Normandie*. It seemed inconceivable, but they knew it was true, that in a storm waves could roll high enough to crash across the upper decks even of a vessel as large as this one. The wind was tearing spray off the crests of waves, which was a bad sign.

"I have ordered two armed guards to remain at the door of the vault," said Ouzoulias to Captain Colbert.

"Yes. Picard told me."

"Somewhere aboard, someone has in his possession ten fortunes in jewels," said Ouzoulias.

"Including mine," said Nina bitterly.

"Experience tells us," said Captain Colbert, "that if we dock in New York without recovering the jewels, they will be carried ashore, will not be discovered by customs, and will disappear forever. Whoever was clever enough to open the safe is clever enough to have discovered a way to smuggle them ashore."

"I fear so. It has happened before," said Ouzoulias. "Never before in so large an amount, actually."

Captain Colbert was distracted from the conversation by the impact of *Normandie* against a mountainous sea that crashed against the forward starboard quarter. The ship shuddered.

He glanced at Mrs. Roosevelt and Jack Kennedy, his eyes glittering. "No danger," he said. "But such a discomfort! God from time to time reminds us that we are a ship at sea."

Mrs. Roosevelt, Ouzoulias, Kennedy, and Nina Rozanov descended into the ship's winter garden, which was located just below the bridge. There they sat down on wicker chairs, in the midst of a veritable forest of lush greenery and flowers. The fountains had been turned off and drained because of the rolling of the ship, but the birds still fluttered in the aviaries, chirping, oblivious to the rolling. Attentive stewards offered bouillon, which only Jack and Nina accepted. Ouzoulias ordered a glass of red wine.

The Captain had changed course, turning *Normandie* into the seas, so that they struck the sharp bow head-on instead of slamming against the sides. The rolling gradually subsided, replaced by bow-to-stern pitching. Heavy sheets of water poured over the forward decks and splashed against the windows of the winter garden.

"The essential now," said Ouzoulias to Nina, "is to find the man who came to your cabin last night."

"A man who. . . ?" asked Mrs. Roosevelt. She had not been told of the visits to Nina's tourist-class cabin, either that by Kennedy or that by the mysterious stranger. Nina explained about the stranger, omitting once more to mention Jack.

"Possibly the murderer . . ." breathed Mrs. Roosevelt.

"Let us not omit from consideration," said Ouzoulias, "the possibility that we are talking about three people— the person who has poisoned the Ambassador, the person who broke into the purser's safe, and the man who visited Mademoiselle Rozanov's cabin. It was no great secret, apparently, that Ambassador Troyanoskii was carrying all these marvelous jewels with him. It is possible that half the passengers on this ship were interested in them."

"Plus the crew," remarked Jack Kennedy dryly.

"Oh no, Monsieur," Ouzoulias protested. "All the crew of *Normandie* are entirely honest. Yes . . . A thousand members of the ship's crew. Seven hundred of them, approximate, are hotel-type workers who have access to all decks."

"And of course you can have no idea as to who all of them are," said Mrs. Roosevelt.

"I have already mentioned what we try to keep away— the thieves, the gambler cheats, the prostitutes. Besides those, the Communists—because they might try to destroy the ship."

Jack grinned. "So you find yourself carrying a Soviet ambassador who is reputedly a Chekist, plus his two aides, who probably are, too."

"Plus who knows?" said Ouzoulias, turning down the corners of his mouth and turning up his palms—another emphatic Gallic gesture. "Murderers—" ("Moor-dair-airs") "—burglars, arsonists . . . uh, what else? Can we prevent? The ship is a small city, hmm?"

"But somewhere aboard," said Mrs. Roosevelt, "a fortune in jewels lies hidden. It cannot go beyond the bounds of the ship until we reach port. That's an advantage, is it not, Monsieur Ouzoulias?"

Ouzoulias shook his head. "Where would we start a search?" he asked. "*Normandie* is more than three hundred fifty meters long, almost forty wide. It has *thousands* of compartments. There is cargo in the hold—crates, barrels, bundles—also passengers' automobiles, theirs trunks in storage below, besides what trunks they have had placed in their staterooms and cabins. Also we carry tens of thousands of pieces of mail. All this is to be searched? It will be searched in New York? No."

"Then we must identify the murderer," said Mrs. Roosevelt simply.

"As simple as that," said Jack Kennedy to Moira Lasky.

They sat in the first-class smoking room in the middle of the afternoon. The room was all but deserted. Moira was smoking a cigarette in her amber holder. If she made any concession at all to the pitching of the ship, it was that her glass of whiskey sat all but untouched on the table before them. Jack was not making that concession.

They were talking about the murder of Ambassador Troyanoskii, and he had just told her Mrs. Roosevelt's confident little statement that all Agent Ouzoulias had to do, really, was identify the murderer.

"Simple optimism," said Moira. "I saw it in her when I ran around New York and Washington with her in 1935, trying to figure out who killed Alfred Hannah. She is amazingly shrewd, but her optimism is almost simple-minded."

"I am amazed," said Jack, "that you know her. You *do* get around, Moira."

"When I told her I know you, I explained quickly it was on a social, not a professional, basis."

"Oh, thank you," Jack laughed. "Uh . . . You mean she *knows* about you?"

"Bob Hannah was desperate to clear his father's name, to find out who killed him. I guess I was flattered to be asked to help. Anyway, I was even invited up to Hyde Park. I had dinner with the President and his mother, as well as with Mrs. Roosevelt. The President's mother was *very* impressed with me."

"Proves how democratic the Roosevelts are," said Jack. He was amused, hardly able to contain his laughter.

"No more democratic than the Kennedys," she said.

"Ah, well . . ."

"Your father offered to lend me money," she said. "To help me find an honest way of life. I would have accepted, except that I'm not sure an honest way of life would let me live in the style to which I am accustomed."

"My father is a man of many interests," said Jack.

"Well, I'm not one of them, in case you wondered. I met

him through mutual friends, not— Well, not the way I meet a lot of men."

Jack grinned. "I'm about halfway disappointed," he said.

Moira glanced away from him. She did not like the comment. She crushed out her cigarette and cleared it from her holder, which she returned to her purse, and she picked up her glass and sipped Scotch.

"Where is your . . . companion?" Jack asked.

"In bed. Suffering ten thousand tortures."

"He speaks English like an American," said Jack.

"He learned it in America," said Moira. "He lived in Chicago for a year or two, with an uncle."

"I noticed you were invited to Troyanoskii's party last night," said Jack. "Did you know him?"

"Ernst did," she said. "He invited him, and Ernst invited me. I did know Troyanoskii in Paris, though. He pretended last night that he didn't remember."

"I guess I shouldn't pursue that," said Jack. "I mean, I guess I shouldn't ask for an explanation."

"No. But . . . Look at this." She held out her hand and showed him a small gold ring set with a modest-sized but very pure blue-white diamond. "He gave me that. I never wore it until today."

"Why today?"

She shrugged. "Suddenly it's more interesting," she said. "Incidentally, I told Mrs. Roosevelt I didn't know Troyanoskii. He was still alive when I said that, so she wasn't yet poking around in the investigation into his death. I see no significance in the fact that I knew him—and no reason why you should tell her."

"I won't. But do you know anything about Troyanoskii? I mean, do you know anything that would help the investigation?"

Moira lifted her glass in her right hand and put her left

on Jack's knee. "You're not a little boy, Jack," she said. "You can understand why I want *no* contact with Monsieur Detective Ouzoulias."

"But do you know anything? Anything I could tell without saying where I found out?"

She smiled tolerantly and shook her head. "No. What can I say? When I was with Troyanoskii he asked me about some American idioms— How did Americans say this? What was the correct way to say that? I was with him twice, and we spent practically the entire time on his American-English lessons. That's why he gave me the ring—because I was a good little teacher."

"How did you come to meet Troyanoskii?" Jack asked. "What was the connection?"

"Ernst knew him," she said simply.

"But—"

Moira smiled. "Don't be naive, Jack," she said quietly.

"Remer. . . ?"

"He's not in love with me, for heaven's sake!"

"Are you saying Remer introduced you to Troyanoskii and—"

"Let Troyanoskii have a relationship with me?" Again she smiled. "He encouraged me," she said.

"Just what *was* the relationship between Ernst Richter Remer and Boris Troyanoskii?" Jack asked.

"I think Ernst was selling him a large quantity of wines and brandies," she said. "That's Ernst's business, after all. I can't help but suspect the amount was too great to have been for Troyanoskii's personal use. I rather imagine it involved a government purchase or a purchase for a large importer."

"Something illegal?"

Moira shrugged. "Ernst has candidly admitted to me he exported tens of thousands of gallons of wines and brandies into the States during Prohibition." She shrugged. "I doubt he is very meticulous about customs duties, that sort of thing."

"Could there have been a deal for Remer to receive payment in the form of gold, platinum, and gems?"

She chuckled. "You're pressing, Jack," she said. "Don't let your anxiety to solve the mystery and be a hero lead you into something stupid. Sure, there could have been a deal like that. And there could have been ten thousand other kinds of deals. Hey, don't overlook the little ballerina. She had one *hell* of a motive for killing Troyanoskii."

"What motive?" Jack asked darkly.

"She thinks he arranged the murder of her parents," said Moira.

8

The social high point of the transatlantic crossing was the captain's dinner, traditionally held the second night out. It would be held on this crossing, no matter that hour after hour *Normandie* was plowing through thirty-foot seas, its bow rising ponderously on one wave, where for a long moment the ship seemed to stand precariously balanced before precipitately plunging into the next. When the first-class passengers were due in the great lounge for the pre-dinner cocktail party, a majority appeared—though some only by a brave effort of will.

Tommy Thompson begged to be excused, saying she would probably appear at her table for dinner but dreaded having to stand around for an hour with a glass in her hand. Mrs. Roosevelt was accompanied to the party by Nina Rozanov.

Nina had come aboard as a tourist-class passenger, not expecting to be invited to the captain's dinner, and had not brought formal clothes. ("I have none, in any case.") Mrs. Roosevelt had told the purser and social director of the ship that since Miss Rozanov was now her guest in an *appartement de grand luxe,* she should be added to the list of first-class passengers, assigned to a table in the first-class dining room, and placed on the invitation list for the captain's dinner. For this evening, Mrs. Roosevelt and Tommy had managed to put together an impromptu ensemble for the little ballerina. She had, fortunately, a long black skirt; every dancer had a long black skirt, she said. Mrs. Roosevelt contributed a white silk blouse. It was a bit too large, but they secured the sleeves at her wrists with two gold bracelets, and Tommy contributed a wide gold-finished belt to cinch the waist. Nina mourned the loss of her diamond necklace, which she thought would be very suitable for the occasion, so Mrs. Roosevelt fastened around the girl's throat for the evening a delicate gold chain set with small pearls—a gift from her husband many years ago.

In the *grand salon* amidships, the pitching of the *Normandie* was not nearly as pronounced as it was in the bow and stern. Nina remarked immediately to Mrs. Roosevelt that the ship was much steadier here than it had been in the winter garden forward or in the suite aft. People tended to stand with their legs a bit separated, to steady themselves, and the stewards carried their trays with special care; but none of this detracted from the elegance of the party. To the contrary, it added an element of shipboard adventure to what otherwise would have been simply a gathering of sumptuously dressed people in an extravagantly opulent room.

Mrs. Roosevelt was of course immediately recognized. A few Americans made it a point to turn their backs and walk away. Everyone else looked for an opportunity to approach and greet her, and she was immediately surrounded.

Nina wandered away from the crush around the American First Lady. She recognized a person here and there in the room—Jack Kennedy, Agent Edouard Ouzoulias, the brilliant American entertainer Josephine Baker. She kept an eye out for the man with the pencil mustache.

Jack Kennedy was one of a group of three, standing, talking, sipping from cocktails. He saw her, grinned, and broke away from the others to invite her to join them. Taking her by the arm, he led her back to the other two.

"Miss Rozanov, allow me to introduce Miss Moira Lasky and Mr. Henry Luce," he said.

"How very nice to meet you," said Moira. "I saw you dance in Paris."

"Ah . . ."

"Pleased to meet you," said Luce distractedly.

"Where did you see me dance?" Nina asked Moira, as though suspicious that Moira was not telling the truth.

"*Ballets Russes,*" said Moira. "Of course."

Nina smiled woodenly. "I hope you enjoyed it," she said.

"I understand," said Moira, "that for a few hours you were suspected of the murder of Troyanoskii."

"Yes. I was. But . . . why should I want to kill Boris Vasilievich?"

"Perhaps," said Luce, "because he is suspected of complicity in a great many crimes committed by the Bolshevik régime." He had suddenly taken an interest in Nina and in the conversation. "I asked my office in New York for information about him. I received word that Boris V. Troyanoskii was a member of the Cheka."

"That has long been suspected," said Nina.

"Suspected . . ." Luce shrugged. "It is true. He is a personal friend of Stalin."

"Not possible, I think," said Nina. "I don't think 'Comrade' Stalin has any friends."

"Accomplices, then," said Luce.

"A very risky thing, that," said Nina scornfully. "His accomplices have a way of dying soon."

"Miss Rozanov," said Moira to Luce, "is actually Countess Nina Nikolaievna Rozanov."

"A countess," Luce said, inclining his head to one side and frowning under his big, threatening brows. "One of the old Russian aristocracy. One of the class that Troyanoskii and his friends murdered in their thousands."

"In their thousands . . ." Nina muttered bitterly.

"Including Countess Rozanov's family," said Moira.

Jack tried not to stare at Nina, tried not to make it too conspicuous that he was watching for her reaction to talk he wished Moira would stop. He saw Nina's face redden.

Luce helped to close Moira's conversational trap. "You had reason to hate the Ambassador, then," he said to Nina.

"Not exactly," said Nina with cold precision. "I was his mistress."

Luce darkened. "Well . . ." he said gruffly. "You will excuse me." He strode away purposefully, as though he had spotted someone he had to talk to—though, watching him, they could see he had not.

"He doesn't want to hear that, hmm?" asked Nina.

"He's a rotten excuse for a human being," said Moira.

"You baited him, dear," said Jack.

Moira smiled. "Yes. It's very easy."

Jack spoke to Nina. "Mrs. Roosevelt arranged for you and me to be at the same table for dinner," he said.

Mrs. Roosevelt was the only guest at the captain's table both the first and second nights. As before, she sat to the captain's right. To her right sat Robert Logan, president

of Logan Motors, Inc., of Detroit. Across the table from her
sat Leonard Cooper, publisher of the *London Daily Advertiser*. Mrs. Cooper sat to the right of Logan. To Mrs.
Cooper's right was Colonel Charles Lévèque, newly
appointed military attaché to the French embassy in
Washington. Colonel Lévèque was accompanied by his
daughter, Mademoiselle Renée Lévèque, who sat to the
left of Leonard Cooper. To her left was Mrs. Logan and
then the Italian banker Emilio Bonaventura.

"I should like to propose a toast," said Leonard Cooper
when they had been served champagne. He rose. The men
followed suit. "To Mr. Chamberlain and Monsieur
Daladier, who have brought us safely through a war-
threatening crisis. Mr. Chamberlain announced today that
he has brought home 'peace in our time.' I believe it is so.
God bless him and God bless Monsieur Daladier."

"Hear, hear," murmured Robert Logan as he drank the
toast.

"Do you think it is true, Madame Roosevelt?" asked
Mademoiselle Lévèque, an exquisitely beautiful blonde
French girl Mrs. Roosevelt judged to be perhaps twenty-
one years old.

Innocently the girl had put Mrs. Roosevelt in an awkward position. "There is reason to hope so," she said.

"Have you been in contact with the President today?"
Logan asked.

"I have," she said. "He is grateful that war has been
avoided. I am sure he would gladly join in our toast."

"I should hope so," said Logan firmly. He was a bald,
strong-jawed, flush-faced man. "I fought in France in 1917
and '18. God forbid we should ever have to do it again."

"Hear, hear," said Leonard Cooper.

"Could France and England have won if they had gone
to war over Czechoslovakia, Colonel Lévèque?" Logan
asked.

The gray-mustached French colonel frowned and shook his head. "A difficult question," he said. "Yes, we could have prevented invasion of France, by our Maginot Line. But the bombing from the air . . . I don't know."

"England is not ready for war," said Cooper. "Even if necessity required it, we are not ready."

"Surprise," said Moira to Jack.

It was a surprise. She had arranged to be seated with him and Nina. He could conceal his vexation. Nina could not.

They had been placed at a table for six. Their dinner companions were a couple from St. Louis, called Hewlett, and an elderly Swiss businessman who spoke only French but had no interest in their conversation and made it clear he did not care if they translated anything for him or not.

Moira favored black. For this dinner she was wearing a bold, off-the-shoulder gown that exposed more skin than was customary among the silk-swathed women in the first-class dining room. Deep Vs in front and back were more acceptable—for some reason not fathomable by Jack Kennedy—than a dress that left the shoulders and upper chest uncovered, yet displayed nothing of the cleavage that was common throughout the room, among young and old. Moira was comfortable, anyway. Jack guessed she would not have been uncomfortable if she had been naked.

"Ambassador Kennedy's son, huh?" said Hewlett. "Well, he's a good Catholic anyway—I guess."

Jack nodded. "He's a very good Catholic, Mr. Hewlett. Very devout."

"Yeah. Democrat, then. We all are."

"Particularly the Irish," said Jack.

"Irish. . . ? Oh, you're Irish. Sure. I guess . . . the name. Yeah, right. And you Irish! Escorting two lovely young ladies to dinner."

Moira had pressed a cigarette into her amber holder and let Jack snap her lighter. "Actually," she said, "we might say I am escorting Jack to dinner. Keep his Irish hots down. Keep him out of trouble."

"Oh . . ."

"And the Countess Rozanov is helping me."

Hewlett's jaw dropped. So did his wife's. "Countess. . . ?"

"Countess Nina Nikolaievna Rozanov," said Moira. "Also, one of the world's most distinguished ballerinas. She is traveling, incidentally, in one of the *appartements de grand luxe* on the top deck."

"God! I understand a Russian ambassador was murdered in one of those apartments last night."

"Yes," said Nina, affecting great calm. "Boris Vasilievich Troyanoskii. I was his mistress."

"Ah . . . Ah . . . So you occupy his suite, then?"

"No, his servants occupy that," said Nina. "I am staying in another one."

"You have visited my country?" Emilio Bonaventura asked Mrs. Roosevelt.

She had to speak diagonally across the whole spread of the table to answer him. "I have, indeed, Signor Bonaventura," she said. "Many years ago. I went there on my wedding trip, in fact, and traveled in Italy with great pleasure. I have fond memories of it."

The Italian banker nodded. Asking the question had tested his English. Understanding her answer—more than that she had visited Italy—was beyond him. "Good," he said. "Good."

"I hear you were in the room with Ambassador Troyanoskii when he was murdered," said Robert Logan to Mrs. Roosevelt.

She glanced sympathetically at Captain Colbert. It had

been impossible to conceal the fact of the murder; it was the talk in every room, at every table. So far, though, word had not escaped that the purser's safe had been opened. "Yes," she said to Logan. "The poor man. It was a very upsetting thing to witness."

"The wife and I received an invitation to that party," said Logan. "We would have stopped in a little later. In fact, we came up to your deck and only turned back when we found out that something horrible had happened."

"Well, I'm glad they decided to kill him with poison and not by blowing up the ship," said Leonard Cooper, the English publisher.

"Not your usual Bolshevik," said Logan. Like many Americans, American businessmen in particular, he had a habit of speaking in absolutes. He didn't have *opinions;* whatever he believed became a fact, and he was only stating it. "Had respect for the capitalist way of doing things."

"You knew him?" asked Mrs. Roosevelt.

"Oh, yes. I met with him in Paris. Twice. About the possibility of importing Sixes into the Soviet Union." He was talking about the automobile that had made his company's fortune—the Columbia Six. "Damn Communists can't manufacture cars, you know. Or anything else, much. They need cars, and he talked about their government buying some of mine."

"What impression did you gain of him, Mr. Logan?" asked Mrs. Roosevelt.

"Too damned bad he was a Communist, was the impression I got of him," said Logan. "He had a business head on him. He knew exactly what he wanted."

"What *he* wanted?" asked Mademoiselle Lévèque innocently. "Or what his government wanted?"

Logan read her question as cynical. He laughed. "Both," he said. "Definitely both."

"Since every effort is being made to solve the crime before we reach port, perhaps you should expand on that statement, Mr. Logan," said Captain Colbert. "I mean, we should know as much as possible about Monsieur Troyanoskii."

"Oh, it's nothing ominous," said Logan. "We talked about shipping Sixes to Leningrad—maybe five hundred of them at first, then thousands more as time went on. I told Troyanoskii we could let him have them for seven hundred and seventy-five dollars plus shipping. He said no, they would have to be sold to the Soviet government for eight-fifty plus shipping. The extra seventy-five dollars would be paid over to a numbered account he would establish in Switzerland."

"Nothing terribly unusual, what?" asked Cooper.

Logan shrugged. "Nothing unusual for capitalists," he said. "A little odd, I thought, for the workers' paradise."

"He gave you, I suppose," said Mrs. Roosevelt, "no suggestion as to where the money would eventually go?"

Logan grinned and laughed. "I thought that was obvious enough," he said.

"Not necessarily," she said. "The Soviet government uses transactions like that to accumulate hard currencies for NKVD operations in Western Europe and around the world."

"You mean I'd have been helping to fund—"

"Espionage," interjected Cooper. "Assassination. Corruption of labor unions and political parties. A range of activities they can't fund with rubles, because nobody in the West will accept them as payment for anything."

Logan spoke directly to Mrs. Roosevelt. "When your husband extended diplomatic recognition to the Soviet government," he said, "I supposed that meant an American businessman could conduct business with it."

"If you would look at the list of governments to which we extend diplomatic recognition, Mr. Logan, I think you will find a great many whose activities you would not wish to fund."

The Hewletts had withdrawn from conversation with Jack Kennedy, Nina Rozanov, and Moira Lasky and were struggling to exchange pleasantries with the Swiss, who really didn't want to be bothered but seemed to feel bound by common courtesy to attempt conversation with two Americans who couldn't speak anything but English.

"It is a pity," said Jack to Moira, "that Herr Remer couldn't have made it to dinner."

"Not really," said Moira. "If he had, I couldn't have chosen my table."

The menus with which they had been presented were nearly as large as newspapers, and it was possible to talk behind them, screening conversation. Jack did so behind his, to Moira. "Why don't you tell Nina what you said to me this afternoon?" he asked.

Moira's eyes at first flashed with anger, then relaxed into hard derision. "Countess," she said thinly. "You say you were Boris's 'mistress'—old-fashioned word. But isn't that inconsistent with what he did to your family?"

"What do you think he did to my family?"

"Well, was he not responsible for their deaths?"

Nina flushed. Her eyes fell. "Not my father," she said. "He was shot by a Red Army unit in Byelorussia. My mother? Well, maybe he shared in the responsibility."

"Why did he take you as his mistress?"

"Maybe he felt some obligation," said Nina quietly.

Mrs. Roosevelt circulated for only a few minutes among the people who assembled in the *grand salon* for the dancing and after-dinner drinking that capped the evening's entertainment. As soon as she courteously could, without being accused of being abrupt or haughty, she returned to her suite, to see if Tommy were ill. She found that Tommy had in fact made it to the dining room and had eaten— before hurrying back, feeling unwell. The weather was gradually improving, and the pitching of the *Normandie* was subsiding. Mrs. Roosevelt went to the little galley of the suite and made herself a pot of tea.

Jack and Nina danced. Oddly, the little ballerina was a bit awkward at social dancing. She did not know the steps. He instructed her, at first diffidently, and she learned quickly.

"I cannot enjoy your friend Moira," she said as they danced. "She pretends to know much that she does not know."

"She can be a good friend," said Jack noncommittally.

Moira had said she must go to Remer's stateroom to see how sick he was, probably also to entertain him. Unless he were overcome by his seasickness, he would be lonely.

Later Jack escorted Nina back to Mrs. Roosevelt's suite. They found the First Lady sitting with a big yellow pad in her lap, writing something.

"I'm glad to see you," she said to them. "I've made some tea. Tommy's gone to bed, and I've no one to share it with. Or maybe you'd rather have brandy."

"I would love some tea," said Nina. "And—" She smiled shyly. "—a bit of that good vodka I see on the table."

"Of course. Jack, would you pour?"

"Happy to," said Jack.

"You will perhaps excuse me for a moment," said Nina. "I will step into my room and remove your so-very-lovely blouse and jewelry, Madame. I fear I should spill anything on it."

"You needn't—" Mrs. Roosevelt began, but Nina had already disappeared through the door to her room.

Jack Kennedy poured tea for Mrs. Roosevelt and Nina, then a small brandy for himself.

"Moira had herself placed at our table," he said.

"An intelligent young woman. With a wit that can be abrasive sometimes," said Mrs. Roosevelt.

"Yes. Uh . . . Do you suppose Nina wants ice in her vodka?"

"You will have to ask her."

He stepped into the short hallway and to the door to Nina's room and knocked. "Nina. Do you—"

The wood of the door shattered, punched out by a bullet that tore through it, missed Jack's shoulder by inches, and slammed into the wall behind him. Nina screamed. He lunged through the door.

The tiny ballerina was on her knees on the floor at the foot of her bed, screaming. Jack stared at her for an instant, long enough to see she had not been hit; then he glanced quickly around the room. A window was shattered. The shot had been fired from outside, through the glass. He ran across the room and tore open the door leading onto the suite's private promenade.

He was just in time to see a black-clad figure drop over the rail from the private promenade to the first-class promenade deck. Because of the rain and wind the promenades were deserted, and no one obstructed the gunman as he ran down the broad, curving stairway to the starboard afterdeck and then forward. Jack last saw him when he paused for an instant to throw his pistol over the side, into the dark, heaving ocean.

Jack turned and went back into Nina's bedroom. She remained on her knees on the floor, moaning in terror. She had taken off Mrs. Roosevelt's blouse; and, since she had been wearing nothing under it, her little breasts were exposed. Mrs. Roosevelt had come in and stood just over her, with a hand on her head, trying to soothe her. She reached for the blouse and draped it over Nina's shoulders, to cover her.

Shaken, Jack grabbed a telephone to call the ship's security office.

9

"You saved my life," Nina said to Jack when she had recovered a fraction of her composure.

"Actually I—"

"When you rapped on the door, I was half undressed, and I thought you were about to open the door and would see me. I jumped toward the bed to snatch up again the blouse and cover my nakedness. So the bullet missed me. Otherwise—"

"The old-fashioned virtue of modesty seems to have some value even today," said Mrs. Roosevelt quietly.

Nina was still shuddering, still tearful. Two armed security men had arrived within a minute after Jack's call, and they guarded the suite. Ouzoulias was on his way, as was the ship's doctor.

"Someone wants to kill me," Nina wept. "They will try again."

"You will have protection," said Mrs. Roosevelt.

The girl trembled. "They will try again. And again."

*   *   *

After examining her, Dr. Grasse administered a sedative to Nina. The drapes were pulled in her room, Tommy Thompson came in to sit with her until she was soundly sleeping, and two armed men stood guard on the private promenade.

"If any question remained," said Jack Kennedy, "I guess this settles it. She can't possibly be thought of as a suspect any longer."

"*Au contraire,*" said Agent Ouzoulias with lifted eyebrows. He tucked his burning pipe into his apparently fireproof jacket pocket and sipped from the brandy he had poured himself immediately on arriving. "Why should someone want to kill a poor innocent little ballerina? Why, indeed, unless she is not so innocent? Ambassador Troyanoskii was murdered for a reason, Monsieur; and I wager Nina Rozanov knows that reason, if she did not kill him herself."

"Or," said Mrs. Roosevelt, "someone wants to kill her *because* she killed Ambassador Troyanoskii—or someone thinks she did. I am afraid this shooting does *not* simplify the investigation."

"The two Russians," said Jack. "Ignatieff and Goldinin."

"Yes," said Ouzoulias. "I have detained them. They were found in the Ambassador's apartment, apparently asleep. One of my staff is performing paraffin tests on both of them. You know this test?"

"To discover if one of them has recently fired a pistol," said Mrs. Roosevelt.

"Yes. If one fires a pistol it is impossible to avoid having some of the burnt gunpowder adhere to one's skin. It cannot be washed away. We will know soon if Monsieur Ignatieff or Monsieur Goldinin fired a pistol tonight."

"It must have been a very small pistol," said Jack.

"Specifically, a twenty-five-caliber automatic," said Ouzoulias. "The bullet recovered from the wall demonstrates that."

"The man was not wearing gloves," said Jack. "But we'll never see the fingerprints he left on the pistol, because he threw it overboard."

Mrs. Roosevelt glanced toward the closed door of the bedroom where Nina was sleeping. "She said something that I find curious—that whoever tried to kill her will try again and again. 'They' will try again and again, she said. I wonder who she meant by 'they'?"

"If she meant the NKVD," said Jack, "her fears are real. They hunt down the people they decide to kill."

"Even outside Russia?" asked Mrs. Roosevelt.

"This is true," said Ouzoulias. "They have many agents in Paris." He rose and poured himself another splash of brandy. Then he took his pipe from his pocket and sucked hard on it to bring the fire back to life. "Maybe we are looking at a political crime."

"It is sometimes useful, I think," said Mrs. Roosevelt, "to write things down in order. I mean, to make a chart. Do you ever use that device, Monsieur?"

Ouzoulias shook his head.

"Will you, then, indulge me?"

"Of course."

"We can start with sheets of tablet paper," she said. "Later we can perhaps transfer our scribblings to a blackboard or poster board, if you can supply such a thing." Ouzoulias nodded. "Of course," he said again.

"All right," she said. "Why don't we start with the murder of Ambassador Troyanoskii. Is it not true that a rational way of approaching a murder investigation is to look for two factors—opportunity and motive? So . . . Who had opportunity to kill the Ambassador?"

"Mademoiselle Rozanov," said Ouzoulias.

"Very well. We start—"

She printed on a sheet of yellow tablet paper:

OPPORTUNITY

Miss Rozanov.

"And?"

"Anyone who had access to that bottle of vodka, or the glass," suggested Jack.

"We don't know who all had access," said Mrs. Roosevelt. "Obviously the steward did—Philippe LeClerc. We must add his name. Who else?"

"The strychnine was obviously not in the bottle," said Ouzoulias. "If it had been, Messieurs Kennedy and Benny would have been poisoned, too. The poison was therefore either in the glass when the vodka was poured in, or it was added to the drink after it was poured."

"I've reconstructed the scene in my mind a hundred times," said Jack. "As much as I hate the idea, I don't see how anyone but Nina could have put poison in that glass. She was the only one who handled it. Though I was watching her, I wasn't staring at her." He smiled. "I have to think of the old movie trick—opening a tiny hidden compartment in a ring and releasing poison into a drink."

"She wasn't wearing a ring," said Ouzoulias firmly. "I looked for one."

"What of the glass?" asked Mrs. Roosevelt. "Did she just pick it up from the table, or did Philippe LeClerc hand it to her?"

Jack shook his head. "I think he handed it to her."

"His fingerprints were on it," said Ouzoulias. "His, hers, and the Ambassador's."

"And she poured the vodka into the glass," said Mrs. Roosevelt.

"How did LeClerc know that Nina Rozanov was coming to the bar to get a drink for the Ambassador?" asked Ouzoulias.

"Oh, it was because he called to her, from across the room," said Mrs. Roosevelt. "He called across the room and asked her to bring him a glass of vodka."

"Uhmmm . . ." murmured the detective, turning down the corners of his mouth. "So we are where we have been from the beginning—we know nothing."

"May we continue to make our little chart?" asked Mrs. Roosevelt. "If we examine the question of motive, that may suggest another line of inquiry as to opportunity."

"Very well," said Ouzoulias. "Once again, we start with Mademoiselle Rozanov. She may have had several motives. Revenge for a real or imagined wrong. She was his mistress. Perhaps he was abusing her. Perhaps he had promised her something and now was failing to do it. Maybe she wanted to steal the jewels."

"I think not," said Mrs. Roosevelt. "I can't believe the Ambassador was killed by someone who wanted to steal the jewels. Why? Because the murder only made the theft more difficult."

"Perhaps not," said Ouzoulias, "since the jewels were so easily removed from the purser's safe."

"Really," said Mrs. Roosevelt, "it would have been easier to steal them from the Ambassador's suite."

"Maybe his two Russians were there to guard them," Ouzoulias suggested.

"Apparently not," said Jack. "They were out in the sitting room, enjoying the party. Did they go to dinner?"

Ouzoulias nodded. "Yes, I inquired. Both of them were at a table in the dining room. During that period the jewels were in the suite unguarded."

"So why didn't a thief just enter the suite and take them?" asked Mrs. Roosevelt. "Why kill the Ambassador?"

"I can think of a reason," said Jack.

"Please tell us."

"The thief had to be someone who knew the Ambassador was carrying the jewels. Probably very few people knew, don't you agree? And probably the Ambassador knew who did. If the jewels had disappeared from his suite while he was alive, I think it's very likely he would have guessed who took them. At least he would have known it had to be one of a very limited number of people."

"It's a point," said Mrs. Roosevelt. "A somewhat strained one, I think—but a point."

"I return to the motive of revenge," said Ouzoulias softly. "And with it I return to the motives of Mademoiselle Rozanov. I should like to know a great deal more about the history of the Rozanov family—particularly their history as it was affected by the Chekist Troyanoskii. What role, if any, did he play in the downfall of the Rozanovs? What role does she *imagine* he played?"

"Let me raise a point," said Jack. "We've been talking about someone wanting to steal the jewels from Troyanoskii. What if it's the other way around—that Troyanoskii was the thief? What if someone was trying to *recover* the jewels?"

"And who might that have been?" asked Mrs. Roosevelt.

"Well . . . Were the four Soviets we know about — Troyanoskii, Nina, Goldinin, and Ignatieff—the only Russians on board?"

"There are others," said Ouzoulias. "We have examined the passenger list. I would like, in fact, to have someone other than Mademoiselle Rozanov as my interpreter when I question Ignatieff and Goldinin further."

"If in fact Ambassador Troyanoskii is what everyone seems to believe—that is, a Chekist, more recently an officer of the NKVD—then there may be many people with real or imagined motives to kill him. We might categorize their reasons as political."

"He was an officer of a criminal government," said Ouzoulias. "It is possible Stalin had him killed. Stalin has had many of his former associates killed."

"We are speculating," said Jack glumly.

"Which can be very useful," said Mrs. Roosevelt. "Sometimes speculation leads to the truth. Now, who had opportunity to fire a shot at Miss Rozanov, and why did someone do that?"

"It was a man," said Jack. "I didn't get a look at his face, but he was a man. What's more, he was pretty athletic. He jumped from the promenade down to the deck below and came up running. Then he took off like a rabbit. A strong fella. Agile."

Mrs. Roosevelt printed a note to that effect on her growing chart.

"So, *why?*" asked Jack. "Why try to kill Nina?"

"It could be," said Ouzoulias, "that someone thinks—or knows—she murdered Troyanoskii and wants revenge."

"Ignatieff or Goldinin," said Jack.

"Possibly," said Ouzoulias.

"Nina thinks those two are themselves agents of the NKVD," said Mrs. Roosevelt. "If they are and they think she killed the Ambassador, they would perhaps be moved to kill her."

"Another possibility is that Nina knows something that someone does not want her to disclose," said Jack.

"Such as who murdered Troyanoskii," said Ouzoulias.

"Or what he was going to do with the jewels," said Jack.

"I can think of something more ominous than that," said Mrs. Roosevelt. "The identity of the man she says came to her cabin last night."

Ouzoulias shook his head. He put his pipe down on the ship's newspaper, which lay on the table beside his chair, and pulled from his pocket a fat pouch of tobacco. To Mrs. Roosevelt's amusement, and Jack's, he proceeded through an elaborately careful and protracted process of knocking an immense quantity of black and gray ash into an ashtray, then loading the cavernous bowl of the pipe with greasy-looking dark-brown tobacco.

"Well, we have the beginning of a chart," said Mrs. Roosevelt. She laid out her sheets to form a rectangle on the coffee table.

OPPORTUNITY TO MURDER T
Miss Rozanov   Philippe LeClerc   Others?
Anyone who had access to the bottle or glass.

MOTIVE FOR MURDERING T
(1) Revenge. For what?
  (a) Nina. Abused by T? Some other motive? What of her
    family?
  (b) Someone else, for something T did as Chekist.
(2) To steal the jewels.
  (a) But how would that make stealing the jewels easier?
  (b) Maybe it did, because T would have known who knew he had jewels.
    (Jack's idea.)
(3) To recover the jewels if T stole them.
(4) Political motives.

OPPORTUNITY TO SHOOT AT NINA
(1) A man. Agile.

MOTIVE FOR SHOOTING AT NINA
(1) Revenge for murder of T.
(2) To keep her quiet.
  (a) As to who killed T.
  (b) As to what T meant to do with jewels.
  (c) As to identity of her midnight visitor.

As she was running her eyes over the chart, the telephone rang. Jack picked it up. The call was for Ouzoulias.

He talked for a moment, then put the telephone down and shook his head.

"How is the American expression?" he asked. "If something it is not, something else is?"

"If it's not one thing it's another," laughed Mrs. Roosevelt.

"Yes. First, a simple matter. The paraffin test exonerates the two Russians of firing the shot at Mademoiselle Rozanov. But, the second thing is more difficult. Your friend Mademoiselle Lasky has telephoned my office to say that her friend Herr Remer has been assaulted and injured."

"Badly?"

"Not badly. He insists, in fact, he will not see Dr. Grasse. But he says he has been struck and his wallet taken. *Zut!* This kind of thing is never before on *Normandie*. People shooting guns, hitting on heads . . . *Zut!*"

Ernst Richter Remer was in the shower when Agent Ouzoulias and an assistant arrived at his stateroom.

"He insists a hot shower will do more for his head than a doctor could," said Moira. She shrugged. "What can I say? Germans are stubborn, you know. They also have a mystic obsession with the good things hot mineral water can do. This isn't mineral, but—"

She was still wearing the daring off-the-shoulders gown she'd had on at dinner, and it was obvious to the two detectives that she had consumed a considerable quantity of wine and brandy during the evening and night.

"What can you tell us, while he takes his bath?"

She sighed. "Well . . . He was feeling ill at dinner time. *Mal de mer,* you know. I went to dinner without him. After dinner I came back here to see how he was feeling, and he wasn't here. He— Uh, he and I are good friends, you see."

"Miss Lasky," said Ouzoulias—pronouncing her name "Lah-SKEE." "I know perfectly well the nature of your relationship with Herr Remer—as well as that of your relationship with several other gentlemen who have befriended you, on the *Ile de France,* the *Paris,* the *Queen Mary,* the *Queen Elizabeth* . . ." He grinned. "The *Nieuw Amsterdam* . . .

"Jesus Christ!" she whispered.

"You have never created a problem," he said. "And as long as you don't, you are welcome aboard our ships. You are welcome on the Cunarders, of course. They are grateful for your assistance in exposing the extortionists Malcom and Helen Johnstone aboard *Queen Mary.*"

"Oh, God . . . Word of that?"

"You know your line of work. You are good at it. You probably understand something about mine. You realize, then, that I do expect *complete* cooperation from you."

Moira nodded.

"All right," said Ouzoulias. "You dined with Mr. Kennedy and Mademoiselle Rozanov. What do you know of the death of Ambassador Troyanoskii?"

"Nothing," she said. "I swear I know nothing. Troyanoskii did befriend me in Paris. But I know nothing of what happened to him. He wanted to improve his English, and I helped him, and he gave me this ring."

"How did you meet him?"

She nodded toward the bathroom door, from where they could hear water still splashing in the shower. "Herr Remer introduced us."

"Ah. Herr Remer knew him?"

"Herr Remer is a factor dealing in wines, champagnes, brandies. Boris Troyanoskii must have bought from him. I know of no other explanation."

"Ah. So you returned to this stateroom after dinner and found that Herr Remer had gone out. So you—?"

"Waited," she said.

"For how long?"

"I . . . In terms of hours and minutes, I don't know. A considerable time. I drank some of his brandy. I became impatient, to tell you the truth. I wanted to go back to the salon and dance. Instead, I waited here."

"Then he returned."

"She nodded. "A few minutes before I telephoned your office. He was angry. He said a man should be able to travel on the *Normandie* without being hit on the head and robbed. He ordered me to call you."

"Yes. And I arrive here . . . fifteen minutes later."

Moira shrugged. "Whatever. Herr Remer was impatient. After a little while he went in the shower. Dr. Grasse arrived. Herr Remer refused to come out and see him. He insists he will be all right, after he pours a few more hundred gallons of hot water on his head."

Ouzoulias nodded. "Go in and tell him we are waiting, will you please."

A few minutes later Ernst Richter Remer emerged from the bathroom, all pink and damp from the hot water, and wearing a heavy, white terry-cloth robe. His black hair lay in wet disarray. He was barefoot.

Moira sat on the bed, and Remer took one of the two armchairs in the stateroom—Ouzoulias having taken the other—and confronted the French Line's detective with a kingly air.

"Monsieur. . . ?" said Ouzoulias.

"I was ill," said Remer. "But I felt better after a while. Not good enough to go to the dining room, you understand, but good enough to go on deck and take the air. I thought that might help, even if I got wet with salt spray. So . . .

So, I've got one of these veranda staterooms, so I could just open the doors there and walk out on deck."

"Yes. Nice stateroom. Immediate access to the ocean air."

"If you like that sort of thing," said Remer. "So I thought maybe I'd actually walk forward and all the way around the ship. I, uh . . . I guess I got too ambitious with that idea, so I turned around and started back. I got back. I came past my door. I thought maybe I'd keep going a little. I walked toward the stern. And all of a sudden . . . *thump!* I went down on my knees, and I felt somebody feeling around me. Whoever he was, he got my wallet, out of my jacket. He got my money."

"How much money, Monsieur?"

Remer shrugged. "Oh, not so awful much. Maybe a thousand marks. I don't carry a lot of money on me."

"Did you at all see the man who struck you?" asked Ouzoulias.

Remer shook his head.

"I am looking for a man dressed in black," said Ouzoulias.

"He could have been dressed in purple, for all I could see."

"Ah. You saw him not at all."

"Not at all," Remer agreed.

"Then you have nothing more to contribute to the information I must use to attempt to identify this criminal?"

Remer shook his head. "I am prepared to offer a reward for him, if that will help."

"It would not help, Monsieur," said Ouzoulias.

"Well, then . . . I have a bit of a headache."

"Yes. We will inform you of whatever we learn. And, on behalf of the *Compagnie Générale Transatlantique,* our most abject apologies. Never before has such a crime been committed aboard *Normandie*. We would, of course, appreciate your not discussing the matter with other passengers."

"Not a word," said Remer.

"Thank you, Monsieur."

Ouzoulias and his assistant left the stateroom.

Remer, sitting in his chair, regarded Moira with a skeptical, almost hostile eye. "All right, kitten," he muttered. "Blow. I'm gonna get my beauty rest."

10

By Saturday morning the wind had subsided, the seas reached no more than eight or ten feet, and *Normandie*'s powerful steam turbines drove her through gray-green water under a cold blue sky. Shreds of high cloud alternately let the sun shine on the sea, then blocked it. From time to time the great ship and the white-capped sea around were dramatized by brilliant sunlight; then it ran through gray and out again into the light. Thick streams of oil smoke from her slanted red stacks were whipped away and quickly dissipated by the wind. The churning white wake behind the ship was like a highway stretching toward the horizon astern.

Passengers strolled on the decks. The men wore overcoats and scarves and sporty wool caps—the women furs and silk scarves and hats held in place with ties or by pins. A few even chose to sit bundled in deck chairs, attended by stewards offering hot bouillon as well as coffee and tea.

Most of the passengers were oblivious to the news from the Europe they had just left. One of the attractions of a voyage on a great ship was a sense that one was living in suspended time, or in an unreal warp of time measured by the rhythm of the ship's life, totally detached from that being lived by ordinary mortals on either side of the Atlantic.

Those who listened to their shortwave radios heard newscasters in a dozen languages describing how the German army was moving across the Czech border. The invasion had been agreed to at Munich, and the Czech forces could only stand aside while thousands of trucks and half-tracks, and a few tanks, crossed their frontier carrying tens of thousands of soldiers in field-gray to occupy the Sudetenland, the German-populated areas of Czechoslovakia.

The Sudeten Germans lined the roads, the broadcasters said—cheering and waving Swastika flags. Many other citizens of the region—Czechs—were sadly driving toward Prague, having elected not even to attempt living in their former homes.

It was the end of Czechoslovakia, one Czech statesman said. Already Poland was demanding a province in the eastern part of the country, and the Germans would gobble up the rest. But in London a British spokesman said no, the Czechs had nothing to worry about—Herr Hitler had specifically promised Prime Minister Chamberlain that the Sudetenland was his last territorial demand in Europe.

In the salon, Wilhelm von Heinroth could not contain his satisfaction. He didn't try. Talking to Henry Luce, he said—"You see? The Führer said he would move into

Czechoslovakia on the first day of October, and he has. He has! Whatever you may think of the man, you see how he does what he says he will do."

Luce only nodded. His personal statements and his magazines' editorial policies had been so confused on the subject of Czechoslovakia that he could hardly speak without contradicting himself.

"You have to congratulate us," von Heinroth persisted. "You have to appreciate what we have achieved. Germany will stand as the great bulwark against Bolshevism."

"Yes," said Luce thoughtfully. "That's important."

In another part of the salon, another German businessman was talking to Jack Benny—

"I have been in the States before, Mr. Benny, and have heard you on the radio. You are a very funny man. It is a pleasure to meet you."

"Thank you," said Benny.

"You have heard this morning's news? We will know peace in Europe. Europe's Spaniards now live inside the borders of Spain, its Italians within the borders of Italy . . . and so on. Now a German population that was abused by a foreign government has been returned to the Fatherland. Only justice, hmm?"

"I can't help wondering what will happen to the Jews who live in the Sudetenland," said Jack Benny.

The German grinned. "Well, we don't need to worry about that, do we, Mr. Benny?" he laughed. "Not you and I anyway. Hmm?"

"Actually, I do worry about it."

The German's grin remained. He clapped Benny on the shoulder. "I do, too, really," he said. "I also worry about the Eskimos and the Hottentots. But there are none aboard the *Normandie*. And no Jews either, I should think—at least none in first class."

Jack Benny looked at the man for a long moment, his chin gradually rising. "Well . . ." he said at last. "I guess it's not likely."

"For reasons of diplomacy," said Agent Edouard Ouzoulias.

"Yes, of course," Mrs. Roosevelt agreed. "Otherwise—"

"Otherwise it would be of questionable . . . ah, *éthique*," said the detective.

"Questionable ethics," she agreed.

"Ethics, yes. Questionable."

"But in the circumstances . . ."

"In the circumstances," said Ouzoulias, puffing on his pipe, "I think we are justified" ("Zhoos-tee-fied-uh").

They were in his office on B Deck and adjacent to the ship's hospital. He had found an interpreter who could translate the Russian spoken by Ignatieff and Goldinin into French, and he had suggested that Mrs. Roosevelt might like to listen in on the interrogation of the two aides to the late Ambassador Troyanoskii. He had offered a man who could translate the French into English, but she had explained to him that she had learned fluent French when she was a schoolgirl and could almost certainly understand everything that was said.

She would, however, listen from an adjoining room, and neither the two Russians nor the interpreter would know she was present. Ouzoulias had suggested that diplomatic nicety because he understood that the government of the United States emphatically did not want to be involved in any way in anything relating to the murder of the Soviet Ambassador.

"It is, of course, not at all necessary that I should listen," she said to Ouzoulias. "I should not want to inconvenience you, or to create any possibility of embarrassment."

Ouzoulias sucked on his pipe. "I have come to respect your insights, Madame," he said. "Some of us have logical minds that assist us in penetrating to the truth of matters. Others . . ." He shrugged. "You have demonstrate the shrewdness of insight."

"Thank you, Monsieur Ouzoulias," she said. "I try to be objective."

He smiled. "Except that you do not wish to believe that the so-beautiful little ballerina could be involve in crime."

"Well . . . I could wish that not prove true."

"Ah. So, we make you comfortable—at least, to the best of our poor ability."

She had taken careful note of the contrast between the luxurious appointments of the passenger facilities of *Normandie* and the functional rooms where members of its staff and crew did their work. She had been aboard naval vessels during Franklin's tenure as Assistant Secretary of the Navy during the World War, and the quarters afforded Agent Ouzoulias reminded her of what she had seen on battleships and cruisers.

His office, in the middle of the ship and without windows, was small. The walls were painted gray. A variety of pipes ran across the ceiling. His furniture was Spartan—a steel desk, two oak chairs, a filing cabinet, a typewriter. He dragged one of the wooden armchairs into the smaller room next door, for her to sit in while she listened. She realized, once in there, that it was his cabin, his sleeping quarters. It was shabby; yet, she had never seen such a collection of toiletries, even in a woman's room. The walls were lined with shelves, all with railings to prevent bottles and cans from crashing to the deck when the ship rolled, and these shelves were crammed with containers of hair dressing, shaving lotion, cologne, creams, powders, and soaps. He left the door ajar, so she could hear the talk in the office. She was glad for that, since it afforded a little more air and a little relief from the oppressive odor of his huge collection of perfumes.

Ouzoulias had identified a Russian-speaking passenger in third class, a Lithuanian businessman named Kazys Urbays, and had asked him to act as interpreter for his interrogation of Ignatieff and Goldinin. Mrs. Roosevelt could not see Urbays, but she heard Ouzoulias welcome him into the office and tell him the ship would reward him with some fine champagne in payment for his services. Happily, Urbays spoke polished French. Not only that, he spoke it with the deliberation of a man to whom it was not a native language; so she found she could understand everything he said.

All the talk was now in French, and shortly also in Russian:

—"Monsieur, I am now going to call in Grigorii Ignatieff. I wish to interrogate him on several points. You should be warned that there is reason to believe he is an agent of the Soviet secret police, the NKVD."

—"In that case, you will perhaps not object if I sit facing the wall. I should not care to have the NKVD know of my participation in anything they consider a disadvantage."

—"I have a better idea. I shall simply have him blindfolded. And I assure you he will not be told who did the translating."

—"Thank you, Monsieur."

Mrs. Roosevelt frowned over this. She had not thought of any possible danger from the two Russians. On the other hand— Anyway, she heard some shuffling in the office as Ignatieff was brought in and led to a chair. She could imagine the scene. She remembered Ignatieff as the younger of the two aides to Ambassador Troyanoskii. He was, she judged, about thirty. He was rather handsome in a rugged way. She recalled, though, her impression that his face had been scraped with a dull razor, and the skin seemed to glow as if in protest—as if it was not accustomed to being shaved every day.

—"You have been blindfolded, Monsieur Ignatieff, to protect the identity of my interpreter. Do not touch your blindfold. If you do, I shall handcuff your hands behind your back."

Urbays translated into Russian, heard Ignatieff's answer, and translated the answer into French.

—"Monsieur Ignatieff wants to know why he should be subjected to any indignity and why he should answer any questions at all."

—"Tell him that if he does not cooperate fully I will have him thrown overboard tonight. Tell him also that if I detect any lies in his answers I will have him castrated without an anesthetic and *then* I will have him thrown overboard."

Mrs. Roosevelt was uncertain if she should be shocked or amused. Ouzoulias had spoken in such a calm, matter-of-fact tone that she could not be sure he didn't mean the threat to be taken literally. Perhaps he understood that the Russian, whose own government was entirely capable of such acts, would not know that an agent of a civilized government would not think of doing what Ouzoulias had described. . . . Or would he?

Ignatieff did not reply to the threat.

—"Now, Monsieur Ignatieff . . . Let us go directly to the nub of the matter. Ambassador Troyanoskii was carrying in his luggage a very large quantity of precious stones set in gold, silver, and platinum. Why?"

—"That is the property of the government of the Soviet Union."

—"Where was he taking it, and why?"

—"He was going to sell it to the Jews in New York."

—"What Jews in New York?"

—"The jewel merchants. He believed he could obtain a higher price for the property there than he could obtain in Paris or London. Rich Americans—"

—"Would pay dollars for the jewels. Now, what was he going to do with those dollars?"

—"That is a state secret of the government of the Soviet Union."

—"Yes. The government of the Soviet Union has ways of extracting state secrets from people—which you yourself have probably applied. And so do I."

—"I cannot reveal a state secret. No matter what you do."

—"For fear of what would happen to you when you went home. You have two choices, Monsieur. You deny me your cooperation—in which case you are not going home. Or you cooperate—in which case you have my assurance that your government will never learn that you told me anything."

—"In the Soviet Union the French have a reputation for using the utmost cruelty against political prisoners."

—"Is that true?" asked Ouzoulias innocently. "I didn't know that."

Mrs. Roosevelt frowned to herself and shook her head. It was odd that Ignatieff, whose government had the most unsavory reputation in the world for savage brutality against its political prisoners, should think the French were even worse. Apparently Ouzoulias suspected he might think so, and he was playing on the Russian's fear.

—"Monsieur Ignatieff. The question is, what did Ambassador Troyanoskii intend to do with the money he obtained by selling the jewels?"

—"The money was to be turned over to the Soviet embassy in Washington, to be used to fund various operations that must be paid for in dollars."

—"Is it correct to say, then, that Troyanoskii was just a courier?"

—"No. He was more than that. Comrade Troyanoskii was a very highly placed man."

—"He was going to see the President of the United States."

—"That was his cover, his ostensible reason for visiting the United States. He was carrying a message to President Roosevelt from Comrade Stalin."

—"Ambassador Troyanoskii lived in great style in Paris. He was traveling in one of the most expensive apartments *Normandie* has to offer. Why?"

—"That was his style. Our government tolerated it because it made him a very effective agent. Capitalists always suspected he was corruptible."

—"But he wasn't?"

—"He was an example of the new Soviet man—wholly dedicated to our system and the world revolution."

—"Who killed him? And why?"

—"Nina, of course. The ballerina."

—"Why?"

—"Probably paid to do it. She is a White Russian, a traitor to her country and a running dog of capitalism."

—"She was his mistress, was she not?"

—"Yes. She wormed her way into his affections, using the means a woman has for that purpose. She gained his confidence. And, when the opportunity arose, she killed him."

—"A rather silly way for her to kill him, don't you think? In a crowded room, in the presence of twenty-five or thirty people."

—"That is only evidence of how cunning she is. Observe.

She has now worked her way into the confidence of Mrs. Roosevelt and is living in her apartment."

—"Where are the jewels now?"

—"In your safe, Monsieur. And my government will demand their return, you may be certain."

—"How did your government obtain them?"

—"They are the confiscated property of traitors, capitalist enemies of the people, aristocrats . . ."

Ouzoulias continued the interrogation of Ignatieff for some more minutes, but it became obvious that the aide had not been taken into Troyanoskii's confidence and accepted his government's official story as to what Troyanoskii was doing with the jewels. And maybe—Mrs. Roosevelt thought—it was the truth. His hostility to Nina Rozanov was interesting. If neither of the two official aides to the Ambassador had fired the shot at Nina, then maybe there were other Soviet agents aboard, incognito. Maybe— She could speculate, but she wanted more facts.

Ouzoulias brought Vladimir Goldinin to the office. He too was blindfolded, he too protested, and he too was cowed by the French detective's cold threat to throw him overboard—having mutilated him first.

She remembered Goldinin as a somewhat older man than Ignatieff, heavier, with the crude features of a peasant. She particularly recalled his stainless-steel teeth—manifestation of a grimly utilitarian dental practice that, so far as she knew, existed in the Soviet Union and nowhere else.

—"Why were you sent with Ambassador Troyanoskii on this voyage?"

—"To guard Comrade Troyanoskii and the jewels. My government feared he might be murdered and the jewels stolen."

135

—"So . . . And Troyanoskii is dead, and the jewels are gone."

—"You have the jewels."

—"No. They were stolen from the purser's safe."

—"This is true?"

—"Yes."

Mrs. Roosevelt could guess the meaning of a long silence. Then she heard again the voice of Goldinin—

—"This condemns me to death."

—"Yes. Your government will regard you as a failure."

—"I have no family. The Party has been my family. But Comrade Ignatieff does. He *must* return, to face whatever punishment the comrades decide he should suffer. I—"

—"You are going to need help."

—"Yes."

—"I can arrange it."

—"I should be grateful."

—"Very well. Let's begin by returning to something you said a moment ago. You were sent to guard Troyanoskii. But I judge 'guard' was the right word—not 'protect.' Am I correct? Your government was worried that the Ambassador might defect, taking the jewels with him. No?"

—"You judge correctly."

—"Then who killed him?"

—"Nina Nikolaievna Rozanov."

—"Why do you say that?"

—"She hated Comrade Troyanoskii. And she had good reason."

—"Ah. The reason is what I want to hear. You tell me, Goldinin. Tell me the whole story."

Mrs. Roosevelt tensed and leaned a little closer to the door. She wanted to hear every word of this. Goldinin began to speak, in muffled Russian. Fortunately, Kazys Urbays spoke up distinctly—

—"She was wrong to hate him. She was wrong . . . How to explain?"

—"Simple, direct words will suffice."

—"Well . . . To begin with, the relationship between Comrade Troyanoskii and the family Rozanov is old, very old. It began long before Nina Nikolaievna was born. I could wish, Monsieur, for your understanding of what I am going to tell you, that you could have known the Countess Andrea Leovna Rozanov. She was an exquisitely beautiful woman."

—"As is her daughter."

—"The Countess Andrea Leovna was petite and lithe, like Nina Nikolaievna; but she had also a poise and presence that her daughter lacks."

It was odd, Mrs. Roosevelt reflected, to hear the peasant-like Goldinin using such terms to praise the beauty of a wealthy aristocrat. He went on—

—"Count Nicholas Alexandrovich Rozanov was a coarse man. It was difficult to understand why a beauty like the Countess would have married him, or how such a man could have become the father of a girl like Nina Nikolaievna. I must tell you, Monsieur, that many people marveled at it—and did not marvel, then, when Countess Andrea Leovna took lovers."

—"Are you about to tell me that among those lovers was Boris Vasilievich Troyanoskii?"

—"Beyond any question."

—"But he was not an aristocrat, and he was not—"

—"He was a student. A young student. Rich. And maybe you think he was not handsome. We are talking about things that happened more than twenty years ago. He *was* handsome. And clever. An engaging companion. He became her lover. They were the same age. He was all her husband wasn't."

137

—"Including a soldier, which the Count was. I fail to see why he didn't discover what was happening and—"

—"Count Nicholas Alexandrovich went to war, to fight the Germans and Austrians. He was gone three years."

—"Without leaves?"

—"No, he came home for short periods from time to time."

—"Ah."

—"Then came the Revolution. The Count, an aristocrat with everything at stake in the old system, joined the Whites and fought for counter-revolution. Eventually he was captured and executed."

—"And in the meantime Troyanoskii had become a Bolshevik—not only a Bolshevik but a Chekist."

—"That is true. He gave good service. So good that he came to the personal attention of Comrade Felix Dzerzhinsky himself, who made him one of the original agents of the Cheka. And it was well for the Countess and her daughter that he was, since he was able to use his influence to save them—for a time. You understand, as the wife and daughter of a White-Russian general executed for—"

—"For treason. Their lives were forfeit."

—"Were forfeit . . . You are exactly right, Monsieur Ouzoulias."

The placid accents in which all this could be discussed by these two men horrified Mrs. Roosevelt. Even the interpreter spoke calmly, blandly conveying the narrative and questions and comments back and forth in French and Russian without his voice disclosing that he was either surprised or troubled by what he was hearing.

—"If Nina was the beneficiary of all this kindness, why do you now say she hated him and probably murdered him?"

138

—"She has been indoctrinated by her uncle and other Whites. She believes that Comrade Troyanoskii toyed with her mother only long enough to learn where she had hidden a fortune in jewels, then had her seized and shot."

—"Does she know he was her mother's lover?"

—"She thinks her mother offered herself to Comrade Troyanoskii to save their lives—and was viciously betrayed by him after he had used her."

—"Is it not possible that is exactly the way it was?"

—"Who knows what passed between two people in their private hours? But I don't think so. I saw as much as a man not admitted into their intimate hours could see. I am a peasant, Monsieur, born and bred. I worked as a stableboy at the Troyanoskii estate. I came to the attention of Boris Vasilievich Troyanoskii. He made me his body servant. In time, I became as close to him as a servant could become."

—"And observed? What did you observe?"

—"I became a 'clerk' to Boris Vasilievich. My duties were the same, but comrades of the new order did not have body servants. I saw him . . . Monsieur Ouzoulias, I saw him do all he could—all that was not inconsistent with his own survival—to save the Countess and Nina Nikolaievna."

—"So . . ."

—"You have guessed the rest of it, have you not, Monsieur Ouzoulias? You have perhaps guessed what Nina Nikolaievna has never guessed."

—"Do you mean to tell me—"

—"I cannot tell you for a certainty. I can tell you it is extremely probable that when Nina Nikolaievna Rozanov murdered Boris Vasilievich Troyanoskii, she murdered her own father."

11

What was it, some Byzantine Soviet scheme to complicate the investigation and divert suspicion from the real murderer? The suggestion Vladimir Goldinin made had angered Mrs. Roosevelt. She had never been quick to anger; from her childhood she had been taught that anger was an emotional extravagance inconsistent with her place in the world. But now she was angry. If what Goldinin said were true— Or if it were not true— She was angry.

The exchange in the adjoining office—French to Russian, Russian to French—continued—

—"What, exactly, was the fate of Countess Andrea Rozanov? And how did Nina escape?"

—"The Countess suspected Comrade Troyanoskii could not save her. Or maybe she thought he wasn't really trying. In either event, she could not have told Nina Nikolaievna of her suspicions. The girl was only four years old. Anyway, the Count's brother, Count Mikhail Alexandrovich Rozanov, offered to take the girl. He was scheming to escape from the Soviet Union, and—"

—"Offered to take the girl? Why not the Countess as well?"

—"I don't know. I am sure he gave Nina Nikolaievna some reason in later years."

—"He was—? I mean, what kind of man was this Count Mikhail?"

—"He was no soldier, though he was given a command by the Czar. The fact is, he had always taken great interest in the ballet, and he had kept a succession of elegant ballerinas as mistresses. He was more committed to this sort of thing than to war—or to his country, for that matter. He did not fight for the Whites, to his credit. Instead, he schemed at leaving Russia, taking as much money with him as possible. And, when his chance came, he took it."

—"And became a ballet master in Paris."

—"That dignifies what he is, doesn't it? He tried to be an impresario of the ballet. He failed, lost what money he had managed to bring out of Russia. He teaches dancing."

—"But what happened to the Countess?"

—"Nina Nikolaievna believes Comrade Troyanoskii betrayed her mother, who was then arrested and shot. The truth is worse. She was arrested—and I insist it was in spite of his efforts to prevent it—and was sent to Siberia. My mother and father were sent there, too, by the Czar— and survived it. The Countess did not. She died after four years there."

—"The Rozanov family jewels?"

—"There weren't so many. The two counts had borrowed money against them, for gambling. Count Nicholas was carrying some sewed inside his uniform when he was executed. The Countess gave some to Comrade Troyanoskii, maybe to bribe him, or maybe for him to use to pay bribes."

—"She says she found some of her mother's jewels in those Troyanoskii was carrying."

—"It is not impossible. He gave her the large diamond pendant, of course."

—"Which?"

—"The diamond pendant she was wearing the night he was murdered. He gave her that. In Paris. When she became his mistress. It is ironic, is it not, Monsieur, that both mother and daughter were Comrade Troyanoskii's mistresses?"

—"Especially if she is his daughter."

—"Yes. And he knew of the possibility, you may be sure. He was an interesting man, was he not?"

"I am appalled," said Mrs. Roosevelt. "I am utterly appalled."

They had returned to her suite, where they would be more comfortable. Ouzoulias had dismissed Kazys Urbays with a renewed promise of a gift of vintage champagne, after extracting from him an absolute pledge of secrecy. (Mrs. Roosevelt had been appalled by how he did that, too—by telling the Lithuanian that his promise never to allow the NKVD to discover how Urbays had cooperated was conditioned on Urbays's keeping his silence.)

"Do you not suppose," she said, "that the whole wretched story could be Goldinin's way of confusing us, turning our attention to untruths and—"

"I have not yet deciphered what advantage the NKVD would find in that," said Ouzoulias. "Although, I must tell you, I would not believe anything a Bolshevik said."

"I am prepared to believe," she said, "that Goldinin or Ignatieff murdered Troyanoskii."

"I hope that is the case," said Ouzoulias. "On the other hand, we now know that Mademoiselle Rozanov has not been entirely truthful, either."

"In that—?"

"She claimed, did she not, that the diamond pendant was all she had managed to bring out of Russia? Goldinin says—"

"Would you rather believe *him*?"

"I find it difficult to believe people live in straitened circumstances for many years, with an extremely valuable diamond in their possession. Sentiment has its limits, does it not?"

"Do you suppose she *does* believe Troyanoskii had her mother killed?"

"It would be a motive, wouldn't it?"

Mrs. Roosevelt drew her hands down her cheeks. "Yes . . . A compelling motive."

"Do you wish to tell Mr. Kennedy any of this?" asked Ouzoulias. "I sense that he is falling in love with the girl."

The question lifted Mrs. Roosevelt's spirits. She smiled. "Jack is young," she said. "He comes from a family of high-spirited men. I understand he is in and out of love three or four times a month—which is only half the number of girls who fall in love with him in the same month."

"But he is emotional . . . He is *commit* to the girl."

"No more than I am, I suspect—though of course in an entirely different way," said the First Lady. "Let me say, Monsieur Ouzoulias, that I am satisfied we may place our confidence in Jack Kennedy in any way we wish." She paused, and her smiled broadened. "That doesn't say we must confide in him everything we know."

"His father is an ambassador. But also a—how you say?—*homme politique,* is he not?"

"A politician. Yes, he is. The whole family is very politically oriented."

"This young man . . . You think he will pursue a career in American politics?"

"I doubt it," she said. "His father has made it very clear that he expects Jack's elder brother, Joseph Junior, to enter politics. I should expect Jack to follow a different career. He's a bit too much the playboy to take politics very seriously."

"Time changes us all," said Ouzoulias.

"Well . . . That is possible. Actually, it is likely. Who knows what future lies ahead of such a young man? Indeed, my husband . . . Who would have suspected of him, when he was Jack Kennedy's age, that he would become President of the United States? Or, more to the point, who would have thought of me, when I was twenty-one years old, that I could cope with—" She paused and smiled again. Her voice fell almost to a whisper. "There are those who think I do it well."

"Any man," said Ouzoulias quietly, "in no matter what line of endeavor, should wish to have such a . . . uh, *compagnon* as you. I could only wish so great a privilege had been mine."

Mrs. Roosevelt blushed. "Oh, thank you, Monsieur Ouzoulias," she said. "How very nice of you to say—"

"I am perhaps too personal."

"I am honored," she said.

"You and I," he said. "We are of the same age."

"Uh, we can trust Jack Kennedy, I assure you," she said. "But I hope you will agree that we should not tell any element of this to Nina Rozanov."

Edouard Ouzoulias nodded gravely. He extracted his

pipe from his pocket. This time it was cold, and he packed it and lit it with a big wooden match.

"A message from the President," said Tommy Thompson as soon as Ouzoulias had left the suite. "I've decoded it."

A MESSAGE FROM MOSCOW ADVISES THAT AMBASSADOR TROYANOSKII WAS MURDERED ON NORMANDIE THURSDAY EVENING STOP ALSO EXPRESSES GRATITUDE THAT YOU ARE ASSISTING FRENCH AUTHORITIES IN TRACKING DOWN MURDERER ALSO ESPECIALLY IN SEEING TO IT THAT MATTER IS TREATED CIRCUMSPECTLY STOP CURIOUS THAT THESE TWO IDEAS SHOULD BE COMMUNICATED STOP PLEASE EMPHASIZE SECOND ELEMENT STOP SOMETHING ODD IN ALL THIS STOP DO NOT SUPPOSE ANYTHING IS AS IT APPEARS STOP MYSTERY IS MORE POE-IAN THAN CONAN DOYLE-IAN I SUSPECT SO USUAL ELEANORIAN LOGIC TECHNIQUES MAY NOT SOLVE THE PROBLEM STOP SERIOUSLY TREAD MOST CIRCUMSPECTLY STOP

"They are coming, you know," said Tommy.

"Coming. . . ?"

"Mrs. R.! You invited the people you've met at the captain's table to lunch today. They will be here shortly."

"Oh, yes, of course. Of course. It escaped my mind because of the distressing things I've heard this morning."

She had asked Tommy to arrange with the stewards to offer a simple buffet in her sitting room. It was always difficult to have a simple lunch in France, and the *Normandie* was emphatically a French ship. Stewards now began to arrive, first with the tables it would take to set the simple buffet, then with the food, which included assorted hors d'oeuvres; stuffed eggs; rabbit and duck patés; onion soup and consommé; coquilles Saint-Jacques; sliced beef, ham, and turkey; a lobster salad; assorted hot and cold vegetables; cheeses; fruits; pastries; coffee; tea; and assorted wines.

Mrs. Roosevelt made a casual inspection of the buffet. Elaborate food had never been a matter of great interest to her, and she marveled at the emphasis some people placed on it—including sometimes her own husband, who appreciated good food and drink and could complain testily when something from the White House kitchen impressed him as tasteless.

"Qu'est-ce que c'est que ça?" she asked one of the stewards behind the table as she pointed to a dish. What is that?

"C'est une anguille sautée à la bordelaise, Madame," he said.

An eel sautéed in butter and wine. She hoped someone among her guests would try it.

"Vous êtes Monsieur LeClerc, n'est-ce pas?" she asked. Wasn't he Philippe LeClerc, the steward who had handed to Nina the glass from which Ambassador Troyanoskii drank strychnine? She would not have forgotten him, of course, but once again she was impressed by his nearly white blond hair; and now she noticed that the blue of his eyes was coldly pale.

"Oui, Madame," he said. Although as a steward he was not supposed to show any emotion, he smiled as though he were flattered that the great lady remembered him.

She smiled and nodded at him, then went on along the table, impatient to return to Tommy, who was typing a draft of the newspaper column in the few minutes they had before guests arrived.

The first to arrive were Colonel Charles Lévèque and his daughter Renée. Mrs. Roosevelt urged Nina to come out from her bedroom and meet the guests, and Nina was soon chatting comfortably with Renée Lévèque.

Henry Luce arrived, and shortly he was talking amiably with Robert Logan, the American automobile manufacturer.

Jack Benny and Mary Livingstone came in.

"I'm sorry if we're late," he said, "but I had to wait for my hair to dry."

"I told him not to hang it in the shower," said Mary.

Mrs. Roosevelt had also invited Moira Lasky, and she appeared alone, without Ernst Richter Remer. "The bop on the head did him more harm than he wanted to admit last night," she said. "He's got a headache now and is lying in bed."

"That's too bad. Dr. Grasse—"

"He doesn't want to see a doctor. He gets testy every time I suggest it. Anyway, he asked me to thank you for the invitation and convey his regrets."

Across the room, Jack Kennedy—whom Mrs. Roosevelt had also invited—was filling his plate at the buffet.

"I say, Kennedy. Good to see you."

The greeting came from Leonard Cooper, the London newspaper publisher, who was studying the food with interest and enthusiasm. He was a ruddy, bald, paunchy man—the sort the Victorians would have called typically English.

"Ah, thank you. Mr., ah . . ."

"Cooper. Leonard Cooper. *Daily Advertiser.*"

"Oh, of course. Forgive me."

"I'd understood Lindbergh would be here. Have you seen him?"

Jack Kennedy shook his head. "No. You understand that Colonel Lindbergh is a shy fellow who has never learned to enjoy parties. He's a charming man one-on-one, but—"

"Yes. I thought he might regard this luncheon as a command performance."

"Well, I'm sure Mrs. Roosevelt doesn't think of it that way."

"Tell me, Kennedy, isn't the slight girl there the ballerina who was traveling with Ambassador Troyanoskii?"

"Yes. Nina Rozanov."

"Ah. A beauty. Of course, that's to be expected. Her mother was a great beauty."

Cooper pointed at the lobster salad, and the steward behind the buffet table spooned a generous portion onto his plate. Cooper nodded—a signal that he wanted more.

"You saw her?" Jack asked. "I mean, the Countess Rozanov?"

"Yaas. As a young journalist, I went to Leningrad in 1917. Just in time to see catastrophe befall the Rozanovs. Not very sympathetic people, I might say; but it was a shame to see such a fall from the heights to the depths."

"What about Troyanoskii? Did you see him at that time?"

"Yes. An errand boy, he was. For the Bolsheviks to accept the son of a rich man into their ranks, he had to do conspicuous service. And he did."

"What service did he perform?" Jack asked.

"Wealth," said Cooper. "His function was to find the wealth the aristocrats and capitalists were squirreling away and to seize it for the Bolsheviks. Since he was a friend of the wealthy—in fact *one* of them—he had some pretty good ideas about where they were hiding their wealth. He would come back from a four-day venture into the countryside, bringing back a whole lorry load of jewelry, art, furniture, even clothing—anything worth money. He went to the country estates and looted them. For the Revolution, of course."

"For the Revolution," Jack repeated thoughtfully.

Cooper sneered. "For the *revolutionists*. Some of the loot went to support the cause, I suppose. Most of it went into the pockets of the looters. It's not widely known, but Vladimir Ilyich Lenin loved silk underwear and wore it under his clothes."

Jack smiled.

"I mean, *women's* silk underwear," said Cooper. "Countess Rozanov's would have been too small for him, but—"

"Are you serious, Mr. Cooper? How did you learn all this?"

Cooper raised his big eyebrows. "I believe I heard from your father than you have some interest in becoming a journalist. If so, you must learn to use sources. Sources, Kennedy. Every famous man has someone who hates him and will betray his secrets."

"Troyanoskii . . ."

Cooper walked away from the buffet, seeking a place where he could sit down and enjoy his food. Jack followed him, carrying a plate half full but not willing to lose contact with the man.

"The aristocrats lived extravagantly," said Cooper. "Why can't the upper classes learn not to flaunt their wealth in the faces of the poor? Jewels and furs cause revolutions, Kennedy. And big cars, yachts, flamboyant mansions. It is bad enough to be poor and hungry without having constantly to see women wearing on their fingers and wrists value that would buy your family food for seven years. Anyway, the Bolsheviks captured immense loot. But most of them had the sense to conceal it. They live today with vast wealth concealed. Even today most of them don't believe their revolution is permanent. They expect to be driven into exile, at best—only when they flee they will carry with them enough loot to support them comfortably for the rest of their lives. Most of them have number accounts in Zurich, too. That's one reason Stalin murdered so many of the old Bolsheviks. He wanted to get his hands on their booty."

"Troyanoskii," Jack persisted.

"The smartest of them," said Cooper. "He knew they would turn on him sooner or later. So he lived abroad as much as he could and hid his loot where they couldn't find it."

"And the Countess?"

"Pretty little thing," said Cooper. "Delicate. Exquisite. With the morals of a cat. She meant to be a survivor. And for a long time, she was—until her interests ran counter to those of another professional survivor."

"Troyanoskii."

"Troyanoskii."

"Was he responsible for her death?" asked Jack.

"The Rozanovs had two principal homes," said Cooper. "One in St. Petersburg—Leningrad, now—and one in the country outside. The country place was safe for a while. The uncle stayed there—the other count, Count Mikhail. When he was there, Countess Andrea could not stay in the country house, if you follow me. I mean, she couldn't stay there unless her husband was there, too. And he wasn't there—hardly ever, after 1914. So she kept to the house in the city, and Troyanoskii moved in with her. He was her protection, from the Bolsheviks and also from Count Mikhail. I've no doubt he took everything he could carry away—the family jewels, the silver, the plate, the art. She handed it all over, to save herself. I have no doubt she told him where more wealth was hidden, on the country estate. I've no doubt, either, that half of what he took—if not more—wound up in his own coffers."

"Then she was arrested," said Jack.

Cooper nodded. "They took her to prison; and, after some of them had their pleasure of her, as the saying is, they shot her."

"Troyanoskii?"

"He kept his mouth shut. It was Dzerzhinsky himself who wanted her dead. The head of the Cheka."

"Why?"

Cooper shrugged. "Why did the Jacobins insist on beheading poor little Jeanne du Barry? Countess Andrea was a highly visible aristocrat. She was politically active, too, I might tell you. Who knows what enemies she had? Dzerzhinsky was always happy to kill someone, to accommodate a friend."

"How did Count Mikhail arrange to escape?"

"I've always had a theory about that," said Cooper. "Mind you, Kennedy, it's just a theory, and you must not mention it to Nina Rozanov. But frankly, I've always suspected that bringing Nina out of the Soviet Union was the condition on which Count Mikhail was allowed to escape."

"Why?"

Cooper tipped his head to one side and smiled slyly at Jack. "Because someone other than Count Nicholas Alexandrovich Rozanov was the girl's father."

"Everyone seems to be so happy," said Margot von Heinroth to Josephine Baker. Because she spoke no English and Baker spoke no German, they were conversing in French. "No one wanted war. But when Adolf Hitler says he will redress a grievance, everyone should know he *will* redress that grievance. Anyway . . . We shall have peace."

Josephine Baker nodded and made no comment. She would let this plump little German woman talk. She was conscious of the contrast between herself and Margot von Heinroth—that she was dark and svelte and had a reputation for iconoclastic humor, while the little frau was plain and pale and unstylish. Frau von Heinroth was more than twenty years younger than her husband, and her deference to his opinions disgusted Baker. She had been glad when von Heinroth walked away from them, suggesting the two women would find more to talk about when he wasn't listening. Margot von Heinroth had not understood Baker's dry question—"I wonder what he thinks that is?"

Moira walked up. "Nice to see you again," she said to Josephine Baker. "You remember we met at the party the other night, just before Troyanoskii—"

"Miss, uh . . ."

"Lasky. Moira Lasky. I'm an old friend of Mrs. Roosevelt's."

"Yes. Well, meet Frau Margot von Heinroth."

"Pleasure," said Moira. "What city are you from?"

"She doesn't understand English," said Baker. *Ou vivez-vous en Allemagne?"* she translated.

"Berlin," said the German.

"My friend is from there," said Moira. "Ernst Richter Remer?"

"Connaissez-vous peut-être Monsieur Ernst Richter Remer, un ami de Mademoiselle Lasky?"

"Berlin est une grande ville," said Margot von Heinroth innocently.

"I get it," said Moira. "Ernst is a wine broker."

"Monsieur Remer est un brocanteur des vins."

The little German woman smiled and shook her head.

"Okay, it's a big city," said Moira.

"Mon gran' père est un brocanteur des vins," Margot von Heinroth volunteered. *"Herr Heinrich Schiller."*

"I'll ask Ernst if he knows him," said Moira. "And so much for mutual acquaintances."

"Les grands negociants des vins sont une fraternité tres limité," said Margot von Heinroth.

"She says the fraternity of big wine merchants is very limited," Baker translated.

"I'm sorry I mentioned it. Ask her how she likes the weather."

"It is odd how small the world can sometimes be," said Mrs. Roosevelt.

"And to others, how very, very large, Madame," said Ouzoulias.

"It seems everyone we meet knows someone who knew Ambassador Troyanoskii or knew Countess Rozanov," she said.

"I hope you will not be offended if I suggest that you and the Countess traveled in similar circles," said the detective.

"Yes . . . I do remember Russian girls at my school in England."

"You see? There are two worlds, and oddly enough the one with the small number of people is commonly called the great world. Wherever people from that world go, they encounter people they know, or mutual friends. I need hardly mention that aboard *Normandie* is a place where the people of the great world congregate."

"But so many people seem to know so much . . ."

As soon as he could, Jack Kennedy had told Mrs. Roosevelt what Leonard Cooper had said about the Rozanovs— particularly that Nina might be the daughter of a man other than the Count. Mrs. Roosevelt did not tell him that Goldinin had said she was probably the daughter of Troyanoskii.

Elliott Roosevelt

"It might be nothing more than gossip," said Jack.

They were talking inside Mrs. Roosevelt's bedroom. Some of the luncheon guests were still in the sitting room.

"It is of no difference," said Ouzoulias. ("Deef-ay-RAWNTZ.") "The odd problems of the parentage of Mademoiselle Rozanov do not answer the three questions on which our attention must be focused—which are: first, who poisoned Ambassador Troyanoskii; second, who stole the jewels from the purser's safe, and, third, who fired a shot at Mademoiselle Razonov?"

12

"Never," said Edouard Ouzoulias angrily. "Never before in my experience have such things happened aboard a vessel of *Compagnie Générale Transatlantique*. Is this voyage cursed?"

He had been called down to D Deck, to the fish-preparation room, in mid-afternoon, to see what frightened chefs had discovered there a few minutes before—the body of a steward, dead of stab wounds. The room was of course equipped with a variety of razor-sharp knives, and one of these had been driven between the steward's ribs from behind his back.

Not one knife was missing from the rack. "Whoever did it," said one of his subordinates to Ouzoulias, "cleaned the knife and replaced it. It may be impossible to discover which was used."

"A matter of great moment," said Ouzoulias scornfully.

The assistant shrugged. "The crime was committed by someone who knows the work schedule here," he said. "There is a period of about two hours between the time when this room is used to prepare fish for lunch and when chefs return to begin cutting fish for dinner. During that time, the room is abandoned."

A chef in white coat and tall white hat spoke. "Because fish must be prepared immediately before it is served, it is not brought in from the refrigerated room until just before the lunch or dinner hour. Then we work quickly. When we have finished the lunch work and go to eat our own midday meal, a crew moves in and cleans this room thoroughly. A room where fish is prepared must be painstakingly cleaned, you know."

"Why would a steward be in here at all?" asked Ouzoulias.

"He should not be," said the chef. "He has no business here."

Ouzoulias sighed disgustedly and glanced around. "Who saw him come in here? Who saw someone else come in? Who saw that someone else leave this room?"

The chef shook his head. Another chef, who until now had hung back, trembling with horror at the sight of the bloody corpse, also shook his head, more emphatically.

"What's his name? Where's his bunk?"

The name of the dead steward turned out to be François Flavigny, a twenty-nine-year-old Parisian who had served aboard the *Normandie* since her maiden voyage. He was regarded by his superiors as a reliable, though unimaginative, man—one who did his job quietly and made no trouble, but never did more than was asked of him. The other stewards who had shared a cabin with him said that Flavigny had a handsome girl in Le Havre, one in New

York, and one in Paris—and that he often borrowed money to buy gifts for these several young women. He was always in need of money, but he always repaid his loans, usually on the next voyage.

Ouzoulias could confirm the young man's attraction for women. Among his possessions there were seven photographs. Each bore an affectionate inscription. The girl from New York had been photographed half naked—that is, in her underwear.

Also found in Flavigny's gear was a key to a first-class stateroom. This proved to be that of Mrs. Foster Duggins, an Englishwoman who was traveling alone to join her husband in the United States. Ouzoulias was faced with the problem of whether or not to interrogate Mrs. Duggins.

After he conferred with Dr. Grasse, he decided to question her only very gently.

Flavigny, the doctor said, was killed by a powerful blow with one of the larger knives in the fish-preparation room. The blow struck just below the shoulder blade and entered the body almost horizontally. The knife-wielder had to be at least six feet tall, said Dr. Grasse—and he had to be powerfully muscled.

"We found something else also, when we stripped the body for the examination," said Dr. Grasse. "A money belt. A few English pounds. A few marks. A few American dollars. And—" He paused for dramatic emphasis. "—more than ten thousand French francs."

"A lot of francs," said Ouzoulias, "for a man described by his fellow stewards as constantly in need of money."

"I hesitated to tell you about this at all," said Ouzoulias to Mrs. Roosevelt. "It does seem unrelated to the matter of the Ambassador and the missing jewels. Yet, I must tell you that in all my experience with CGT—the company you call French Line—I have never been aboard a voyage during which two people were murdered, an attempt was made to kill a third, and a vast fortune in jewels was taken from the purser's safe. I cannot believe it is a coincidence that these things all happened on this voyage. I simply cannot believe it. There *must* be a connection."

"I agree with that," said Mrs. Roosevelt.

"The Englishwoman, Mrs. Duggins, took my gentle questioning rather hard," said Ouzoulias. "I had to tell her, of course. I had at least to inquire if anything was missing from her stateroom."

"Their relationship was. . . ?"

"I needn't say more."

It was late afternoon now, and Mrs. Roosevelt found she was beginning to show the effects of late hours, attention to duty, and the tension of the kind of events she had witnessed these three days. In a week she would be fifty-four years old. It was said of her, both by those who admired her and those who fervidly did not, that she worked harder than any First Lady who had ever preceded her, bar none. Her stamina was acknowledged, both by those who found it hopeful and helpful and by those who decried it as hazardous to the Republic.

She had received another invitation to be at the captain's table—the third night in succession, something almost unique. She had sent Captain Colbert a handwritten note, saying she was a little tired and would, with his kind consent, take her dinner in her suite this evening. She was certain he would be glad to have that note. It would solve a delicate problem of protocol with which he must have been struggling manfully.

She focused her mind on the possible connection between this latest atrocity and the things that had happened before. "I may tell you, Monsieur Ouzoulias," she said, closing her eyes for a moment, "that I was hoping this voyage would afford me a bit of a chance to relax. I—"

"You face congressional election next month," said Ouzoulias.

"You know that?"

He lofted a great Gallic shrug. "We know something of the *politique* of most nation," he said. "After all, was it not we French who invented *politique?*"

She hadn't really thought the French invented politics, but she did not elect to argue the point. So she nodded.

Agent Edouard Ouzoulias was apparently somewhat pleased with his claim to French preeminence. He pulled his pipe from his jacket pocket, and once more she was surprised to find it still held flame deep in its reservoir of ashes and tobacco and that he could bright it to life without touching fire to it. He must have spent half a lifetime learning to pack a pipe to do that. She wondered how many holes he had burned in jackets, but she decided not to ask.

"There is no reason why you should continue to concern yourself," he said. "Your assistance has been valuable, but these crimes are *my* responsibility after all."

"Promise me, Monsieur Ouzoulias," she said, "that we will solve this mystery before we dock in New York on Monday. If you can promise me that—"

"I cannot promise it, Madame," he said. "I cannot, indeed, promise that five years from now we will know who murdered Ambassador Troyanoskii."

Mrs. Roosevelt ran her fingertips over her eyes, and her palms down her cheeks. "The game is afoot, Monsieur Ouzoulias," she said. "Do you know that expression—'The game is afoot'? Sherlock Holmes—"

"Of *course.*"

"Well . . . When the game is afoot, I could no more withdraw than I could withdraw in the middle of a campaign when my husband is a candidate for President. Do you understand?"

"Then I fear you share with me much hard labor, dear Madame," he said.

"Non sine mag—"

"Not without great labor did God overcome death," said Jack Kennedy, who had been in Nina's room talking with her and now came out just in time to interrupt Mrs. Roosevelt's Latin quotation.

"I thought," she said, "you got little Latin and less Greek at Harvard these days."

"No Latin, no Greek," the young man laughed. "But always an ample supply of all the world's best clichés. I'm sorry. I guess I'm interrupting something."

"It may be well," said Mrs. Roosevelt, "if we all sit down at dinner together this evening."

So it was at seven-thirty. Four gathered around a table in the sitting room—the First Lady, Edouard Ouzoulias, Nina Rozanov, and Jack Kennedy. Mrs. Roosevelt had insisted that Tommy Thompson go on to the grand dining room for dinner at her elegant table. How many evenings, after all, did one have the opportunity to dine aboard *Normandie?*

"Mademoiselle Rozanov," said Ouzoulias. "You remain a suspect, I must tell you. We cannot be satisfied with some elements of what you have told us. Many questions remain to be answered. Perhaps you cannot answer all of them, but we have to suspect you can answer some."

Nina had brought few clothes on the voyage, so she was dressed for dinner in the simple black skirt she had worn the night the Ambassador had introduced her—with a tight black sleeveless knit bodice. Her hair was tied back very tightly, shaping itself to her head. She looked, Mrs. Roosevelt reflected, like a sculpture of a young dancer, by Degas.

Probably, Mrs. Roosevelt reflected, Nina regarded the people around the table as so many accusers—except, perhaps, Jack Kennedy, with whom she seemed to have established a sort of rapport. It seemed brutal for Ouzoulias—perhaps all of them, in fact—to be challenging the tiny girl. She played so large a role in everything happening that it was difficult, when she was not in your sight, to remember that she was so tiny. It was equally easy to forget that within that tiny body there was a strong, determined personality.

"Of what am I accused, Monsieur?" she asked quietly. "Of the murder of Boris Vasilievich? Of the theft from the purser's safe? Of firing a shot at myself?"

"Mademoiselle," said Ouzoulias. "You would assist us if you would explain why we found in your cabin the jewels that seemed to have come from the treasure the Ambassador had in his stateroom."

"They were mine," she said firmly. "Rightfully mine."

"Mademoiselle," said Ouzoulias gently, "you told us that Ambassador Troyanoskii allowed you to search through jewelry he had stolen—or his government had stolen—and recover what was your family's. Please, Mademoiselle. You left Russia when you were a child. How, then, could you have recognized articles of jewelry in a great collection of similar articles?"

Nina glanced around the dinner table, her eyes passing hurriedly past Ouzoulias but pausing on Jack's eyes and Mrs. Roosevelt's, as if she thought there she might find some sympathy. Then she lowered her eyes. "He admitted to me," she said, "that some of the jewelry had been my family's. I *demanded* he make some of it mine. I could tell which pieces—some, anyway—were mine. I had studied the old insurance photos many times. Many times . . ."

"The lovely diamond pendant. . . ?" asked Mrs. Roosevelt.

"It *was* my mother's," Nina whispered. "Boris Vasilievich gave it to me in Paris, not long after we met."

"Why?" asked Jack Kennedy simply.

"He was an evil man," she said in a hushed, small voice. "He was capable of murder." She nodded. "Yes. Maybe worse. And he wanted me. He *wanted* me. But he loved me, too. He was gentle." She closed her eyes and squeezed out tears. "Ugly man . . . Evil . . . But kind to me."

"He gave you—?" Ouzoulias started to ask.

"The diamond," Nina whispered. "I . . . I think I remember it. My mother wore it. I *think* I remember. I believe he gave me what was really my mother's." Then she shrugged. "The rest of it, who knows? He was generous. Oddly generous. I don't know why. He said the things he gave me would help me in America. He said I should sell everything immediately—all but the diamond pendant. I stole nothing from him, Monsieur! Nothing!"

"How did you come to meet him?" asked Jack.

"He came to Paris," she said. "It was . . . what? It was 1933, I guess. He was a Bolshevik, of course. My uncle hated him. I was eighteen years old and my uncle would not let me see him. Then he came to the ballet. He— He was not to be resisted."

"Do you think he was responsible for the death of your mother?" Ouzoulias asked.

Nina pondered for a moment, pressing tears from the corners of her eyes with the tips of her fingers. "No . . ." she whispered finally. "My uncle insisted he was. But Uncle Mikhail is a fanatic in his hatred of the Bolsheviks."

"You must forgive me, Mademoiselle," said Ouzoulias, "but I am going to ask you an indelicate question."

Nina glanced into his eyes, then shrugged. Having grown up in Paris, she could shrug as meaningfully as any Frenchman.

"You have described yourself, Mademoiselle, as Ambassador Troyanoskii's mistress. On one occasion you described your relationship with him as 'intimate.' I must ask you, then, to be specific as to the nature of that relationship. Did you, in fact—"

"No."

"No?"

"He was very affectionate to me," Nina said solemnly. "I used the word 'intimate.' He did treat me in an intimate way, as though I were his mistress. He would enter a room where I was dressing. On public occasions where we were together, he treated me as a mistress, most openly. But— I wondered why he never in fact demanded . . . the ultimate act."

The other three—Mrs. Roosevelt, Ouzoulias, and Jack Kennedy—exchanged glances. Maybe Troyanoskii *had been* her father.

"Why did you consent to this, Mademoiselle?" asked Ouzoulias. "Surely, your reputation—"

"Almost from the time I met him," she said, "Boris Vasilievich talked about taking me to London or New York, where I could establish my career free of the impediment of being a White Russian."

"Surely that's no impediment in ballet," said Mrs. Roosevelt. "Some of the finest companies in Europe are peopled with Russian refugees."

"As I grew up," said Nina quietly, "I came to understand that my uncle Mikhail was an impediment. He had no great reputation as a ballet master. In fact, he had none at all. He was more interested in politics. He and his friends sat around, drinking vodka, talking endlessly of the day when they would return in triumph to St. Petersburg."

"Was there, then, a conflict between your uncle and your new friend Troyanoskii?" asked Jack.

"Yes. Uncle Mikhail hated Boris Vasilievich."

"Troyanoskii created the distinct impression that he had made you his mistress," said Jack. "That must have—"

"It made my uncle furious," said Nina. "At me, also. Uncle Mikhail reminded me repeatedly—as he had ever since I was old enough to understand—that it was he who had brought me out of Russia and so saved my life. How, then, could I ally myself with a notorious Bolshevik, even a Chekist?"

"And you did it because—"

"Because I could see there would never be anything for me—no kind of life—if I were forever bound to Uncle Mikhail. I owed him loyalty, of course. But I wanted to leave him. He took my earnings, directly from the ballet company. At the end, I was supporting him. Boris Vasilievich represented opportunity. And freedom."

"Had you no alternatives, child?" Mrs. Roosevelt asked gently. "Surely a beautiful young girl like you—"

"Oh, yes," said Nina. "Dancers. Impoverished egomaniacs. They had ideas. And . . . rich men. They, too. Disgusting ideas."

"When your uncle learned that you were leaving him, leaving France in fact, with Ambassador Troyanoskii, how did he react?" asked Mrs. Roosevelt.

"I don't know," said Nina. "Boris Vasilievich sent him word, after I had moved into his flat—about two weeks ago. Boris Vasilievich was afraid Uncle Mikhail and his White Russian friends would try to restrain me if he learned that I was planning to travel to America. So, one day I took a few things in a small bag and left Uncle Mikhail's flat. Boris Vasilievich was waiting for me in a car. I never returned. I never saw Uncle Mikhail again."

"Did he try to—?"

"Yes. Both in person and through others. But Ignatieff and Goldinin lived in Boris Vasilievich's flat. They had guns."

"Others?" asked Ouzoulias. "What others? What did they do?"

"Uncle Mikhail came to demand my return. When he was turned back by Goldinin, he went away and came back with two men. That was when Goldinin and Ignatieff showed them their pistols."

"I do not understand, Mademoiselle," said Ouzoulias, "why, even after the Ambassador was dead, you continued to say you were his mistress and had an intimate relationship with him."

Nina reached for a glass of champagne Jack Kennedy had poured for her. She drew a deep breath and for a moment held it while she hesitated to answer. "Boris Vasilievich," she said gravely, "did not intend to return to Europe. He had decided to desert the Bolshevik cause and live in America. He wanted to take me with him—I am sure to be his mistress there, maybe even his wife. But he could not allow the NKVD to see that he was doing something very different from anything he had ever done before—such as take with him a girl he respected . . . maybe loved. It was essential to the scheme that he take me as a plaything, his mistress of the moment. He emphasized that."

"But after he was dead?" Ouzoulias asked.

"Monsieur," she said solemnly. "Someone *murdered* Boris Vasilievich. Someone tried to murder me. Doesn't it occur to you that whoever killed him also tried to kill me? And will try again?"

"Do you believe he killed your mother?" asked Ouzoulias.

165

Nina shook her head. "Who knows? *He* knew. Maybe he was kind to me because his conscience troubled him."

"My dear," said Mrs. Roosevelt. "Do you think it is possible that Ambassador Troyanoskii was murdered by friends of your uncle? It is possible that the White Russians—?"

"Possible," snapped Nina. "Did I not say before that Bolsheviks will continue to rule in Russia because the Whites are no better than they? They have no country, those men. They dream of taking again the wealth and power they lost twenty years ago. They are *conspirators*. Nothing but conspirators. What else have they to do but dream and scheme? Yes, they could have put someone aboard this ship to kill Boris Vasilievich. And—"

"And they might," said Jack Kennedy, "have considered it to their advantage to try to make it appear that *you* killed him."

Nina closed her eyes and nodded. "Of course," she said. "Have you," she asked Ouzoulias, "taken *that* into consideration?"

Ouzoulias spoke to Mrs. Roosevelt. "Must we accept yet another theory about the crime?" he asked plaintively.

Mrs. Roosevelt nodded and smiled. "Any theory, Monsieur Ouzoulias, that turns suspicion away from Mademoiselle Rozanov."

13

Jack Kennedy was less comfortable than anyone suspected. No one knew it but a few members of his family and his closest friends, but he had only recently been circumcised— a painful operation for an adult male—and he was still experiencing some resulting tenderness. Also, from time to time he suffered bouts of sinus headache; and a headache had developed over the dinner with Mrs. Roosevelt, Nina, and the detective— perhaps because of the dry heat aboard the ship. He decided, when he left Mrs. Roosevelt's suite, to go to the ship's gymnasium for a session in the steam room, perhaps followed by a swim in the pool.

In the steam room he sat with a towel across his lap, otherwise naked. He was a pale, gawky young man whose dogged tenacity in pursuit of athletic recognition surprised nearly everyone who knew him. It had been no wonder he hurt himself at football; he always extended himself too far, trying to excel—or trying to compete with his elder brother, Joe, or other young men who were stronger than he. Excellence was expected of him, he knew. His parents would tolerate nothing less. But his unprepossessing appearance at age twenty-one did not suggest a star athlete or a star anything else.

His mind, during his twenty minutes in the steam room, did not focus on the murder of Boris Vasilievich Troyanoskii or on the attempt to kill Nina that had almost killed him. Rather, he was thinking about his father and about what had happened in Munich in the past few days.

The problem, as Jack saw it, was that his father's attitude toward the European problem was far apart from President Roosevelt's. Any man was entitled to his opinion, of course, but Ambassador Kennedy was, after all, a Roosevelt appointee, and the President and the State Department expected an ambassador to voice administration attitudes, not his own. Another problem was that his father was being mentioned here and there—not yet widely—as a possible candidate for President or Vice President in 1940. President Roosevelt could not, of course, stand for a third term. Prominent among those being suggested as his successor was Vice President John Nance, Garner, and an Irish Catholic from Boston would balance the ticket nicely—particularly if that Irish Catholic from Boston were a committed isolationist.

Colonel Lindbergh had been a guest at the embassy in London. He had briefed Ambassador Kennedy on the strength of the German air force. The Ambassador had sent a summary of that briefing to the White House. He had done more. He had given the same summary to Prime Minister Chamberlain, who had undoubtedly read it before he went to Munich and surrendered Czechoslovakia to Hitler. This afternoon, listening to the shortwave radio in his stateroom, Jack had heard his father's voice, telling an interviewer how very wise Chamberlain had been to let Herr Hitler have his way about the Sudetenland. Jack was not sure his father was right. In fact, he doubted it. He was not supposed to hold an opinion independent of his father's, so he kept his doubts to himself; but he suspected the President's opinion of the Munich agreement was one-hundred-eighty degrees opposed to Joe Kennedy's view.

Other than that— Well, he had to finish his degree at Harvard. The professors expected a level of performance, no matter that a man's father held an important position in London and that a man had opportunities to move in the world they studied and wrote about but—most of them—could only dream of touching. Academics liked people who stood aloof and studied events. They were suspicious of—jealous of?—those who participated.

And— Girls. To his amusement, he found himself a "catch." In Boston and London, mothers worried over ways to arrange for their daughters to meet John Fitzgerald Kennedy. Better than that, the daughters often proved interested in more than a polite relationship. This past summer he'd had several relationships that had passed beyond the polite, and as he returned to the States he found himself in the embarrassing position of being obligated to untangle some of those relationships.

Nina Rozanov. God, if he had only been the Czar! The Czar had been privileged to enjoy as many ballerinas as he wanted. Unhappy Nicky the Second, though, had never had the imagination to take full advantage of the privilege. Nina . . . She would almost be worth running away with, forgetting you were a Kennedy. Almost—

* * *

The pool. Though narrow, it was seventy-five feet long.
The pool itself and the ramps and walls surrounding it
were lined with blue-and-white Sèvres porcelain tiles. At
this hour only a few people were there, all of them nearly
uniform in their swimming suits—blue knit shorts and
vests for men, blue knit suits for women, both men's and
women's outfits cinched at the waist with white web
belts.

The pool bar—similarly decorated with blue-and-white
tiles—remained open.

Jack climbed down a ladder into the water—a descent of
some six feet, since the water had to be low enough not to
splash out when the ship pitched and rolled. He swam
three lengths of the deep part, then paused in the middle,
treading water, working his legs, exhilarated by the exercise.

"Mr. Kennedy, isn't it?"

A woman was in the pool beside him, treading water as
he was. He hadn't noticed her until she spoke, and he
didn't think he knew her—at least, he couldn't place her.

He smiled at her. "I'm afraid you have me at a disadvantage," he said.

"We met at a reception, where one meets so many people
it is no gaffe not to remember. I'm Pamela Duggins. We
met at The Savoy, at the reception for Vivien Leigh."

"Oh, yes." He didn't remember.

"There is no reason why you should remember," she
said. "You were introduced as the son of the American ambassador. I was on the arm of my squirrely little husband,
who was introduced as a corn broker. We were not a very
impressive couple."

"Oh, I—"

She grinned and playfully slapped water at him. "If you

want to make it up to me, you can come over to the bar and have a drink with me."

They climbed from the pool and walked to the adjacent bar. Except for the tiles covering the floor, the walls, and the bar, it was an ordinary semicircular bar, faced by leather-topped stools. Some of the people wore wet swimming clothes. Others had donned white robes. Still others had come down to the bar from the decks above and drank at the pool bar in street clothes or the formal clothing they had worn to dinner in the grand dining room.

Pamela Duggins was a tall, husky blond, maybe thirty-five years old. She was as tall as Jack and maybe as heavy. Her face was oddly flat—sharp but short nose, sharp but receding chin, a broad mouth with thin lips, pale blue eyes. She had elected not to wear a rubber bathing cap in the pool, and her short, wet hair clung tightly to the contours of her head. Before they reached the bar she had entangled her arm in Jack's, and he was aware that she had been to the bar before.

"Whiskey?" she asked. She turned to the bartender, pointed a finger at herself, and said—"A large whiskey, please."

Jack nodded at the bartender. A large whiskey, as the English said—a Scotch.

"I wish I had waited for one of the Queens," said Pamela Duggins. She meant she wished she had chosen the *Queen Mary* or the *Queen Elizabeth* for her transatlantic crossing. "Something wrong with this ship."

"It's the most beautiful ship in the world," said Jack.

"Something wrong with this crossing, then," she said dully.

"I find it delightful."

"The ship . . . Yes. Elegant. But it is a tragic ship—or at least this is a tragic crossing."

He wasn't sure what she knew or what she referred to, so he kept silent and waited for her to explain herself.

"I am sure you know two men have died during this crossing," she said. "Both of them murdered. The Russian ambassador . . . and a steward named François Flavigny."

"Steward?" Jack asked. He hadn't known it.

The woman nodded. "A handsome young man. Killed with a knife."

"A fight?"

She shook her head. "Simply murdered. The ship's detective came to tell me. He doesn't know who did it."

Jack frowned and shook his head. He did not ask the question that had come instantly to his mind.

"I've been indiscreet again," she sighed. "Why, you must wonder, did the detective feel he had to tell *me*?"

"I, uh— I wasn't wondering," he lied.

She shrugged. "You can guess why."

Before he could shake his head and lie again by suggesting he had no idea why, the bartender interrupted by placing their drinks before them.

"He had a key to my stateroom," she said as she lifted her glass. Her eyes rose to Jack's. "I'll give *you* that key, if you want it."

"The offer . . . uh, is an honor, Mrs.—"

"Pamela, dammit!"

"Uh, okay. It's an honor, Pamela."

"Which you do not wish to accept."

He frowned and searched for words. "My father is a political man, you know. That imposes . . . It imposes, shall we say, rules of discretion? You're a handsome woman, Pamela. Any other man at all would—"

"Would he?" she asked coldly.

"I would think so. And if your husband— Well . . . For someone else, it might be a scandal. Maybe an amusing scandal. For me . . . Please try to understand."

Pamela Duggins tilted her head and regarded Jack Kennedy with a knowing smile, half sarcastic, half genuinely amused. "In London it is supposed you are a bed-hopper," she said. She put her hand on his bare arm and ran her fingers down it. "I thought, if that is the case, why not Pamela? We can add each other to our trophy collections." Now she shrugged, and her smile broadened. "You are not very graceful, Jack, in saying no. I wonder if you ever make the proposition yourself—and if you do, do you make it more gracefully? If you don't, you must be a virgin."

"I—"

"Do you have any sense of how *boring* this voyage is?" she asked, her mood switching rapidly to irritation. "Big damned ship. Loaded with thousands of dull people." She glanced around and gestured angrily. "Look at the men! Carbon copies of my husband! So I gave my key to the steward who brought me a quart of whiskey and invited him to return when he was off duty." She smiled. The liquor facilitated her swings in mood. "And he did return. Big French boy. No more than half literate. And I don't give a damn who finds out, my husband or anybody else. Except that—"

"Except that somebody killed him," said Jack.

"An oddly clean end to a brief affair," she said.

Jack looked around to see if anyone seemed to be listening to their conversation. No one was, though she was no more discreet about keeping this kind of talk hushed than she had been—apparently—about the truncated liaison she'd had with a steward.

"Let's take our drinks over to the pool," he said.

They walked into the terraced shallow end and sat down in the warm water, well apart from anyone else.

"Can you think of any reason why the murder of your steward might be related to the murder of the Russian ambassador?" he asked. "It is an odd coincidence that two murders should happen on the same ship on the same transatlantic crossing, don't you think?"

Pamela Duggins stretched her legs out before her and settled her body deeper into the comforting water. "I think it's odd that I pay all the pounds I paid to cross the ocean on the *Normandie* and have my little love partner stabbed to death after only two nights. My husband is not on board, so it could not have been him. Maybe François had another lover who was jealous. In that case, I'm in danger, too, don't you think?"

"I don't know," said Jack. "I don't think so. I don't imagine jealousy was why your friend was killed."

"Oh, *thank you*. More flattery. You really are a charming young man."

"Two murders are not the only crimes that have been committed aboard this ship during this crossing," he said gravely. "If no one else has told you, let me tell you—in complete confidence, Pamela, please—that there has also been an *attempted* murder and a burglary. There is reason to think all these crimes are related. Didn't Monsieur Ouzoulias ask you questions about a possible connection?"

She shrugged and drank Scotch. "The French Sherlock Holmes? He announced the death regretfully and respectfully left me to mourn my loss."

"Well, then . . . Will you allow an American Sherlock Holmes to ask you a question or two?"

"Why not? It's the funnest game I'm likely to get to play tonight."

"Well, tell me," said Jack, "was there anything about your steward that struck you as unusual?"

Pamela Duggins gulped the last of her whiskey and waved at the bartender to bring her another. "I have some little experience with affairs like this," she said. "Jack . . . darling. My husband is a wealthy man, a self-made man. He deals in what we English call corn, what you call grain. I'm on my way to the States to join him in New York, from where we will travel to the damned Great Plains, yours and Canada's, where he will meet with brokers in wheat and maize and God knows what other dusty little granules that people grind up and eat—and I will have the high privilege of entertaining their Baptist and Methodist wives. Jack, I do amuse myself as I can. When I can. Where I can. With whom I can. When you ask me if François struck me as unusual, I can answer from experience."

"Please do."

"They all ask for money," she said grimly. "I mean . . . hotel boys, ship's stewards. I mean— God, Jack, I am as handsome as Lady Chatterly was described as being, don't you think? Then why can't I— Well, never mind. They ask for money. Sooner or later. And maybe François would have, if he had lived."

"But he didn't?"

She shook her head. "No."

"He didn't steal?"

"All that French idiot—Ouzoulias—could think of. Had my murdered lover stolen anything from me? No. Nothing."

"Do you have any sense," Jack asked, "that he was maybe not really a steward but was someone else working as a steward to get him a place aboard this ship?"

"Well . . . He wasn't like any other steward who ever served me aboard ship."

"Did he speak English?"

"Not a word. And since I speak no French, and neither of

175

us spoke any other language, communication between us was . . ." She smiled happily. "Delicious."

"You speak no French. Then you couldn't know if he spoke French with an accent?"

"What do you have in mind, Jack?"

"Could he have been a Russian?"

She shrugged. "Who knows? The ship must have his papers."

"What else, Pamela? What kind of man was he?"

"A moody man," she said reminiscently, sadly. "The first night he was gay, happy. That was Thursday night. Then Friday— He was . . . How can I say? He was dutiful. But distracted."

"Maybe he was afraid. Maybe he knew he was in danger."

"That's a guess," she said. "Your guess."

"Well . . . Is there anything more you can say? Do you have *any* clues?"

"No Trichinopoly ashes, Sherlock," she said sarcastically. "No red mud from Belgravia. No tearful confession to make. I'm afraid you've learned nothing."

"Well . . ."

"And since I cannot nail you on my stateroom wall, my young friend— *Adieu. Bonne nuit. Bonne chance.*"

He encountered Josephine Baker on his way back to his stateroom.

"Ah, Kennedy," she said. "Give me an arm. I have imbibed too freely of the juice of the grape and am happy to have a strong young American arm to help me return to my door."

He gave her his arm and squeezed her hand in his to help support her, and they set off sternward, toward the first-class staterooms on the upper deck.

"Believe it or not," she said, "the night is not unkind. Let's venture out in the air. I could use a breath of the fresh stuff."

Shortly they were at the rail on the first-class promenade on the boat deck, looking back at the ship's faintly luminescent wake. She stood silent for a while, staring. He put his arm around her—out of a sense that she might be cold, wearing as she was a clinging silver lamé dress which left her back bare—and became very quickly aware of her warmth, which she communicated generously to him.

She was thirty-two years old. (That was how old she was, actually, though he guessed thirty-five.) She knew the world better than he did, he understood. She was wise, he had observed, in a way he could hope to become. And she was . . . a Negro.

His hand lay on her arm, and he realized it was the first time he had ever touched a black person. He couldn't recall ever even shaking the hand of a Negro. There was no reason why he hadn't; certainly he felt no reluctance about it; but, strangely, in his experience the occasion for it had never arisen. And now— Josephine Baker! He was standing here in the moonlight on the deck of the world's most luxurious ocean liner with his arm around the exotic, world-famous Josephine Baker!

"Boring, isn't it?" she asked suddenly. "Even if it is the *Normandie*. Dull people . . . God, how *dull* the rich can be!"

"The ship has facilities," he said. "I've been swimming this evening."

"I'm not sure the fabled French tolerance for dark skins would extend to my going in the swimming pool," she said. She didn't look up at him; she stared out to sea as she spoke. "If I weren't asked to leave, I might find myself swimming alone."

"Really?"

"Yes."

"I never thought of it."

"*You* don't have to."

Now she looked up at him. Her dark eyes were partly playful, partly solemn. He had never before seen anything like this mixture of impudent comedy and profound tragedy in anyone's eyes.

"It's not fair," he said softly.

"'Not fay-uh,'" she mimicked him. She smiled. Solemnity retreated. "The world isn't fay-uh, Kennedy. It isn't getting any fairer, either, what with this fellow Hitler rampaging all over Europe. If his ideas take over everywhere, then where will *I* go?"

"Come home to America," he said innocently.

"Not bloody likely," she muttered, staring away toward the horizon.

"I wish I could do something better than say I'm sorry."

She returned her eyes to him again. "I'll tell you what's better," she said. "Have a good time. That's what I try to do, mostly. It's what your old man does, too. He's known for it."

Jack wanted to change the subject. "Do you hear any talk about the murder of Ambassador Troyanoskii? I mean, what are they saying in the salon?"

"Oh, that he was a Bolshevik and good riddance. They say unkind things about Mrs. Roosevelt because she's trying to help the French solve the mystery. They say the Bolsheviks themselves probably killed him. They say she took the ballerina into her apartment to provide a place for you and the girl to sleep together. They say also it's a good thing that Hitler took part of Czechoslovakia, because that will make a stronger Germany, better able to stand against the Russians. The boring opinions of boring people."

"I'm sure Mrs. Roosevelt would be happy to see you more often," said Jack. "Unless you object, I'll suggest she invite you to lunch or dinner tomorrow."

"That's nice of you, Kennedy. I'll come and be on my best behavior."

14

Mrs. Roosevelt and Agent Edouard Ouzoulias were alone in her sitting room. Ouzoulias had arranged for the chart Mrs. Roosevelt had made on tablet paper to be transferred to a big rectangle of yellow poster board, and the new chart was at their feet on the floor. Mrs. Roosevelt had added some writing to it, and it now looked like this:

OPPORTUNITY TO MURDER T
Miss Rozanov   Philippe LeClerc   Others?
Anyone who had access to the bottle, glass, ice.

MOTIVE FOR MURDERING T
(1) Revenge. For what?
  (a) Nina. Abused by T? Some other motive? What of her family? *But what if he was her father?*
  (b) Someone else, for something T did as Chekist. *Count Mikhail Rozanov? White Russians?*
(2) To steal the jewels.
  (a) But how would that make stealing the jewels easier?
  (b) Maybe it did, because T would have known who knew he had jewels. (Jack's idea.)
(3) To recover the jewels if T stole them.
(4) Political motives. *Was T defecting?*

OPPORTUNITY TO SHOOT AT NINA
(1) A man. Agile.

MOTIVE FOR SHOOTING AT NINA
(1) Revenge for murder of T.
(2) To keep her quiet.
  (a) As to who killed T.
  (b) As to what T meant to do with jewels.
  (c) As to identity of her midnight visitor.

MURDER OF FLAVIGNY
Connection?

"It seems to make no difference how many times we stare at this," sighed the First Lady wearily—it was after midnight—"we only seem to add complications, not eliminate possibilities."

Ouzoulias twirled his snifter to set up a whirl in his brandy. "In it somewhere is the answer," he said.

She reached out with a long black pencil and tapped the top of the chart—"Opportunity to Murder T."

"It is here," she said. "If Miss Rozanov didn't do it, then who did?"

"And how?" he asked, his fatigue manifesting itself in the slight impatience that betrayed itself in his voice. "If the strychnine was not in the vodka bottle, then how did it get in the glass? How could it have been sneaked in, between the bar and when Mademoiselle Rozanov handed the glass to Troyanoskii?"

Mrs. Roosevelt sighed. "I'm losing sleep over the puzzle. Tomorrow is—" She paused and glanced at her watch. "Today is Sunday. Monday afternoon we dock in New York. Are we to concede we haven't been able to identify the murderer of Ambassador Troyanoskii?"

"My dear Madame," said Ouzoulias. "I have spent my life doing this kind of work, and I have had to concede many times that I could not solve a mystery. It is only the detectives of the fiction who solve all their problems. In real life—"

"Many criminals go free," she said.

"And some innocent men are convicted," he added.

She stared at the chart once more. "We—"

A knock on the door. Ouzoulias stepped over and opened it.

"Monsieur Kennedy, good evening." He turned and smiled at Mrs. Roosevelt. "It seems we are not the only ones who have difficulty sleeping."

"Come in, Jack," she said. "I've a pot of tea—or you can
have a shot of brandy if you prefer."

"Thank you," said Jack. "I do prefer."

"Nina went to bed long ago."

"I didn't come to see Nina."

Ouzoulias frowned over his pipe. Squinting and twisting
his mouth, he searched in its bowl for some suggestion of
the spark of fire he could coax into glowing life. Unhappy
with what he saw, he nonetheless clamped the bit between
his teeth and sucked, making a wheezing, gurgling sound
that seemed to promise little. But after a moment a thread
of smoke rose. He sucked harder. Soon he was smoking
contentedly.

Mrs. Roosevelt and Jack had watched him curiously.
Jack broke their silence—

"I went swimming after I left here. In the pool a Mrs.
Duggins, an Englishwoman, introduced herself to me. And
she told me a curious story."

"About Flavigny?" asked Ouzoulias.

Jack nodded. "About a steward named François Flavigny. It seems Ambassador Troyanoskii is not the only
man murdered on the *Normandie* during this crossing."

"We are trying to keep it confidential," said Ouzoulias.

"Then you had better throw Mrs. Duggins overboard.
She's drowning her grief in whiskey—and talking."

"Did she tell you anything that we should know?" asked
Mrs. Roosevelt.

"Two things," said Jack. "First, he didn't ask her for
money. She has flings with waiters, hotel porters, ship
stewards, and so on, and—"

"Of course all of them ask for money," said Ouzoulias.
"They blackmail women like her."

"Well, she says he didn't. Maybe he died before he got
around to it."

"You say she told you *two* things about the young man," said Mrs. Roosevelt

Jack nodded. "The other was that his mood shifted radically between Thursday night when he first came to her stateroom and last night when he visited for the second and final time. During their first . . . occasion he was jolly, lighthearted. During the second he was saturnine, nervous—as if he were afraid. Well, maybe he had reason to be."

Mrs. Roosevelt leaned over her chart and wrote at the bottom— "F nervous Fri. nt. Had money."

"He *didn't* ask for money," Jack said, amending her note. "She said what was curious was that he *didn't* ask."

"But he *had* money," she told him. "A great deal of money was found on his body."

"Maybe Mrs. Duggins was lying when she said she didn't give him money," Jack mused. "Maybe she did, after all."

"Ten thousand francs, you think?" Ouzoulias asked, puffing on his pipe.

Jack frowned. "No. Unless . . ."

"Unless he extorted the money from her somehow," Mrs. Roosevelt suggested.

"Why would an Englishwoman pay an extortionist in French francs?" asked Ouzoulias. "Why would she be carrying that much money in francs? She boarded *Normandie* at Southampton, not at Le Havre. If she changed that much money aboard ship, the purser will have a record."

"Where was François Flavigny when Ambassador Troyanoskii was murdered?" asked Mrs. Roosevelt.

"I inquired about that," said Ouzoulias. "He was off duty. He had been scheduled to serve at the bar in the Ambassador's suite, but he reported sick that afternoon. Philippe LeClerc replaced him."

"He wasn't sick," said Jack fervidly. "He went to Mrs. Duggins's stateroom and— Well, we know what he did. And he was happy and lighthearted, she said."

"Then he lied," said Ouzoulias grimly.

"A line of inquiry," said Mrs. Roosevelt. "I think it's worth finding out why François Flavigny, who was supposed to serve at that party, didn't—and why Philippe LeClerc, who was not supposed to, did."

"Would you like to pursue that line of inquiry now?" asked Ouzoulias.

"I shall not sleep," said Mrs. Roosevelt.

"Let me find out which stewards are on duty," said the detective.

He lifted the telephone and dialed a number. He grunted a few words in French, so curtly that Mrs. Roosevelt could hardly pick up the sense of what he was saying. Then he put down the telephone, turned to her, and said—

"*Bonne chance.* Philippe is on duty. When he returns to his station, he will be sent here with a bottle of *eau minerale*. It might be well, Monsieur Kennedy, if you would carry the bottles of water from the table into a bathroom, so Philippe will not suspect anything at first."

Ten minutes later Philippe LeClerc arrived bearing a tray laden with two bottles of mineral water, plus one of champagne, compliments, he said, of the captain.

"*Ah, oui,*" said Ouzoulias. "How fortunate that you should be our steward this evening. We have been discussing the unfortunate events aboard *Normandie* during this crossing, and it may be that you can supply a bit more information."

LeClerc nodded deferentially. "Monsieur. . . ?"

"François Flavigny," said Ouzoulias. Apparently not wanting to be distracted by his pipe, he shoved it, fire and all, into his pocket. "You knew him?"

LeClerc nodded. "Not good. I *travaille* . . . uh, work . . . with him."

"What do you know of him? What characteristics did you notice?"

LeClerc's blue eyes shifted suspiciously from Ouzoulias to Mrs. Roosevelt to Jack Kennedy. Jack made an effort to seem casual. He found LeClerc's almost-white hair difficult to believe. He had seen actresses who had stripped the color from their hair with chemicals and achieved some such effect, but he had never seen hair that color on a man.

"Flavigny . . ." said LeClerc hesitantly. "He . . . he like the lady. You know? *Les mademoiselles. Les madames, aussi. Un homme tres amoureux, n'est-ce pas?*"

"When he died," said Ouzoulias, "he had a great deal of money on him. What do you know about that?"

"Uh . . . *Pardon?*"

"*Argent. Beaucoup d'argent.*"

"*François?*" LeClerc asked skeptically, with a faint smile. "*Impossible.*"

"*Pas impossible,*" snapped Ouzoulias. "*Dans une centuire d'argent.*" In a money belt.

LeClerc smiled broadly and shook his head. "*Il a emprunté d'argent,*" he said. He borrowed money. "*Tout les types.*" From all the guys.

Ouzoulias sighed and glanced at Mrs. Roosevelt and Jack Kennedy. "The night Ambassador Troyanoskii was murdered," he said. "You understand? You worked. Why you? Why not François? He was on the list. Why the change?"

LeClerc frowned hard. "He . . . The lady. She want François. François want to go lady. François . . . *a demandé.*"

"He asked," said Ouzoulias. "He asked—*demandé*—you go to Troyanoskii's *appartement?*"

LeClerc nodded. *"Oui.* He . . . go lady. I work."

"Why?" Ouzoulias asked. *"Pourquois?"*

LeClerc shrugged. *"Cent francs,"* he said. *"Il m' a donné cent francs."* He paid me a hundred francs.

Ouzoulias settled a hard eye on LeClerc. *"Qui a tué François Flavigny?"* he asked bluntly. Who killed François Flavigny?

"Monsieur, je ne sais pas." Sir, I don't know.

"Even if he is lying," said Mrs. Roosevelt. "Even if he is somehow involved in the death of François Flavigny, even if he put the strychnine in Ambassador Troyanoskii's vodka, that still leaves unexplained who fired the shot at Nina and who stole the jewels from the purser's safe."

"Obviously the man who was working behind the bar when the Ambassador was poisoned has been a suspect all along," said Ouzoulias. "LeClerc has been under surveillance from that night—not constant surveillance, but we have been keeping an eye on him. I know where he was when the shot was fired at Mademoiselle Rozanov. It is not perhaps impossible he went to the purser's office the night the safe was open, but I can assure you it is most unlikely."

"If only we could find out where the damned jewels are," said Jack. "Who has them . . ."

"Of course," said Ouzoulias. "But where would you have me search?"

"Think of it a moment," said Jack. "Since the ship can give word to customs officers in New York—and I assume it will—that a vast fortune in jewels has been stolen and is coming off the ship in the port of New York, they will search thoroughly. Won't they? And whoever has the loot must know that. So—"

"Which means?" Mrs. Roosevelt interrupted. "Where does this lead, Jack?"

"Well . . ." he said. He glanced at the bottle of vintage champagne Philippe LeClerc had brought, compliments of the ship. "That's open, slowly losing its character. Shouldn't we—"

"Pour," said Mrs. Roosevelt. "A glass for me, too, please."

He went to the table and began to pour the champagne. "Anyway . . . Isn't it likely that all luggage coming off the *Normandie* in New York will be searched more thoroughly than the luggage off any other ship? And, remember, the quantity of jewelry we are talking about is not a few gems that can be folded into someone's dirty underwear. My point is that the jewelry is very likely to come off the ship some way other than in passenger luggage."

"Then how, Monsieur Kennedy?"

"How many automobiles are in the hold?" Jack asked. "I saw a dozen put aboard at Southampton. How many more were put aboard at Le Havre? Does the ship not also carry freight?"

"Yes . . . A quantity of freight in the lower hold."

"If I were going to try to carry a substantial bulk of gems and precious metals off the *Normandie,* I believe I would smuggle it in the automobile I have shipped, or in something being carried as freight. Is it not true that most of the freight being carried has been shipped by passengers who expect to recover it on the dock in New York?"

"Eh bien."

"Could the purser check to see which passengers have freight in the hold? And automobiles?"

Ouzoulias nodded. "Yes . . ."

"Forgive me," said Jack. "May I suggest you order that check performed?"

Elliott Roosevelt

*   *   *

The hour . . . Jack Kennedy looked at his watch and
could hardly believe it was after three. Worse. It was almost four A.M. He had drunk too much—much too much—
in the past eight hours. To his very great surprise, Mrs.
Roosevelt had taken an interest in the champagne Philippe LeClerc had brought with the mineral water and had
drunk three glasses. He and Ouzoulias had finished the
rest of the bottle, and on top of the whiskey and brandy
and the other wine he had had during the night, it had
been too much. He felt— Well, he felt what people always
feel in such circumstances.

It required a moment's study and then effort even to get
his key into the lock and open the door to his stateroom.
He did not remember if he had left the lights on, but they
were.

He *did* remember he had not left a woman on his bed!

Yet, there she was, dressed in black—black dress, dark
stockings, black shoes—asleep on his bed. It was Moira
Lasky.

"Moira . . ."

She opened her eyes. "Ah . . . Jack. Ummm . . . I went to
sleep. You keep strange hours."

"How did you get in here, if you don't mind my asking?"

She sat up and threw her feet over the edge of the bed.
She smiled. "Jack. It's an odd hotel room or ship's cabin I
can't get into. A dutiful steward let me in. I told him you
were expecting me."

He walked into his bathroom and drew a glass of water.
Back in the bedroom he opened a drawer, found a bottle of
Alka-Seltzer, and dropped two of the big tablets in the
glass. He frowned over the roiling water, waiting for the
tablets to dissolve. He sat down heavily in an armchair,
glad to be off his feet.

188

"When the fizzing of Alka-Seltzer is too much for a man's head," said Moira, "he's had too much of . . . well, *something*."

"Champagne," he said.

"Headache juice," said Moira. "When you've had a few more years' experience, you will know that champagne is meant to be taken in small quantities on elegant occasions. In bulk, it generates memorable hangovers. If you want to drink too much, Jack, drink gin."

"Is it the champagne," he asked, "that makes me think I've come back to my stateroom to find a beautiful brunette lying on my bed?"

"No. I just came to talk with you, and when I found you weren't here, I got myself let in. I had no idea you'd be out till dawn. I stretched out to wait and went to sleep."

The Alka-Seltzer was ready to drink, and he grimaced and downed it in a few heavy gulps. "To what do I owe the privilege?" he asked.

"I wanted to talk to you."

"You said that."

"Well, do you want me to leave?"

"No," he said. "What did you come to talk about?"

Moira closed her eyes and sighed. "Actually, I just wanted a shoulder to cry on. And now that I've slept a couple of hours, I have no desire to cry at all, on a shoulder or otherwise. I really—"

"What's the problem, Moira?"

"That bastard . . ." she said. Her face hardened, and a little hot color came to her cheeks. "He told me he didn't want to see me anymore."

"Ernst Richter Remer?"

"That Kraut idiot," she muttered. "He's just as much a Nazi as any of the rest of them."

Jack Kennedy rose from the chair into which he had

sunk so gratefully a minute or two before. Moira still sat on the edge of the bed, her head down a little; and he put his hand on her silky black hair. He had wondered how she could maintain an arrangement with a man like Remer.

"I don't mind being called a hooker," she said. "I *am* a hooker. Why did it hurt? I mean, when *he* did it, why did it hurt?"

"You don't, for God's sake, love the guy?"

That lifted her spirits. She looked up and showed Jack a bitter grin. "Are you kidding? But the deal was supposed to last till we dock in New York."

"So? Your passage is paid for."

Moira straightened her back and shoulders. "Damn right," she said. "You know, it's . . . it's just the experience of *rejection,* I guess, that hurts. You know, when you do what I do— Well, you know. I have a certain pride about myself. Believe it or not, I do. I know I'm attractive. I'm *good* at what I do. And to have a guy tell me he doesn't like me, doesn't want to see me anymore . . . Well, it does get to me."

"I'm sorry," said Jack.

"Every trade has its drawbacks," she said with a little shrug.

He loosened his necktie and took off his jacket. "I wish I could ask you to stay the rest of the night—what little of it's left," he said.

"I wish you could, too. And I wish I could accept that proposition. But it wouldn't be a good idea for either one of us."

He began to unlace his shoes—an unsubtle suggestion that she should return to her own stateroom and allow him to get some sleep.

"Remer is weird," she said. "You wouldn't believe."

"Moira . . ."

She grinned. "I'm not talking about— C'mon, Jack. What I mean is, he's holed up in his stateroom and won't come out. He's having his meals brought in. I thought he was seasick, but he's not, really. He's just weird. He shaved off his mustache this morning—that is, yesterday morning, Saturday morning. And he's drinking— I mean, he's pouring down wine like it was going out of style. And still not getting very drunk. A strange man, Jack."

"How much wine can a man drink?" Jack asked conversationally, not terribly interested in the idiosyncracies of the slick German he had disliked from the moment he met him.

"Well, you know he's a wine broker. He has twenty cases of wine in the hold, that he's taking to New York. He had three cases brought up to his stateroom. Can a man drink three cases of wine between now and Monday?"

Jack frowned. "Is he drinking that wine, really? Have you seen him drinking it?"

"No. I told you, he put me out of his stateroom. Out of his life. In fact, it was when I asked him if he was going to drink all that wine that he got mad and told me to get out."

"The bottles of wine are in wooden boxes, I suppose."

She nodded. "All snuggled in sawdust. Dusty old wine bottles, in sawdust." She lifted her chin and regarded Jack with a skeptical eye. "I can hear wheels going around in your head. Are you grinding up an idea?"

He sighed. "Well, a thought. Just a thought. Let me keep it to myself for now. I'll feel foolish if it turns out to be meaningless."

15

"I'll feel foolish if this turns out to be a bad idea," said Jack to Agent Ouzoulias. "Still . . . I think it's worth checking."

"Bien sûr," said Ouzoulias.

"Is there any way to find out what he is putting in those boxes? I mean, can we find out without intruding on him and of course alerting him?"

Ouzoulias puffed thoughtfully on his pipe. "I believe so," he said again. "We can find out."

A few minutes later Ouzoulias and Kennedy were in the stewards' common room, on D Deck, in the bow of the ship. This was the room where the stewards came to catch bites of food and relax between calls to serve the passengers. It was, Jack noted, a functional room, not luxurious, yet comfortably appointed. Even the stewards lived better on *Normandie* than they did on other ships. A dozen white-jacketed stewards sat at the tables, eating croissants with butter, or pastries, and drinking coffee. As the chief security officer entered their common room, the stewards rose to their feet. Ouzoulias gestured them back to their seats.

"Messieurs," he said. "I will address you in English for the benefit of Mr. Kennedy. I have already learned that one of you, that is, Marcel Dubois, served breakfast this morning to Herr Ernst Richter Remer. Which of you is Dubois?"

One of the stewards raised his hand. He was a young man of no particular distinction of appearance.

"Ah," said Ouzoulias. "I would like to ask you, Dubois, what you observed in Herr Remer's stateroom this morning. Anything unusual?"

Dubois was capable of a Gallic shrug. *"Rien,"* he said. Nothing.

"Was Herr Remer ill? Was he suffering *mal de mer?*"

Dubois turned down the corners of his mouth. He shook his head. *"Il a faime,"* he said. He was hungry, which Dubois supposed negated seasickness.

"Did you see anything unusual in his stateroom?"

"Rien."

"Cases of wine?"

Dubois frowned as if the suggestion mystified him. *"Non, Monsieur."*

Ouzoulias glanced at Jack. Jack shrugged. Both of them wondered if Moira Lasky had been telling the truth.

"Monsieur . . ." One of the other stewards put down his cup of coffee and spoke. "I served Monsieur Remer last evening, and he had in his stateroom the three cases of a fine Bordeaux."

"Not there this morning," said Dubois emphatically.

"So . . ." murmured Ouzoulias. *"Messieurs. Merci."*

* * *

Below the waterline a great ship like *Normandie* was filled with the equipment that drove it across the waters—immense tanks of fuel oil, furnaces that heated the water in huge boilers, gigantic turbo-alternators driven by the steam generated in the boilers, and the enormous electric motors that turned the propeller shafts. It was a part of the ship never seen by passengers—a special, dramatic world of smoothly turning machinery attended by sweating engineers who stared at a thousand gauges and attended a thousand wheels and levers.

As Jack followed Ouzoulias through this world, he was impressed by its quiet. The machinery did not clank or rumble. The pervasive sound was a deep-throated hum. The world of coal had long since died on ships like this; and the furnaces that boiled the water were fed by engineers who turned valves, not by stokers who shoveled coal. On *Normandie* the ducts that exhausted fumes from the engine rooms ran up the outside of the ship, then back amidships to the funnels, and were hardly apparent to the passengers. The engine rooms were hot, and the engineers sweated, but they were clean, in white uniforms, and attentive to their valves and gauges.

Forward of the engine rooms were the garages in which the *Normandie* carried its passengers' cars—and on this voyage even a small airplane, its wings folded back against its fuselage. Forward of the garages—and below them, just above the keel—were the holds in which the ship's cargo was stored.

Agent Ouzoulias had checked with the supercargo. Ah, yes, he had said. Herr Remer had ordered three cases of his wine brought to his stateroom—and a few hours later had sent them back. No, he had not offered an explanation.

Robert Boulanger, the supercargo, emerged from his office and led Ouzoulias and Kennedy into the cargo hold where Remer's wine was stored.

It was in a vast room piled high with crates, barrels, boxes, and bundles, redolent of everything from tobacco to exotic spices, from oil to sharp acids. This space aboard *Normandie* was totally functional, lighted—when it was lighted, when the supercargo flipped the switches—by dusty bulbs in dozens of ceiling fixtures.

Here, as nowhere else on the ship, Jack imagined he could feel the faint vibration, a faint sound, of the great steel hull of *Normandie* slipping through the icy Atlantic waters. Anyway, he imagined that cold water, just outside the riveted steel he could see a few yards to his right.

"These-uh case of *vin*," said the supercargo, speaking English as best he could as a concession to Kennedy, "is here. In zis hold."

To identify the boxes shipped by Herr Remer, as distinct from thousands of other wooden crates shipped by others, was no great problem for the supercargo, who walked along the ranks of heaped cargo with a clipboard in hand, turning over the sheets clipped to it as he read the numbers chalked on the freight.

"Ah, so," he said after a while. He had stopped before a pile of twenty sturdy wooden boxes, held in place by straps. *"Le vin. La."*

"Which," asked Ouzoulias, "were taken to his stateroom yesterday?"

The supercargo turned down the corners of his mouth, so earnestly that it seemed the question must be impossible to answer. But with his pencil he tapped three boxes. *"Celui, celui, et celui,"* he said. That one, that one, and that one.

"Les ouvrions," said Ouzoulias. Let's open them.

The supercargo had anticipated this order and was carrying a small crowbar. He knelt before the stack of boxes, pulled one away from the others, and pushed the wedge of the crowbar between the lid and the wall of the box. He worked the crowbar, and the nails in the lid yielded.

What was inside was what Moira had described—a dozen bottles of dark red wine packed in sawdust. Ouzoulias ran his hands among the bottles, stirring the sawdust, searching.

"*Rien.*"

Jack ran his hands around the bottles. He lifted one from the sawdust. Nothing. The rich red wine was undisturbed, the cork still in place. Anyway, obviously enough, no one could have pressed rings and necklaces through the narrow lips and down the narrow necks of these wine bottles.

The supercargo pried off the lids of the other two cases he identified as ones that had been taken to Remer's stateroom and brought back to the cargo hold. The same. The dozen bottles in each box nested in the sawdust.

"Are you certain these three are the cases that were taken to Herr Remer's stateroom?" Jack asked.

"I am certain, Monsieur," said Boulanger.

"Then open all of them," said Ouzoulias. "Every one. And report to me."

Mrs. Roosevelt and Tommy Thompson returned from religious services in the shipboard chapel. Mrs. Roosevelt had been interested to note that of the two thousand-odd passengers on *Normandie,* about forty had attended Protestant services, about twenty the Catholic mass held earlier.

On Sunday morning the ship was two-thirds of the way across the North Atlantic, and it was possible to imagine—though imagination it certainly was—that one could detect a faint odor on the air—the scent of the North American land mass. The morning was bright, with a brisk but not oppressive wind, and it was possible to walk comfortably on the decks, if one were well bundled up in coat and scarf. *Normandie* overtook and passed a Dutch vessel in mid-morning. Captain Colbert saluted with his great steam whistle. The white Dutch ship returned the greeting in a brave but higher pitch. Its passengers lined its decks to watch the majestic French ship pass. It was a high point of their voyage, one they would tell their friends on both sides of the Atlantic.

The news was as quiet as the sunny ocean. The German army had completed its occupation of that part of Czecho-slovakia known as the Sudetenland. All the radio reported was the joyous welcome the gray-clad German soldiers received as they rode their trucks and armored cars through the towns and villages. It was as if no one could think of a reason to object to German occupation.

If anyone aboard *Normandie* took the occupation seriously, they did not voice it. Everyone welcomed the smooth Sunday-morning seas. One woman remarked to Mrs. Roosevelt that obviously God had sent good weather for the Sabbath. Few people emerged from their staterooms to attend chapel services. Many more were already at the bars in the grand salon and in the grill room. Everyone had a sense that this was their last full day at sea. Tomorrow about noon the ship would enter New York Harbor, and then the passengers aboard would be compelled to abandon the fantasy of ship life and return through immigration and customs indignities to the dull realities of life on land.

Without her ordering it or offering it, the ship had set up a breakfast buffet in Mrs. Roosevelt's suite, for her and for whomever else she wanted to invite.

Jack Kennedy was there when she arrived, just before
noon. So was Agent Ouzoulias. Jack—for reasons all his
own, at which she could only guess—hurried to her side
and suggested she ask Moira Lasky and Josephine Baker
to join them.

Then the three of them—Mrs. Roosevelt, Ouzoulias, and
Jack—sat down over coffee, and Jack told her about
Moira's early-morning conversation, plus his and the de-
tective's opening of the wine cases in the hold.

"I feel like an idiot," Jack concluded.

"Why?" she asked. "An intriguing question is unan-
swered. Why did Herr Remer have three cases of wine delivered to his stateroom, then taken back to the hold,
without drinking from any of them? I find that an im-
mensely suggestive question."

"We can ask it of Moira," said Jack.

A few minutes later Moira arrived, and a moment after
her, Josephine Baker. Moira was dressed in black as
usual, and Baker was wearing a brown silk dress. Mrs.
Roosevelt called Tommy from her room and suggested she
invite Nina to join them. Now they were seven.

"We have no secrets from each other," said Mrs. Roosevelt as soon as all of them had filled their plates. "All of us
are anxious to find a solution to the mystery of the murder
of Ambassador Troyanoskii—and now that of the steward
François Flavigny—also the attempt to kill Nina and the
theft of the jewels the Ambassador was carrying. It is almost certain that these crimes are related. If we do not
solve the mystery by the time the ship docks in New York,
it may never be solved, since the principals will scatter,
and we may never see them together again."

"I am grateful for the help I am receiving," said
Ouzoulias—though something subtle in his voice suggested to Mrs. Roosevelt that he was speaking at least a
bit ironically.

The telephone rang, and the call was for the detective. He fiddled with his pipe as he listened to his caller. When he put down the phone he turned to Mrs. Roosevelt and the others and said—"Interesting . . . Herr Remer has ordered three more cases of his wine brought from the hold to his stateroom."

Moira shook her head. "I'm sure I have no explanation," she said.

"Is the wine very valuable?" asked Jack.

"The cases we examined are St. Julien, Léoville-Las-Cases," said Ouzoulias. "I would call them very valuable."

"Then maybe he is checking his wines to see if the rolling of the ship has damaged them," Jack suggested. "I've read that motion can damage a fine wine. The rolling would at least stir up sediment."

"Did he say anything about possible damage to his wine?" asked Mrs. Roosevelt.

Moira shook her head. "He never talked about wine. Not to anyone. When the subject was brought up at the dinner table, the first night aboard, he just shook his head and said nothing. He wouldn't even suggest a wine for our table."

"Nina," said Mrs. Roosevelt gently. "Did Ambassador Troyanoskii buy wine from Herr Remer?"

Nina, who was sitting apart as if she did not want to participate in this conversation, shook her head. "I never heard him speak of it."

"But they did know each other," said Moira. "It was Ernst Remer who introduced me to Boris Troyanoskii."

"How long had they known each other, do you suppose?" Mrs. Roosevelt asked Nina.

The ballerina shrugged. "Boris Vasilievich did not discuss business with me."

"Did Troyanoskii buy wine in case lots?" asked Jack.

Nina shrugged again. "I don't know how he ran his

199

household," she said. "Ignatieff or Goldinin should be able to tell you."

"Was he a connoisseur of wines?" asked Ouzoulias.

"I suppose so."

"Then—"

"But perhaps Herr Remer isn't," Josephine Baker interrupted. "Maybe Herr Remer knows nothing of wines—or very little. Maybe that's why he wouldn't talk about wines over dinner, or even select one for the table."

"But he's a broker in wines," Moira objected.

"Do you *know* that? For sure?" asked Baker. "Remember something, Moira. Remember our little talk during Mrs. Roosevelt's buffet luncheon yesterday, when Frau von Heinroth said her grandfather was a big wine broker in Berlin and that the German wine brokers were a small fraternity, and—"

"And she'd never heard of Ernst Richter Remer," Moira finished the sentence.

"Well . . . not exactly. I took her meaning to be that if Remer is a wine broker, her grandfather would know him."

Moira turned to Ouzoulias. "If Frau von Heinroth would cooperate, would it be possible to arrange a radio call to Berlin, patched to her grandfather's telephone?"

Ouzoulias turned the corners of his mouth down and the palms of his hands up. "Why not?" he asked.

Frau Margot von Heinroth was glad to cooperate with the detective, but her officious husband insisted on accompanying her to the radio room where the attempt would be made to put a call through to her grandfather in Berlin. The starchy German stood behind the radio operator, watching critically as the operator spoke into a microphone and listened on earphones.

Conversation was in German, and von Heinroth remarked to Ouzoulias that the operator's accent was so bad that he wondered if the Berlin operator would be able to understand.

"He places calls to Germany regularly, Herr von Heinroth," said Ouzoulias. "We find that telephone operators suddenly become most cooperative when they learn they are speaking to the radio operator aboard *Normandie*."

"Technologically rather difficult, I should think," said von Heinroth.

Ouzoulias heaved a Gallic shrug. He lifted his hands toward the banks of mysterious, dial-and-gauge-covered boxes that stood along the bulkhead of the radio room. The room was warmed by what must have been hundreds of big vacuum tubes glowing in those boxes. Two more boxes stood on the desk before the operator, and as he spoke into his microphone he made small adjustments on several knobs.

The operator looked up at Frau von Heinroth. He handed her a telephone. "You are in contact with the Berlin operator," he said. "Just give her your number."

"I want to hear the conversation," said von Heinroth.

The operator glanced at Ouzoulias, as if to ask permission; and, getting no objection, flipped a switch that put both sides of the conversation onto a small radio speaker that stood at the edge of his desk. Fran von Heinroth spoke English.

"Good morning, Grandfather. I am calling you from *Normandie*."

"I thought you had gone to America."

"I am aboard *Normandie*. The French ship. We are at sea. We land in New York tomorrow."

"Is something wrong?"

"Not at all. I've been asked to inquire about somebody."

"To inquire about somebody? From the ship? In the middle of the ocean?"

"Yes, Grandfather. It's important. A gentleman here, of the French government, wants to know if you are acquainted with a wine broker named Ernst Richter Remer."

"Who wants to know? And why? Does Wilhelm know about this? Does he consent?"

"Wilhelm is standing here beside me. It is part of a police inquiry. There has been a murder aboard the ship."

"You should have sailed on *Europa* or *Bremen*."

"Grandfather, do you know this man?"

"What is the name?"

"Remer. Ernst Richter Remer. A wine merchant, from Berlin."

"Not a wine merchant from Berlin. Unless he just has a little store. I never heard of him."

"On the other hand," said Ouzoulias to Mrs. Roosevelt, Jack Kennedy, Moira, and Josephine Baker—who had waited to learn the result of the radio call—"wine merchants in Paris have heard of him. He is remembered for having bought considerable quantities of fine wines, several times in the past year."

"What quantities?" asked Jack. "Twenty cases is not much wine."

"Perhaps it is," said Moira, "to be carrying on a passenger ship. Do wine brokers carry their wine along with them when they travel, as luggage?"

"If not," said Jack, "then he should have in his luggage the papers that show what he is shipping, and how. He is not on his way to the States to sell twenty cases of wine."

"You could search his stateroom," said Moira bluntly to Ouzoulias.

202

"For what reason?" the detective asked. "Aboard *Normandie,* we do not grossly insult the passenger unless we have the well-establish-ed reason."

"Moira . . ." said Mrs. Roosevelt. "What can you tell us about Herr Remer?"

Moira sighed. "He speaks English too well," she said. "Like an American. He says he learned it in a year or two he spent in Chicago. I wonder if a German could learn English that well in so short a time. Anyway, he doesn't talk like a Chicagoan, more like a New Yorker."

"How can you tell?" asked Ouzoulias.

"Well, for example, he says 'bring' when he means 'take.' Typical New Yorkese. Like, when he talked about this voyage, he said, 'When I go to the States, I think I'll bring my camel overcoat.' Anybody but a New Yorker would say, 'I'll *take* my camel overcoat.' And when we went to the ticket office in Paris, there was a line of people waiting to buy passage on this ship. Ernst said, 'My God, do we have to stand on that line?' Any American but a New Yorker would say, 'Do we have to stand *in* that line?'"

"When he talks with you, he speaks English?" asked Ouzoulias.

"He has to," she said. "I don't speak German. Or much French, either."

"At the dinner table?" asked Mrs. Roosevelt.

"English," said Moira. "Or American, rather. Actually, he didn't talk much at all."

"Can you think of any reason," Mrs. Roosevelt asked, "why he might have wanted to murder Ambassador Troyanoskii?"

"Or any of the other crimes that have been committed on this voyage?" asked Ouzoulias.

Moira shook her head. "I don't think he's who he says he is. Aside from that . . ."

Josephine Baker laughed. "I doubt there are many people on this ship who are who they say they are."

When the others had left—Jack Kennedy to walk with Nina Rozanov in the cold, windy sunshine of the decks, Josephine Baker and Moira Lasky to the grill room—Mrs. Roosevelt and Edouard Ouzoulias laid out her chart again. She created a new heading near the bottom of the sheet

HERR REMER

Who is he? What connection? Why his deception?

"We don't know where he was when someone took a shot at Nina. We don't know where he was when the purser's safe was cracked. We don't know where he was when Flavigny was murdered," she said. "Furthermore, he was in the suite when Ambassador Troyanoskii was poisoned— though he was not near the bar or near the Ambassador at that point. Clearly he didn't put the strychnine in the glass of vodka."

"I am satisfied about something," said Ouzoulias. "Not all these crimes are committed by one man. All are related. But we are dealing with more than one perpetrator."

Mrs. Roosevelt sighed noisily. "Oh, *dear*. I am afraid you are right. Somehow it all fits together and makes sense. These things did not happen by chance. We are not dealing with coincidence."

"Coincidence happens," said Ouzoulias. "If we are realistic, we must accept that coincidence could be an element of our mystery."

"Lord forbid," she muttered under her breath.

16

"Regardless, Picard," said Ouzoulias firmly. "I accept full responsibility, but I demand the box be opened now."

The detective was in the purser's office. Their conversation was in French, and Ouzoulias was demanding that Picard open one of the safe-deposit boxes in the vault.

"If a passenger learned that we can do this—"

"He will not learn it from me, Picard. Will he learn it from you? Dismiss your personnel. This is important."

The purser shook his head, but he rose from behind his desk and walked into the inner office. With a quiet word and a wave of his hand he dismissed the single assistant who was at work on Sunday afternoon. Picard closed the office door and locked it. Still wearing a face that expressed his disapproval, he opened the vault and withdrew from the rack the safe-deposit box assigned to Herr Ernst Richter Remer.

As was customary for such boxes, two keys were needed to open it—one that was issued to the boxholder, one retained by the purser. Like banks, ship's pursers wanted boxholders to believe the boxes could not be opened without both keys. This was in a sense true. What boxholders were not told was that there was a master key that could open all the boxes. Picard removed the master key from the pocket in his vest.

"Your responsibility," he said to Ouzoulias.

"My responsibility."

Picard inserted and turned first one key and then the other. He lifted the lid of the box.

"Rien!"

The box was empty.

"Has he been here since Friday morning when we saw him open the box?" asked Ouzoulias.

"No. I had already checked the log. He rented the box when he boarded the ship. He opened it then. He returned to it on Friday morning. That's all."

"I could not watch him closely that morning," said Ouzoulias, "but I could swear he put nothing in and took nothing out."

Picard shrugged. "Why would the gentleman rent a box and keep nothing in it?"

"I mean to find out," said Ouzoulias.

"Am I under arrest?" Moira asked the detective.

Ouzoulias only shrugged.

"I was taken away from a conversation in the grill room by one of your officers," she said. "He indicated I had no option but to come with him."

Ouzoulias let an ironic little smile play over his face.

They were sitting in his Spartan office, and he was for once scraping the accumulated ash out of his pipe and preparing to reload it with entirely fresh tobacco—which was an elaborate process, requiring tools and a certain vigor of effort.

"I'm always at a disadvantage—"

"Yes," he interrupted. "Young women who choose your style of life must cooperate fully with the police. It does involve a certain vulnerability." He shrugged. "I don't mean to take any unfair advantage of you. I did, however, want to talk to you outside the presence of Mrs. Roosevelt. That dear lady is so sympathetic toward young women in trouble that—"

"Am I in trouble?"

"I don't think so. Not yet, at least. But I want to ask you some questions. They are blunt questions and will require blunt answers—the kind you and I might not want to exchange in the presence of Mrs. Roosevelt."

Moira shrugged.

"How much were you being paid?"

She drew a deep breath. "First-class passage and five hundred dollars," she said.

"Have you been paid?"

"When he told me to stay away from him, he gave me a hundred and told me I was lucky to get it. He said I could sue him if I didn't like it."

"He did pay for your passage?"

"Yes."

"Where did you meet him?"

"In Paris, at the George V Hotel. I . . . ."

"Monsieur the concièrge assisted you in identifying a gentleman who was looking for a nice young lady," said Ouzoulias dryly.

"More than that. He was looking for an American young lady."

"Why?"

"The story was that he was going to America and wanted a young lady to accompany him on the ship."

"Why? Why, that is, apart from the obvious reason? Did you not suspect there was another reason?"

"It has happened to me before," she said glumly.

"What has happened to you before?"

"During a crossing on the *Queen Mary* I discovered that the English gentleman who had formed an alliance with me the first day out of New York was not the Lord Hartington he said he was but a petty gambler named—"

"Leach," said Ouzoulias. "The Cunard Line forgave you. They knew you bore no responsibility. Tell me, though, about your association with Count Emilio Gomez."

Moira nodded. "Gomez was a blackmailer. I met him in Cannes. He entertained me royally, formed an association of the usual kind, and invited me on an Aegean cruise. The ship was the *Champollion*. During the cruise he struck up an acquaintance with an English merchant banker. Shortly the acquaintance was a close friendship. And—"

"And he offered your company to his new English friend," said Ouzoulias.

"You know everything."

"No. I guessed."

"The man's wife was terribly ill, and he was taking this cruise for the rest and an opportunity to recover his equilibrium. It seemed so . . . charitable of the Count to suggest I give the man . . . solace. Then I learned that he blackmailed him. He threatened to reveal to the directors of the man's London bank that he had been engaged in an illicit relationship during his cruise. He told the man I would testify he seduced me."

"Yes."

"I knew nothing of this. I swear I knew nothing. That is—I knew nothing until it was too late."

"I believe you," said Ouzoulias. He was finished reloading his pipe and now lit it with a big wooden match. As he puffed, he said—"It is an old story. Young women like you are often made the unwitting . . . and unwilling . . . accomplices of criminals."

"I am well educated," she said. "I know how to conduct myself in social situations. I am often introduced as a niece, even once as a sister. "I—"

"Your presence with a man lends him a certain air," said Ouzoulias. "Perhaps of sophistication. It makes the man seem . . . How shall we say? A fellow playboy?"

"I try to stay away from scum, Monsieur Ouzoulias. Honestly I do. Ernst Remer—"

"Is not Ernst Remer," said Ouzoulias.

She lowered her eyes and nodded. "No, I suppose he isn't."

"I don't know who he is, Mademoiselle Lasky. I wonder if you and I can make an informed guess. Did you bring anything aboard the ship for him? Anything in your luggage? Anything at all?"

She shook her head. "No. I am smarter than that, Monsieur. I have never trusted a man enough to let him make me his courier as a smuggler."

"He is not a wine broker," said Ouzoulias. "Still, he is carrying nothing but wine in his cases of wine. The seals on his bottles are intact, the corks tightly in place, and there is nothing in the boxes but bottles. Still, can you think of any reason why he has now had six cases delivered to his stateroom, kept them there for a few hours, then sent them back to the hold?"

"No . . . It is a complete mystery to me. It's as if he's doing something to the wine. Could he be putting a needle

through the corks and injecting something into the bottles?"

Ouzoulias turned up his palms. "But what? And why?"

"I have no idea."

"How long did you know the man in Paris?"

"Two weeks, roughly."

"And Troyanoskii?"

"About the same. I met him during dinner at the George
V. He came to our table. He and Ernst obviously knew
each other. Boris Troyanoskii was a congenial fellow—
very social, affable. I did give him lessons in American
English, as I said. But Ernst had some kind of business
relationship with him. He made Ernst nervous, I could
tell. Ernst was anxious to please him."

"You thought he was going to sell the Ambassador a
thousand cases of expensive wine?"

"At first I did. Then I began to wonder if the relationship
were not something else."

Ouzoulias was satisfied now that his pipe was burning
comfortably. "You were with him when the strychnine was
put in the Ambassador's vodka. Is there any possibility
Herr Remer could have done that?"

"No possibility, I swear. I was with him. He did not go
near the bar in the five minutes before Boris was poisoned."

"How did he react to the death of Troyanoskii?"

"He was appalled. Shaken."

Ouzoulias raised his eyebrows. "So shaken that he did
not wish your company that night?"

"Monsieur," she said. "I have not slept with Ernst Remer since we came aboard the *Normandie*."

Henry Luce stood at the window of Mrs. Roosevelt's
appartement de grand luxe, looking out at the sea and the
long wake of the *Normandie* stretching toward the horizon
astern.

"Excellent accommodations," he remarked.

"Not paid for by the government of the United States, in case you are curious on that point," she said. "I had bought passage to and from France at my own expense. The French government asked me to travel on the *Normandie* and converted my ticket. It was only when I came aboard that I found we had been assigned anything other than an ordinary stateroom."

"Entirely appropriate for the First Lady," said Luce.

"Appropriate for a queen," she said. "I'm not sure it is appropriate for the wife of the president of a republic."

"In any event," said Luce, "it is a pleasant voyage, isn't it—apart from the crimes committed on board during this crossing."

"Those have been distressing," she said.

Luce had interrupted a session during which she had been dictating a newspaper column to Tommy Thompson. She was wearing a rose-colored wool dress—what she had worn to services in the chapel—with a string of pearls at her throat, also an orchid sent her by Colonel Lindbergh.

"I said I would get you as much information as I can about the principal characters in your crime drama," said Luce. "I've been in touch with my office on that point."

"I'm grateful," said Mrs. Roosevelt.

"The Soviet government is oddly silent on the murder of Troyanoskii," said Luce. "One might have thought they would have been shrieking that the capitalist government of France had conspired at the death . . . and so forth—the usual Bolshevik you-know-what. But, no. A statement from the so-called Soviet ministry of justice expresses confidence that the French government will do all it can to bring the criminal to justice."

"Which you interpret to mean. . . ?"

"I interpret it to mean they don't give a damn," said Luce. "Or that they killed Troyanoskii themselves."

211

"Can you think of a motive that might have influenced them to murder Ambassador Troyanoskii?" she asked.

"My suspicion is, he was defecting," said Luce. "It is understood that he has money in secret accounts here and there—not just in Switzerland. The convincing part is, he was bringing his young mistress with him—the little ballerina. He had the marks of a man who did not intend to return from his visit to the States."

"Does anything else bolster your suspicion that his own government conspired to murder him?" she asked.

"Yes," said Luce with an emphatic nod. "They're godless, atheistic Communists—capable of anything."

Mrs. Roosevelt nodded. "Ah . . ." she murmured.

Ouzoulias put down the telephone. Moira still sat uneasily facing him across his desk. He lifted his chin and looked at her pensively.

"That was the supercargo on the telephone. Herr Remer has had three more cases of wine delivered to his stateroom and then returned to the hold. At my command, the supercargo has been opening the cases and examining them. In one of the second group of cases a bottle is missing. Can you think of an explanation for that?"

She shrugged. "He drank it."

"He drinks whiskey also," said Ouzoulias. "I've checked the stewards' records of what liquor they have carried to his stateroom."

"What kind of whiskey?" she asked.

"Rye whiskey," said Ouzoulias.

"Are you certain?"

"A brand called Old Overholt."

Moira grimaced sarcastically. "It's unlikely he learned to drink Old Overholt in Chicago," she said. "Midwesterners drink bourbon. New Yorkers drink rye."

"Always?"

"No, of course not. But it's a regional difference."

Ouzoulias sighed. "One bottle missing," he said. "Do you suppose he was searching for a particular bottle and found it?"

"You can always go into his stateroom and find out," she said.

The detective nodded. "I am beginning to think I will," he said.

Jack Benny and Mary Livingstone sat together at a table in the grill room, eating simple cheese sandwiches and drinking beer. Mrs. Roosevelt came in, with Nina at her side; and, seeing them, walked to their table.

"Mr. Benny," she said. "And . . . Mrs. Benny . . ."

"Mrs. Kubelsky," said Mary Livingstone. "Please sit down for a moment—at least for a moment. It's such an honor to have become acquainted with you on this voyage. We had no idea you would be aboard the *Normandie*— much less that we would meet you."

Mrs. Roosevelt smiled warmly. "I resisted changing to the *Normandie* at first, but if I'd known you were aboard I'd have come in a minute. You're a great favorite of the President, Mr. Benny."

"Make his day complete, Mrs. Roosevelt," said Mary Livingstone, "and tell him the President can't stand Fred Allen."

As they laughed, Nina frowned; and Mrs. Roosevelt explained to her the comedy feud between Jack Benny and Fred Allen.

"I think I have much to learn about America," said Nina.

"It's too bad we can't do ballet on radio," said Jack Benny.

"It's too bad you can't play the violin on radio," said Mrs. Roosevelt—and once again Nina frowned while the others laughed.

"I wonder in America how they will like a Russian name like Nina Rozanov," the little ballerina said seriously.

"Well . . ." said Jack Benny. "If they like Benjamin Kubelsky and Sadie Glutz, I think they'll— On second thought, why not change it? Tell me, Nina, how would you like being called, say, Barbara Fairchild?"

Mary Livingstone shook her head. "Angela Stanford."

"Ellen Dallas," suggested Mrs. Roosevelt.

"This is. . . ?" Nina asked.

Mary Livingstone put her hand on Nina's. "Not funny, Nina," she said gently. "Anyway, I tell you what. If you don't have something good set up for you when you arrive in New York, you ask Mrs. Roosevelt to tell you how to get to Beverly Hills. You come and stay with us a week or two, and Jack and I will introduce you around in Hollywood. Countess Nina Rozanov. We'll get you in pictures. It'll be easy."

"Right now," said Nina somberly, "I am not to be allowed to leave *Normandie* in New York. I am to return to France to be put in prison for stealing jewels."

"No," said Mrs. Roosevelt firmly. "Not if I have to bring federal agents aboard ship to take you off." She smiled at Nina. "Don't worry about that, child," she said. "Monsieur Ouzoulias will not charge you with theft. I know he won't."

Nina lifted her chin, and her face stiffened. "Maybe I did take what was mine," she said.

Mrs. Roosevelt nodded. "Maybe you did. Even so—"

"Even so, you have a welcome waiting for you in the States," said Jack Benny. "And new friends."

"I am grateful," said Nina.

* * *

"Ah," said Ouzoulias to Moira as they walked through the grill room. "There is Mrs. Roosevelt and Mademoiselle Rozanov."

"And . . . and, God, Ouzoulias! Look who else!"

Sitting three tables away from the Bennys and Mrs. Roosevelt and Nina, Ernst Richter Remer drank coffee, nibbled on a pastry, and stared moodily out to sea.

He glanced around and saw Moira. With a short, clement gesture he beckoned her to come to his table. She muttered to Ouzoulias that he should accompany her, and together they went to his table.

Remer's appearance had changed radically. Without the mustache, his face was undistinguished. His hair had been suavely stuck to his head with a dressing; now it stood in unruly curls. What was more, he seemed to have rinsed out a black dye; and hair that had been sleekly black was now faintly lightened with gray.

"Moira . . . Monsieur . . ." he said quietly. "Please sit down."

"Thank you, Ernst," said Moira coldly.

They sat for a moment looking out at the sea, which aboard ship was a matter of obsessive interest.

"I have been damned sick," said Remer. "So bad it made me act like an idiot. I hope you'll excuse it, Moira."

"*Seekrankheit?*" asked Ouzoulias.

"Uh? Ah . . . *ja. Ja.* Seasick."

"*Der Arzt hat ein Mittel gegen Seekrankheit,*" said Ouzoulias.

"Uh? Yeah. Sure. Right. Uh . . . Uh, a remedy. Okay. I . . . I carry my own. Didn't work so well."

"Not much better than your German, Ernst," said Moira.

Remer glanced from her to the detective and back again.

215

"All right," he said. "So I'm not German. But you can check my passport with the German consulate in New York, Monsieur Ouzoulias. It is valid. I carry a valid German passport—even if I wasn't born there. I am a citizen of the German Reich."

"And your name, then, is actually Ernst Richter Remer?" asked Ouzoulias.

He sighed. "I have used other names in my life. I was born in the United States. But my passport is good. It's not a forgery."

"And you are not a wine broker."

He flushed. "Oh? No? What are the qualifications? I am involved right now in the shipment of more than a thousand cases of wines, champagnes, and cognacs from France and Germany to the States. The documents are in my luggage. How many cases do I have to export and import to be a broker?"

"You are not a Berlin broker. The Berlin brokers don't recognize you as such."

He shrugged. "Who *do* they recognize? Those old boys are a closed club. If you're not a member, you're not a member; you can't become one."

"Then you are a common . . . manipulator," said Moira. "I suppose there is no Frau Remer."

Remer sneered. "What did *you* care?"

"What is your name, Monsieur?" asked Ouzoulias. "Your baptismal name?"

The man grinned. "Moira and I were never baptized," he said. "Were we, Moira? And who gives a damn? Pretty good joke on the Nazis, isn't it, to have got one of their passports?"

"Give us a name we can use," said Ouzoulias.

"My name is Remer," he said. "A German court satisfied itself of my ancestry, confirmed me in that name, and issued the papers that entitled me to a German passport."

"Why did you have six cases of wine delivered to your stateroom, then carried back?" asked Ouzoulias. "And why is one bottle missing from one case?"

Remer laughed. "*Normandie* rolls and pitches, Monsieur. That ruined one bottle. Maybe others. Do you know anything about fine wines? They don't like the rolling and pitching of ships."

"And why did you cut off your mustache?" Moira asked. "And why wash the dye out of your hair and let it lie naturally?"

He grinned. "Who told me I looked like a gangster?" he asked. "You, Moira. You said I look like a Hollywood version of a bank robber. Stylish . . . *Too* stylish. So? Significant?"

Ouzoulias pulled his pipe from his pocket and jammed it abruptly between his teeth. "What was your relationship with Ambassador Troyanoskii?"

Remer glanced around, as if to see if anyone could be listening to their conversation. "Troyanoskii was taking a powder," he said. "He wasn't going back. He was going to meet Roosevelt—he'd tricked Stalin into sending him to Washington with a personal message for Roosevelt—but what he was really going to say to FDR was 'Help!' Okay. He was going to ask for asylum. So, what he wanted from me was a way to carry a lot of money to the States on the sly. That thousand cases I've got coming over on a freighter is his. I'm bringing it into the States, but he's already paid me for it—with Russky government funds, I wouldn't be surprised. He could've unloaded that thousand cases in New York for maybe fifty thousand dollars—which would've given him a little profit, too, since he only paid me about thirty-eight thousand."

"In other words," said Ouzoulias solemnly, "you provided him a means of taking stolen funds into the United States."

"Hey, I don't know it was stolen. I just guess."

"What about the jewelry?" Moira asked.

Remer shook his head. "I don't know anything about any jewels," he said.

"Why did you bring me on this voyage and send me off to my own stateroom every night?" she asked.

"Hey, I told you, kid. I been sick."

"So you have been alone all night, every night, hmm?" said Ouzoulias.

"Right. I didn't feel like fun and games. *Seekrankheit.*"

17

"Do you believe him?" asked Mrs. Roosevelt.

Agent Edouard Ouzoulias shook his head. "No. But I don't know if he's lying about everything or just about some things."

"Do the stewards keep a log of when they serve each stateroom?" she asked.

"Only when something is ordered that incurs a charge," said the detective. "Anyway, I asked the stewards who were on duty late at night on that deck if they were called to his stateroom at any time during the night. The answer was that none were."

"So he was alone in his stateroom the night when the purser's safe was cracked and the night when a shot was fired at Nina."

"Correct."

The First Lady sighed. "Maybe we are placing too much emphasis on this man," she said. "His conduct is suspicious, but . . ."

"I wish I could find out who he is," said Ouzoulias. "I've radioed Paris. Ernst Richter Remer travels in and out of France from time to time. *Sûreté* has no record on him, not even a set of fingerprints. I included a description of him in my message—of how he looked when he came aboard and how he looks today. Nothing."

"Could we radio the New York police?"

"Perhaps we should."

"I can do better than that, perhaps," she suggested. "Perhaps I should send a radiogram to the Mayor of New York."

The exchange of radiograms read as follows:

WOULD GREATLY APPRECIATE QUICK AND CONFIDENTIAL CHECK OF POLICE RECORDS CITY OF NEW YORK RE ERNST RICHTER REMER A CITIZEN OF GERMANY STOP MAN IS ABOUT FORTY TO FORTY-FIVE YEARS OLD BLACK HAIR SLICKED DOWN ALSO PENCIL MUSTACHE STOP REMER THOUGHT TO HAVE BEEN BORN IN NEW YORK CITY AND TO HAVE OBTAINED GERMAN CITIZENSHIP RECENTLY STOP ALSO DO YOU HAVE ANY INFORMATION RELATIVE TO A POSSIBLE CONNECTION BE-TWEEN THIS SUBJECT AND MOIRA LASKY STOP INVESTIGA-TION INTO SERIOUS CRIMES ABOARD THIS SHIP MAY BE FACILITATED BY INFORMATION STOP

ELEANOR ROOSEVELT

EXCUSE HOURS DELAY IN RESPONDING STOP YOUR REQUEST ARRIVED WHILE I WAS READING SUNDAY FUNNIES STOP YOUR MAN IS ALBERT HAUSHOFER AKA AL HAUSHOFER BORN IN LOWER EAST SIDE FORTY-FOUR YEARS AGO STOP NO RECORD OF CHARGES OR CONVICTIONS HERE EXCEPT FOR PETTY LAR-CENY CHARGE DROPPED TWENTY YEARS AGO STOP NYPD SO CERTIFIED TO GERMAN CONSULATE WHEN INQUIRY WAS MADE IN 1936 STOP AT THAT TIME HAUSHOFER WAS CLAIMING GERMAN ANCESTRY REMER FAMILY AND APPLYING FOR CIT-

IZENSHIP GERMANY STOP OTHERWISE HAUSHOFER WAS SUB-
JECT OF REPEATED SUSPICION AS GENERALLY SHADY
CHARACTER NO VISIBLE MEANS OF SUPPORT FOR COMFORT-
ABLE WAY OF LIFE STOP NOTHING AT ALL IN FILE SINCE 1934
EXCEPT CONSULATE INQUIRY STOP IT IS ASSUMED HE LEFT
NYC IN 1934 STOP MOIRA LASKY ONCE WORKED FOR POLLY
ADLER AND HAS ONE ARREST NY ON MORALS CHARGE STOP
CHARGE DROPPED STOP NO COMPLAINT ON LASKY SINCE 1935
STOP NO RECORD OF ANY CONNECTION BETWEEN THE TWO
STOP WILL BE AT PIER TO GREET YOU ON YOUR ARRIVAL IN
FAIR CITY STOP

LAGUARDIA

"Haushofer," said Mrs. Roosevelt. "Albert Haushofer. Can you radio that name to Paris?"

"Yes, with a request it be relayed to Interpol," said Ouzoulias.

"Is this progress?" she asked.

Ouzoulias shrugged. "Every scrap of information one can obtain represents progress in the investigation of a criminal matter. But . . . We have less than twenty-four hours to solve the mystery before the ship docks and all the people scatter. I feel less and less confident."

Agent Ouzoulias remained in the radio room for half an hour after he sent his message to Paris, hoping a quick answer might come back. None did, not even a message saying *Sûreté* had no record of one Albert Haushofer. As he stood by the radioman's desk, smoking, watching him handle messages, and chatting with him in the intervals, a man from his security office hurried in.

"Monsieur! A shooting! In the cargo hold!"

His man was so confused he did not know who had been shot or how badly anyone had been hurt. Ouzoulias grabbed a telephone and called the supercargo. Unhappily,

221

it was the supercargo who had been shot, according to a frightened sailor who answered the telephone. Monsieur Boulanger was alive, he said. That was all he knew.

Normandie was more than one thousand feet long. Hurrying from one place to another always involved choosing the right stairway or elevator to ascend or descend from one deck to another and then finding a passage through the ship's thousand chambers. Ouzoulias knew where he was going and how to get there, but he required ten minutes to reach the cargo hold.

The supercargo lay on his back in the hold. Dr. Grasse knelt over him, and a dozen sailors stood about, horrified.

"Alive?" Ouzoulias asked.

"Alive," Boulanger grunted. "No thanks to this quack chirurgeon who's trying to kill me."

"Shot in the leg," said Dr. Grasse. "Not in the mouth, unfortunately."

Knowing Boulanger wasn't dying, Ouzoulias took a moment to glance around the hold. A suspicion that had come to him as he hurried down here was conspicuously confirmed not ten meters from where the supercargo lay. Six or seven of Remer's—Haushofer's—wine cases had been forced open. Sawdust was scattered around the deck. Three bottles had rolled across the deck and come to rest against some big packing crates.

So. Someone else suspected something was hidden in those cases of wine.

"Pick up those bottles," he said to two of the sailors. "That's valuable wine. Repack it."

He squatted beside the supercargo.

"Damn that wine," Boulanger croaked.

"Who shot you?" asked Ouzoulias.

"A criminal . . ."

"Yes, I suppose so. Do you have any idea who it was?"

The supercargo closed his eyes and shook his head. His jaw was set, his teeth clenched. What the doctor was doing was painful.

"He was breaking into the Remer wine," said the detective.

The supercargo nodded. "I . . . *Easy, damnit!* I heard a sound in here, looked in, saw light. I switched on the overhead lights. The man looked up, then went on doing what he was doing—only faster. I came running, yelling. And . . . Damn! He had a pistol! He fired once . . ."

"And hit you in the leg."

"Ahh . . . I think that's what he meant to do. I think he could have killed me if he wanted to and didn't. I . . . I don't know why I think that. It's just that— Well, he was so unemotional about it. He pulled the gun, took aim, and fired. I went down, and he took the time to pry open another box and stir around in the sawdust before he stood up and ran. He wasn't afraid. I swear, the man wasn't afraid. It was like shooting a man was something he did every day."

"Wasn't he interested in the fact that you were getting a good look at him?" asked Ouzoulias.

Boulanger shook his head. "Can you believe it? I didn't get a good look at him. What I got a good look at was his gun. Then I got a good look at my leg—with the blood spurting out. I . . ."

"He made a tourniquet," said Dr. Grasse. "He used his brains better than he does his mouth."

"I thought if I looked hard at him, he might shoot me again—to be sure I couldn't identify him later," said the supercargo.

"Well, you got some impression of what kind of man he was," said Ouzoulias, betraying impatience. "I mean, aside from the fact that he had fired a gun before."

Boulanger sighed weakly. "He was young. Light-colored. Big. When he decided to run—which he did when he heard members of the crew coming—he jumped up on a stack of crates and jumped down on the other side of them. In a moment . . . he was gone."

"'Light-colored,'" Ouzoulias repeated. "Not Monsieur Remer, then."

"I have never seen Monsieur Remer."

"'Big.' Not, therefore, a young woman."

"*Woman?* Are you insane? The man could have been King Kong!"

"How was he dressed?"

"Rough clothes," said the supercargo. "At first I thought he must be a member of the crew."

Ouzoulias blew a long sigh and reached into his pocket for his pipe.

"Do you suppose," asked Dr. Grasse, "I could now transfer my patient to the ship's hospital?"

"Yes," said Ouzoulias. "And do me a favor. Take a bottle of wine from those cases. Extract a sample through the cork with a syringe. And— Oh, to hell with that. Open a bottle. Analyze it, please. For strychnine, of course. Or for anything else you can think of that should not be in a bottle of fine Bordeaux."

"As you wish," said the doctor.

Ouzoulias turned to one of Boulanger's assistants. "Place two armed guards in this hold," he said. "Something about that wine is of great interest to someone. Arrest anyone who comes near it."

Jack Kennedy sat at a table in the grill room with Josephine Baker. They were having a late lunch of sandwiches and English beer, and she was telling him—

"So, I sat and waited . . . and waited . . . and waited.

And finally it became clear to me that my meal was not going to be served, that Mister Sherman Billingsley was not going to serve a Negro. So . . . I got up and left."

"Billingsley," said Jack. "A two-bit saloonkeeper. Bootlegger. Scum."

"A social arbiter in New York," she said.

He shrugged. "Among gangsters. Bar-hoppers. If you want to talk about society, people who really *are* society don't befriend the keepers of speakeasies."

"Well, the story was that Walter Winchell objected to my presence."

"Winchell! A real, ethical, professional journalist wouldn't lift a glass with the likes of Walter Winchell."

Josephine Baker smiled. "Thank you, Jack," she said. "It's one way of soothing my hurt feelings."

"Seriously, Josey," he said. "If I were going to have hurt feelings, I'd wait to have them hurt by better people than Sherman Billingsley and Walter Winchell. They're the dregs of the community. They really are."

"Can I quote you?" she asked playfully.

"I've said enough things to you that, if they were quoted publicly, my family would disown me and the Democratic Party would disown my family." He grinned. "So— I'll take the chance."

"I don't know if you've got guts or you're reckless," she laughed.

"A fine distinction," he said.

Josephine Baker lifted her beer, sipped, and changed the subject. "I feel sorry for your friend Moira Lasky. She's terribly vulnerable, Jack."

"To our friend who's coming here," said Jack. He nodded toward the door, at Agent Ouzoulias, who had just entered the grill room and stood looking around. "He isn't a very typical policeman, is he?"

Josephine smiled with real amusement as she regarded the tall, lean Frenchman whose tweeds hung loosely on his bony frame. "A Gallic Sherlock Holmes," she said.

Ouzoulias saw them and came to their table. "Do you mind if I join you?" he asked.

Both of them gestured to him to take a chair.

"Do you know where is Madame Roosevelt?" he asked.

"The Logans arranged a little party for her," said Jack. "In the winter garden. For Americans. Chance to chat with the First Lady. She had to go."

"Chance for Americans in first-class to meet the First Lady," Josephine Baker amended.

"I wish to see her when she has returned," said Ouzoulias.

"Anything new?" Jack asked.

"Well . . . An effort was made to break into Herr Remer's wine. A man broke open several cases. His interest must have been much like ours."

"Look who's coming," said Josephine Baker. "Hans und Fritz. First time I've seen them out of their suite."

Grigorii Ignatieff and Vladimir Goldinin strode purposefully toward their table. It was Ignatieff who spoke, directly at Ouzoulias—

"Must talk," he grunted. "Must Russkii-Franzuskii man. Russkii-Angliskii. *Must!*"

"I believe he's saying he wants an interpreter, Russian to French or English," said Josephine Baker dryly.

"Looks as if he's had an accident," said Jack.

It was true. Ignatieff's face was bruised. A shiny red-blue knot had risen just over his left eye, and he had a distinct red scrape along his jaw.

Ouzoulias stared at the two Russians for a moment—skeptical and hostile. Then he shrugged and said, *"Oui. Nous parlons."*

*   *   *

The arrangement was as before, except that instead of the two Russians being blindfolded to protect the identity of the interpreter, Kazys Urbays, the Lithuanian sat in the room where Mrs. Roosevelt had listened. With the door ajar, he could translate from Russian to French and French to Russian.

"Monsieur Ignatieff wishes to protest most strongly against the outrage that has been done his person and his government," said the voice from beyond the door.

"Tell him I don't give a damn about his protest," said Ouzoulias.

"Monsieur Ignatieff wishes to know why he was subjected to an outrageous and provocative procedure before this meeting began."

"Tell him he was given a paraffin test to discover if he fired a pistol within the last hour or so."

"Monsieur Ignatieff says his government will not tolerate such violations of the rights of its citizens."

"Tell him to go to hell. Tell him when the paraffin test proves he shot the supercargo of this ship he will spend the rest of this voyage in irons—and will be returned to France in irons to stand trial."

"Monsieur Goldinin says Monsieur Ignatieff could not have shot anyone and that your suggestion that he did appears to be nothing more than a tactic designed to divert attention from the international provocation you are committing by maltreating a Soviet citizen."

"I want to know how he got the bruises on his face."

"Monsieur Ignatieff says that is none of your business. Monsieur Goldinin says he struck Monsieur Ignatieff on the face. He says he is Monsieur Ignatieff's superior officer and disciplined him for insubordination."

"Tell them they are liars."

"Monsieur Ignatieff demands the immediate return of the property of the Soviet government, which was illegally seized by you on the night when Ambassador Troyanoskii was murdered."

"Meaning the jewelry."

"Monsieur Ignatieff confirms that he is speaking of a large quantity of jewelry, which he says is the property of the government of the Soviet Union."

"Ask him if he expected to find it in the wine cases."

"Monsieur Ignatieff says he knows nothing of any wine cases but is informed that his government's property has been removed from the purser's safe and secreted somewhere aboard the ship."

Ouzoulias puffed on his pipe and stared hard at the two Russians, at the rude, defiant Ignatieff in particular. He was anxious to have the supercargo face Ignatieff.

Goldinin was calmer, smoother than Ignatieff. Ouzoulias remembered that it was Ignatieff who had a family at home—a family whose members could become the victims of Soviet wrath if he did not recover the jewels he had been sent to guard against Troyanoskii's venality and disloyalty. Goldinin, who had said his family was the NKVD, had less to lose. Indeed, Ouzoulias had wondered if Goldinin had not decided to defect.

Goldinin spoke, and in a moment the disembodied voice beyond the door translated—"Monsieur Goldinin says the property of his government must be returned before the ship docks tomorrow."

There was something odd in Goldinin's voice. It was as if he were trying to communicate something he hoped Ouzoulias would understand and Ignatieff would not detect. Also— Also, he seemed unnaturally rigid in his chair, as if he were reluctant to shift. Could it be that these two had had a fistfight and that Ignatieff had taken bruises on the face, Goldinin bruises on the body?

"Ask the two gentlemen," Ouzoulias said to the interpreter, "if there are other agents of their government aboard this ship."

"Monsieur Ignatieff answers that it is none of your business."

Ouzoulias grunted and puffed on his pipe. "Advise the two gentlemen that I am confining them in third-class cabins under guard."

"Monsieur Ignatieff strenuously protests this illegal and provocative action."

As soon as Ignatieff was led away—still protesting, but protesting in angry Russian to Frenchmen who had no idea what he was saying—Ouzoulias closed the door to his office, keeping Goldinin there.

"Tell Monsieur Goldinin," said Ouzoulias to the interpreter in the next room, "that I want to know what is going on."

Kazys Urbays spoke in Russian to Goldinin. Goldinin replied in Russian. Urbays translated—

"Monsieur Goldinin joins in Monsieur Ignatieff's protest. His government—"

"Never mind his government," Ouzoulias interrupted. "What I want to know is, what made Ignatieff think the missing jewelry might be found in the wine cases stored in the cargo hold."

"Monsieur Goldinin says he does not know. He says he knows nothing of any cases of wine, and he says Monsieur Ignatieff knows nothing of them either."

"Ask Monsieur Goldinin if he wants political asylum, either in France or the United States."

"Monsieur Goldinin says what he wants is to survive this voyage. And he says he will say nothing more. He asks you to place double guards on the cabin where he is to be confined, and he asks that they be armed."

"I want to know why he makes this request."

"Monsieur Goldinin—"

The telephone interrupted the translation of Goldinin's response. Ouzoulias snatched up the instrument.

"Ouzoulias. I am quite busy."

"This is Dr. Grasse. I have some important information for you."

"About the murder?"

"Yes, definitely."

Ouzoulias glanced at his watch. "I have an appointment to confer with Madame Roosevelt. Is this something she can hear?"

"Why not, if she is hearing everything else?"

"Very well. I will see you in her apartment in fifteen minutes."

Jack Kennedy was there, too. Mrs. Roosevelt had returned from the party in the winter garden, where she had greeted more than two hundred Americans who had walked past her in a receiving line that also included Henry Luce and Charles Lindbergh. She was wearing a gray velvet dress, pearls, and a gray velvet hat. In her sitting room she put aside the hat.

Ouzoulias was waiting, talking with Kennedy. The doctor had not yet arrived. Ouzoulias used the time to explain what had happened in the hold and how he was holding the two Russians in confinement.

"Why would Ignatieff and Goldinin have suspected the jewels might be in the wine cases?" asked the First Lady.

"We had reasons for our suspicions, but—"

"We cannot overlook the possibility that Nina Rozanov told them," said Ouzoulias.

"Where is Nina, incidentally?" asked Jack.

"Not in her room?"

"No. I knocked."

Mrs. Roosevelt went to the door of Nina's bedroom, knocked, then opened the door. Nina was not there.

"She's not a prisoner, after all . . . Maybe she wanted to see more of the *Normandie*. How many times does anyone get to travel on a ship like this?"

"I will have a glass of your wine, if you don't mind," said Ouzoulias.

As he was pouring himself a glass of dark red wine, Dr. Jules Grasse appeared.

"Ah, Grasse. Ever the physician. Carrying your medical bag, I see."

"Carrying something significant," said the doctor. He opened the bag and pulled out a bottle of red wine, St. Julien, Léoville-Las-Cases. "A bottle from the cases in the hold."

"Strychnine?" asked Ouzoulias.

"No," said Dr. Grasse. "Something more interesting." He turned the bottle upside down. "Observe—"

He pointed to a fine line, so fine it was all but invisible, and he traced it with his finger, all the way around the circumference of the bottle, just above the bottom.

"It's been cut!" said Mrs. Roosevelt.

"Yes," said the doctor. "The bottom cut off and then, I should judge, cemented back in place. The cut is made so near the bottom of the bottle that the line fades into the natural line made by the thickness of the glass bottom. Now, if you can supply a pitcher or bowl, and a corkscrew."

As they watched, fascinated, Dr. Grasse extracted the cork from the bottle and poured the red wine into a small vase that had held flowers. Inside the bottle, clearly visible now, were two halves of a heavy gold bracelet set with gems. Other stones, maybe a dozen of them, lay about in the bottom of the bottle, in the dregs of the wine.

18

"I've got to place that man under arrest," said Ouzoulias.

"Yes, of course," said Mrs. Roosevelt. "Though— Though what we have learned, thanks to Dr. Grasse, still doesn't explain the death of Ambassador Troyanoskii."

"Monsieur Albert Haushofer can answer many questions," said the detective.

"He has many *to* answer."

Just as Ouzoulias nodded, the telephone rang. He took it and frowned at what he heard from the other end. *"Zut. Zut . . . Bien . . . Merci."* He slammed the telephone down angrily. "The paraffin test," he muttered, as much to himself as to inform the others of what he had heard, "proves that Ignatieff has *not* fired a pistol. Not. So, who shot the supercargo?"

"Every answer generates another question," sighed Jack Kennedy.

Mrs. Roosevelt smiled wryly. "Except when we are trying to solve a mystery, let us be grateful for that."

The distance to the first-class stateroom occupied by Remer-Haushofer was not great, and Mrs. Roosevelt said firmly she wanted to accompany Ouzoulias, to hear what the man would say. Ouzoulias agreed. When Jack Kennedy asked if he could come too, the detective shrugged and gestured that he should follow.

They needed only walk down, outdoors, since Remer-Haushofer's was a veranda stateroom, opening on the promenade deck. Ouzoulias, impatient, strode up to the door and knocked firmly.

No response.

Ouzoulias knocked again. He already had his master keys out of his pocket, and when he knocked a third time and got no response he jammed his key into the lock and turned it. He shoved back the door.

Remer-Haushofer lay facedown on the floor in a ransacked stateroom.

Dr. Jules Grasse stood back from his patient, affecting an arms-akimbo posture akin to that taken by an artist staring at his latest work, and regarded Remer-Haushofer with an air of satisfaction.

"Broken nose," he said. "Two teeth gone. One rib cracked. Bruises that are going to hurt for two weeks." He shrugged. "Otherwise . . . He will survive. You may interrogate him."

Remer-Haushofer lay on his own bed, still in the stateroom. Two maids were still busy cleaning up the ruin of the room—a broken lamp, a broken mirror, drawers and closets emptied on the floor, bloodstains on the carpet and bedclothes.

Ouzoulias poured a generous splash of cognac into a snifter and put it in Remer-Haushofer's hand. "Drink," he said.

Remer-Haushofer looked up groggily. He clutched the big snifter to his mouth and poured the amber cognac over his painfully swollen lips.

Ouzoulias had brought from Mrs. Roosevelt's suite the bottle containing jewels, and now he showed it to Remer-Haushofer, who sighed and nodded.

"What would you rather be called?" asked Mrs. Roosevelt. "Ernst Richter Remer or Albert Haushofer?"

"Legally . . . I'm Remer," the man muttered.

"Unless Monsieur Ouzoulias has a different idea, I think it might be well if you told us your story in narrative fashion, from the beginning," she said. She drew up a chair. "You know all the old things they say to people in your circumstances. It will be better for you if you cooperate."

Remer let his head loll on his thick, luxurious pillow. "Maybe . . ." he said weakly, "there's a deal someplace in this."

"That is entirely up to Monsieur Ouzoulias," said Mrs. Roosevelt.

"I care little for petty jewel thieves," said Ouzoulias loftily. "Or— Or for the great ones, either. I want to know who murdered Ambassador Troyanoskii, who fired a shot at Mademoiselle Rozanov, who shot the ship's supercargo. These things I want to know, and I am prepared to overlook much done by the man who gives me the information that solves these mystery."

"I can solve part of them," said Remer.

"Solve what you can," said Ouzoulias.

Remer let his head settle into his pillow. He stared at the ceiling and began to speak—

"It makes no diff what my name is, to tell the truth.

234

Yeah, I was born in the City . . . What city? *The* city. Hell, there's only one. N'Yawk. Downtown. Lower East Side. Back in Germany, my grandfather Haushofer made hats, in the town of Speyer. Not my old man, though. My dad played the main chance, always. Handsome guy. Slick. He married Fredericka Remer, my mother. The Haushofers were *nothin'* in Germany. But the Remers . . . That was somethin' else again. And when my mother married this slick con man, my father—who was a Jew, to boot—the fuss was so big that they couldn't live with it. In fact, the Remers gave my old man some money if he'd take my mother, who was pregnant with me by now, and go away somewhere, like to the States."

"A remittance man," said Jack. "Send him an allowance if he'll never come back."

"Yeah, right. Only this was a lump-sum payment, just enough for passage. Anyway, I was born in New York. And I was brought up as a Remer, not a Haushofer. I mean, my mother wouldn't let them circumcise me when I was born. My old man didn't care. And my grandfather wouldn't have either. They weren't faithful, you know. Didn't observe The Law. Y' know?"

Mrs. Roosevelt sat in her chair, still dressed in gray, listening quietly. Jack Kennedy stood with his back to the wall, his face taut. Ouzoulias puffed thoughtfully, sending up thick clouds of vile smoke, conspicuously relating every word Remer spoke to what he already knew of the case.

"So I was brought up as a Remer. But I was my father's son. Only more so. He made his living off the fat of the land, so to speak. What I mean is, he flimflammed the fat—so smooth you couldn't believe it. Y' know . . . they actually *loved* him for it. I watched him. I got so I could work it. But I couldn't make them love me for it, and the

235

time came when it was a good idea for me to live some-place else, with a new name."

"So you went to Germany and—"

"Right. And convinced the Krauts I was an heir of Richter Remer and had come back to claim my birthright."

"Property?" asked Mrs. Roosevelt.

"No, just the name. The Krauts never figured it out that the Haushofers of Speyer were Jews. I don't think many people in Speyer knew it. The Haushofers—"

"Yes, you told us they weren't observant Jews," said Jack.

"Okay. So they let me have the name Ernst Richter Re-mer and granted me citizenship under that name. Like I said, my passport is no fake."

"All of which," said Jack, "is interesting history and says not much about how Ambassador Troyanoskii—"

"I'm *comin'* to that," Remer protested. "You said from the beginning. Well, that's where the beginning was."

Ouzoulias frowned unhappily into the bowl of his pipe, where apparently the fire had just ceased to find fuel. He poked at the black ash with his finger. His interest seemed more focused on that than on Remer's recitation. But Re-mer went on—

"I'm not smooth enough to get along on flimflams like my old man. So I got into another line of business. Two or three. More dangerous but a whole lot more profitable."

"You are a dealer in stolen gems," said Mrs. Roosevelt.

Remer smiled—as best as he could with his swollen lips. "Better than that," he said. "I steal them myself."

"That is, you *used to,*" she said.

His smile faded, and he nodded. "Yeah. I'm afraid that's right."

"Tell us about Ambassador Troyanoskii," she said.

"It's simple enough," said Remer. "You've figured it out.

In my luggage you'll find the little machine I use to cut the bottoms off wine bottles, plus the cement I use to stick the bottoms back on again. It's just a glass cutter set in a little cradle. I experimented a long time before I got it just right. And I had to practice. Cutting glass is chancy. You can break the bottles very easy. I broke one yesterday."

Ouzoulias frowned over his pipe and dug at the dead ash with one finger. "Who killed Troyanoskii?" he asked bluntly.

"Well, I didn't," said Remer. "And I don't know who did. His death fouled me up, I can tell you for sure."

"Ah-ha!" cried Jack Kennedy. "*You* are the man who came to Nina's cabin the night when Troyanoskii was killed—when she was in chains. *You* gave her the tool so she could pick the lock and take off her leg irons. Your voice—"

Mrs. Roosevelt interrupted. "Uh, where were *you*, Jack, when Herr Remer was—"

"In her bathroom . . ."

Ouzoulias grinned. "Of course," he said insouciantly. ("Uv gairss.")

Jack ignored Mrs. Roosevelt's question and Ouzoulias's comment. "You said that night that the death of Troyanoskii was a great disadvantage to you. And you wanted Nina to—"

"I needed somebody to translate their damn, incomprehensible gobbledygook into a civilized language," said Remer. "I mean Ignorance and Goldbean—"

"Ignatieff and Goldinin."

"Well, sure. I figured they'd grabbed the loot as soon as they saw Troyanoskii was dead. And why not? I would have, if I'd been them."

"Back up a bit," said Mrs. Roosevelt.

"Oh, you've got this figured out," mumbled Remer

through his broken lips. "Some more of that brandy, old buddy," he said to Ouzoulias. "Ol' Boris Vasilievich had played both ends against the middle for twenty years. And got away with it. But Comrade Josef Visarionivich ain't gonna put up with that forever."

"Stalin," said Mrs. Roosevelt.

"Stalin," Remer confirmed. "People Comrade Stalin takes a dislike to have a way of winding up dead. Comrade Troyanoskii saw the hints and decided to take a powder while the taking was good. You know this. You've figured it out. So he gathers up as many goodies as he can—including, incidentally, the little ballerina—and plans a crossing to the States on the *Normandie*. But he's got a problem . . ."

Remer paused to accept another snifter of brandy from Ouzoulias.

"To put the problem in the crude terms *I* use . . . the Ambassador Extraordinary and Plenipotentiary from the government of the Union of Soviet Socialist Republics needed a *fence*. A *fence*."

"The proceeds from the sale of the confiscated royalist jewelry," said Mrs. Roosevelt, "were to have gone to fund NKVD operations in the United States."

"Yes," said Remer. "Except for what ol' Boris Vasilievich got for the jewels left under his pillow by the tooth fairy. Those were *his*."

"So he made a deal with you," said Jack.

"Informal," said Remer. "I looked over what he was going to carry in his luggage and gave him a rough appraisal. I said I was carrying a few items of my own to the States—which was true, in the wine bottles—and would be glad to put our lots together and see what we could do with them in New York. You see, the Ambassador was a smart fellow in all kinds of flimflams except how to fence the—"

"You expected a percentage, I should imagine," suggested Mrs. Roosevelt.

Remer tried to sneer. It was not easy, through his broken teeth and bloody lips. "No, not me," he said. "I'm a charity."

"Who killed Troyanoskii?" Ouzoulias demanded angrily. His problem with his pipe had erased his patience.

Remer rolled his head over on his pillow and regarded Ouzoulias calmly through eyes swollen nearly shut. "If I tell you, will you drop all charges against me and let me go in New York?" he asked.

Edouard Ouzoulias pondered for a moment, then shrugged. "Perhaps," he said.

"Even if 'perhaps' was good enough," said Remer. "I couldn't tell you. As God is my witness, I don't know."

"Does God as a witness make any difference to you, Herr Remer?" asked Mrs. Roosevelt.

Remer smiled at her. "Not the least," he said. "But getting out of this mess does." He sighed and shook his head. "I don't know who killed Troyanoskii."

"Or how?"

"Or how."

"Tell me," said Mrs. Roosevelt, "what role Moira Lasky had in all this."

Remer laughed weakly. "Having a girl like her on the arm makes a man look square, like a businessman with money," he said.

"But she was not a part of—"

He shook his head. "Leave her alone. She didn't know anything."

"All right," said Mrs. Roosevelt. "You say you didn't kill Ambassador Troyanoskii. Let us assume that is so. How, then, did you come into possession of the jewels he was carrying, that now seem to be submerged in your wine?"

Remer glanced into each of the faces that looked at his

with intense interest—Mrs. Roosevelt's, Ouzoulias's, Jack's. "Okay," he said. "I didn't kill the Ambassador—if that's what you want to call him. I figured Ignorance or Gold-demon did. I needed to talk to them. If Troyanoskii needed a fence to get his profit out of the loot in New York, then so did they. But the idiots seemed to speak Russian only, and nothing else. I did something stupid. I went to see Nina Rozanov that night and offered her a share of the loot if she'd translate for me. I was honest about that. I'd have treated her right."

"But you found out then that the jewelry had been moved into the purser's safe," said Mrs. Roosevelt.

"Right. The two Russians told me that much—mostly by gestures."

"And you cracked the safe."

Remer turned up the palms of his hands. "And didn't touch nothin' else," he said. "Only what was sort of mine anyway."

"You had rented a safety-deposit box to give you a look at the interior of the purser's safe," said Mrs. Roosevelt.

"Smart!" said Remer. "Hey, I had no notion the Troyanoskii jewels would get inside that safe. I just . . . Well, I check out safes wherever I go. I rented the box, which got me inside the vault, and I checked out the lock. Hey . . . Why wouldn't a big, luxurious ship like *Normandie,* which carries rich people and puts their goodies in that vault, have invested in a better vault? A *kid* could crack that safe!"

"Finish the story, Herr Remer," said Mrs. Roosevelt.

"I carried the Troyanoskii loot back here to my stateroom. I ordered three cases of wine brought up from the hold. With my little glass cutter I cut open twenty-four— excuse me, it was twenty-three; I broke one—bottles and stashed the loot inside. I . . . I gotta admit, some of the pieces was too big to go in wine bottles. Them— Well, they went over the side, into the Atlantic."

"Lost forever," said Ouzoulias.

"A man hates it," said Remer. "But he loves his freedom more."

"All of which," said Mrs. Roosevelt, "leaves us without an answer to the question of who fired a shot at Nina."

"Y' gotta forgive," said Remer. "It was me. I was scared that night. I wasn't thinkin' right. I knew she'd recognize me the first time she saw me again. So I—"

"Tried to kill her," said Jack.

Remer glanced around the faces. "I ain't a very nice guy," he said simply.

"Ah, so," said Ouzoulias. He was repacking his pipe. "When you were supposed to be hit on the head and wouldn't let Dr. Grasse—"

"I couldn't let him examine my skull," said Remer. "He'd have found out I wasn't hurt."

"And of course you were never seasick," said Mrs. Roosevelt.

"Hey," said Remer. "I ain't never been seasick in my life. In fact, I been thinkin' of flyin' the Atlantic on one of them new whatchacallit flying boats. I don't think even that would make me sick."

"I have two questions," said Ouzoulias solemnly. "Who shot the supercargo? And who came here and attacked you, broke your nose, and all that?"

Remer stared at Ouzoulias for a long moment, through eyes swollen nearly shut by now. For an instant he switched his eyes to Mrs. Roosevelt, then to Jack Kennedy. "When you find out, tell me," he said. "When you find out, you have your murderer."

"What your attacker wanted was, of course, the jewelry," said Mrs. Roosevelt.

"Yeah," Remer grunted.

"Will you recognize him when you see him again?" she asked.

"No. He had his face covered with a bandanna—you know, like an old stagecoach robber in the movies. And he was wearin' a hat. No, actually it was a cap—a knit cap. He had on dark blue pants and sort of a . . . a sweater. It was dark blue, too."

"How did he speak?" asked Ouzoulias.

"English," said Remer. "With an accent. Like maybe French was what he knew how to speak and English was somethin' he had to work at."

"How did he know you had taken the jewelry from the purser's safe?"

"I don't know. But he knew all right. He didn't ask any questions. He just said he wanted the stuff and wanted it right now, and when I didn't come up with answers he liked he started pounding on me."

"Did you tell him where the jewelry was?"

"You better believe I did."

"Hmm," said Ouzoulias, and a little smile crossed his face. "If he tries to get it from the wine cases, he will be surprised. All is under guard now."

Remer shifted his body and grunted with pain. "Well . . ." he said weakly. "What happens now?"

"You are, of course, under arrest," said the detective. "You, too, will be under guard."

"All very well," said Agent Ouzoulias, as they walked back to Mrs. Roosevelt's suite. "We know who has cracked the safe, who has fired the shot at Mademoiselle Rozanov. We don't know—"

As he paused to sigh loudly, Mrs. Roosevelt offered the rest of the statement—"What we don't know is who killed

Ambassador Troyanoskii, who killed François Flavigny, and who shot the supercargo."

"Yes," said Ouzoulias. "And when we don't know that, what good is it to know who opened the vault and stole the jewels? A small question compared . . ."

"The whole problem," said Mrs. Roosevelt, "returns to one overriding question—*how* did the strychnine get into the Ambassador's glass?"

19

Sunday evening's dinner was the last for this voyage. *Normandie* would enter New York Harbor in the morning and by noon would be berthed at her Hudson River pier. Captain Colbert again invited Mrs. Roosevelt to the captain's table.

As she had done twice before, Mrs. Roosevelt sat at the captain's right. At his left was the American automobile manufacturer, Logan. Colonel Charles Lindbergh once again sat by Mrs. Roosevelt, and Henry Luce across from her. Mrs. Logan sat beside Lindbergh. A professor from the Sorbonne and the mayor of Strasbourg and his wife completed the seating.

"Well," said Luce to Mrs. Roosevelt, "have you solved the murders on the *Normandie?*"

"I'm afraid not," she replied. "The mystery is somewhat complex."

Captain Colbert frowned. He had

hoped the subject would not be raised. He entertained the unrealistic idea that relatively few of his passengers knew there had been murders aboard ship, and he would have liked to keep it that way.

"The weather has been good for this crossing," he said. "Except of course for the one day of storm."

"How could you have flown the Atlantic, Colonel Lindbergh," asked Mrs. Logan, "if you had encountered a storm like that?"

"I couldn't have done it," said Lindbergh. "But of course I had radio reports of the weather before I left."

"I understand it is possible today to fly even in such weather," said Logan.

"Not in storms," said Lindbergh. "You try to fly around them."

"It's an odd damn business," said Luce. "Someplace in the story there's a connection between the late Troyanoskii and the ballerina. I mean, a connection other than what's obvious."

"I wish I understood that element of the mystery," said Mrs. Roosevelt to Luce. "But I don't." Her three last words were meant to dismiss the subject.

"Well, we'll never know the answer till we figure that part out," said Luce.

"True."

"What do you think of the congressional elections coming up?" asked Logan. "Democrats going to lose control of Congress?"

"Oh, I can't imagine that," said the First Lady.

"Your husband is a master politician," said Logan. "A master."

"I have supposed," she said, "that he simply speaks to the interests and concerns of the American people."

Logan chuckled. "Oh, sure—and no offense meant, I

know you understand. What I mean is, I guess he has a sense of what the voters are concerned *about*."

"I would suppose," said Mrs. Roosevelt, "that the chief concern of most voters is having three meals on the table every day, decent clothing, a decent home, and . . . And, well, some hope for a better future."

"Hear, hear," said Lindbergh; then he blushed brightly, embarrassed to have expressed himself.

"Coming up to 1940," said Logan. "What will you and the President do after you retire?"

"Go home," said Mrs. Roosevelt simply. "The President will relax and swim a lot—and write his memoirs. Frankly, Mr. Logan, both of us are looking forward to it. The President is fifty-six years old, you know, and I am fifty-four. I hope we have twenty years left to us, and I hope they can be twenty years of relaxing, enjoying our children and grandchildren, reading and writing, perhaps traveling a bit—and letting someone else shoulder the burdens of national leadership."

"He wouldn't think about a third term, would he?" asked Luce.

She shook her head. "No, of course not. Unless . . . Well, if the country sank into depression again, or if a major war broke out, and if my husband felt a duty—" She smiled. "No. If, in fact, the concessions made at Munich this week mean years of peace ahead, for the whole world, well, we shall enjoy a peaceful retirement."

"May I quote you on that?" asked Luce.

"Why of course, Mr. Luce," she said. "I never say anything you can't quote." She inclined her head to one side and smiled at him. "If I didn't want to be quoted, I wouldn't speak in the presence of an eminent journalist."

Jack Kennedy and Moira were not at dinner in the grand dining room. They sat at a table in the less-formal grill room, alone, eating by candlelight and glancing occasionally out at the black Atlantic, where nothing was to be seen but an occasional flash of luminescence or, rarely, the lights of a distant ship.

Moira was tearful. "Damn him!" she said. "I try *so* hard not to become involved with scum."

"No one is accusing you of anything," he said.

"The *association,* Jack!" she said in a hoarse whisper.

"You may come out well," he said. "The French Line may like you. You have helped, after all."

"Nobody's safe, you know that?" she said. "Whoever it is, he beat Remer badly. He—"

"He killed Troyanoskii, killed Flavigny, and shot Boulanger," said Jack.

"And is at large on the *Normandie,*" she said. "Who's next?"

Josephine Baker was at the purser's table, with Jack Benny and Mary Livingstone, and with businessmen and their wives, from France and Britain as well as America.

"Will you stay in the States long, Miss Baker?" one of the women asked.

"Only so long as it takes me to collect some money that's owed me," she said. "Then back to France."

"Nous regardons La Baker comme une reine," said a Frenchman. We regard Baker as a queen.

"I'm a fad in Paris," she said.

"Oh, I think not," said an Englishman. "Fads are temporary. Like Wallis Simpson. Soon forgotten, let us hope. But you, Miss Baker, are an institution."

Josephine Baker smiled. "Yes, maybe. An institution. In America . . . maybe a sanatorium. Maybe a reformatory. Anyway, an institution."

"En France—"

"The French have been very kind," she said.

"We note that you are a friend of Eleanor Roosevelt," said an American. "Grotesque creature, isn't she?"

"No, sir," said Josephine Baker. "*You are.* She most certainly is not."

The orchestra struck up national anthems—first "La Marseillaise," then "God Save the King," then "The Star-Spangled Banner"—and waiters began to carry in an array of ice sculptures. The largest of these was carried to the captain's table and set on a big silver tray. It was a five-foot-tall model of the Statue of Liberty, standing on its pedestal just as it did in New York Harbor.

The orchestra played "The Star-Spangled Banner." Everyone raised wine glasses. Captain Colbert stood. Mrs. Roosevelt stood. Together, while everyone in the room applauded and toasted them, the Captain and the First Lady drank an unspoken toast to Franco-American amity.

They sat down. Captain Colbert beamed. Mrs. Roosevelt smiled and acknowledged the personal toasts raised to her by her companions at the captain's table.

The ice sculpture of the Statue of Liberty was a bizarre object. It had been cut in two—the fine cut was barely visible—and a hollow cut out in the ice of the pedestal. In that hollow, a dozen or so red and white roses, made of sugar by the ship's pastry chefs, had been arranged on some sugar rose leaves. It was a curious effect: innocently attractive even if it was a little grotesque.

The First Lady's attention returned to it as it began to melt. By the time the dessert was served, the statue's lines were softening rapidly. Inside, the sugar roses slowly dissolved as their ice cavity melted, and their color began to spread: a tint of pink that seeped through the cut in the statue and began to run down into the tray, where it colored the accumulating water.

Captain Colbert noticed Mrs. Roosevelt staring at it. "I hope it pleases you," he said. "My staff wanted to do it."

"It pleases me, Captain, more than I can tell you," she said. "It is the answer to a question that has troubled me for three days."

"I have the answer, I think," Mrs. Roosevelt said to Edouard Ouzoulias. "I could be wrong. The Lord knows I've been wrong many times in my life, but . . ."

"I have some additional evidence," said Ouzoulias.

They were together in her *appartement de grand luxe* after dinner. Jack Kennedy was there, at her invitation, as was Josephine Baker. Nina, who had eaten at a table with Tommy Thompson, was there, too.

"I think," said Mrs. Roosevelt, "it would be well to bring Herr Remer here, if he is not in too much pain."

"*Oui,*" said the detective. "And Boulanger, *n'est-ce pas*? The witnesses."

"The two Russians," she said. "Goldinin and Ignatieff."

"Yes, them. Mademoiselle Rozanov can translate."

"We could be on the verge of making fools of ourselves, Monsieur Ouzoulias," said Mrs. Roosevelt.

"Madame," he said. "I ask you a favor, if you do not mind. Would you be so gracious as to call me Edouard and not Monsieur Ouzoulias? Surely it is not indecorous."

"Of course," she said. "You should call me Eleanor."

"*Merci,* dear lady. And so . . . Let us proceed to make fools of ourselves."

They assembled in the sitting room—Mrs. Roosevelt, Ouzoulias, Tommy Thompson, Jack Kennedy, Moira Lasky, Nina, Goldinin, Ignatieff, the supercargo Boulanger, and the painfully limping Remer-Haushofer. They took chairs. Tommy Thompson sat at a small table with pencils and a

shorthand pad. She would make a transcript of everything
that was said. Nina and Moira sat on the floor. Jack Kennedy
remained standing.

"And one more," said Mrs. Roosevelt. "Edouard, will you
ask your people to bring in the steward?"

Ouzoulias went to the door, gestured, and two uniformed
sailors led in the steward Philippe LeClerc.

LeClerc was handcuffed. Mrs. Roosevelt had been accustomed to see him as a steward, deferential and un-
threatening; now she saw him hostile and defiant: a
troubling contrast. The sailors pushed him down onto a
chair, and he sat tensed, with his shoulders lifted as if to
be ready to lunge.

"A question," said Ouzoulias immediately. "Boulanger,
is this the man who shot you in the leg?"

"Possible," said the supercargo. *"Je ne suis pas sûr."*

"Remer?"

Remer-Haushofer shrugged. "I told you. He was
masked."

Ouzoulias turned toward the two Russians. "Monsieur
Goldinin? Monsieur Ignatieff? Who is this man?"

"I not know," said Goldinin, now disclosing for the first
time that during his years with Troyanoskii he had
learned a few words of a language other than Russian.

Nina translated the question into Russian for Ignatieff,
then translated his answer—"He says he does not know."

"Well, I know some-zing," said Ouzoulias grimly. "The
trace are almost gone, but the paraffin test prove that this
man—" He pointed at LeClerc. "—have fired a pistol not
long ago. Today. And how can it be that a steward can fire
a pistol? What pistol is this? And why? And—"

"I can tells you," said Goldinin. He spoke English—more
than a few words, in his own way. "He the NKVD. He
name no LeClerc. He Feodor Josepovich Svischev."

"*Smert shpionam,*" spat LeClerc.

"What did he say?" asked Ouzoulias.

"'Death to spies,'" Nina translated quietly.

"Well . . ." said Ouzoulias. "Very well. But— Thanks to the very gracious Mrs. Roosevelt, we know how the strychnine got into Ambassador Troyanoskii's vodka. And perhaps the gentle lady will be good enough to explain."

Mrs. Roosevelt nodded solemnly. "I noticed at dinner this evening how a decoration of candy roses had been placed in a cavity in an ice sculpture. When the ice began to melt, the sugar in the roses began to dissolve. Then it occurred to me— Why could not the strychnine have been in the ice cubes in Ambassador Troyanoskii's vodka?"

"Uh . . . Please, are you sure?" asked Moira.

"No, I'm not sure," said Mrs. Roosevelt. "But let's pursue the matter. *Ice cubes.* Ordinarily, the *Normandie* does not offer ice cubes. Look at the bar the ship has been good enough to provide this evening. No ice *cubes.* No chunks of ice. Chipped ice."

"But . . ." said Jack Kennedy breathlessly. "Jack Benny and I—"

"Yes," said Mrs. Roosevelt. "You and Jack Benny drank vodka from the same bottle, also chilled with ice cubes. I believe all the ice at the bar that night was in the form of cubes. And one ice cube—maybe more—contained strychnine, introduced into the water before it was frozen. It was a simple thing for the murderer to segregate the poisoned ice and put it in one glass only."

"*My God!*" said Jack Kennedy.

"The strychnine was in the ice cubes," said Mrs. Roosevelt. "As Ambassador Troyanoskii stood there and drank two or three glasses, the cubes melted, and the poison was dissipated into his vodka. While you, Jack, and Mr. Benny, sampled vodka from the same bottle and suffered no ill effect."

"*Aussi*," said Ouzoulias, "the glass was drop on the floor, the ice melt into the carpet, and the doctor analysis find the strychnine strong in the fiber of the carpet."

"Prove," said Ignatieff—suddenly using one English word, then lapsing into Russian—"*nichto*."

"*Nichto* except for some other facts," said Mrs. Roosevelt. "Philippe LeClerc was not scheduled to serve at the bar in Ambassador Troyanoskii's suite Thursday evening. François Flavigny was. And Monsieur Flavigny is dead—dead, with a great deal of money in his possession. How does that come to happen?"

"Also," said Ouzoulias, "I will ask Monsieur LeClerc to explain why he has been absent from his duty post most of the time since midnight last."

"I have been ill," said LeClerc-Svischev. "I so reported—"

"Thank you," said Ouzoulias. "And how do you explain the paraffin test that proves you fired a pistol within the last twenty-four hours?"

LeClerc-Svischev raised his handcuffed hands and ran them across his forehead and down over his cheeks. "All you are saying is . . . speculative. What can you prove?"

"What do I have to prove?" asked Ouzoulias. "Monsieur Boulanger. Is this the man who shot you?"

Boulanger shrugged. "I have said I could not see the man. But . . . this man it could be."

"Also," said Ouzoulias, "I notice the bloody bruise on the knuckle, Monsieur LeClerc. Did you get the bruise by striking Herr Remer with your fist?"

"A man can bruise a—"

"But a man cannot introduce grains of spent gunpowder into his hand except by firing a pistol," said Ouzoulias.

"I know nothing of all this," said LeClerc-Svischev sullenly.

"Then, of course," said Ouzoulias, "we have the fingerprint on the pistol, plus the ballistics test that will prove the bullet that injured Monsieur Boulanger was fired from the pistol that bears your fingerprint."

"An open-and-shut case," muttered Remer. "I'd try to cop a plea if I was you, buddy. The French execute by lopping off heads."

Svischev raised his chin very high. The tendons in his neck stood out like chords. He turned down the corners of his mouth, and he sucked a deep breath—noisily, as if he had difficulty getting air. He glared at Goldinin. *"Sobaka!"* he growled.

"Dog . . ." Nina translated blandly.

"All right," said Svischev. "I do not murder the traitor Boris Vasilievich Troyanoskii. I do him execute, on behalf of the Soviet state!"

"By freezing ice cubes with strychnine in them," said Mrs. Roosevelt.

"Da. Smart lady."

"And you killed Flavigny," said Ouzoulias. "I suppose that's because you needed to keep him from talking about how you paid him money to give you his job Thursday night."

"Da."

"And you shot Monsieur Boulanger, the supercargo, when he discovered you opening the wine cases."

"Da. And how you find the gun? I hide him. How you find so fast?"

Ouzoulias smiled. "We didn't. We haven't found it. But now that you've confessed, we don't need to find it."

"Now you talk," said Ouzoulias to Svischev. "You tell all."

Svischev had asked for a drink of vodka. He had stared at the glass for a moment before he drank, as though he wondered if they might not feed him strychnine; but he had tossed it back and swallowed five or six ounces of vodka in three or four gulps.

Ouzoulias's admission that they had not found the pistol had shaken Svischev, and for a moment he had slumped in his chair, shaking his head. Shortly he recovered his defiant composure, and now he looked at Ouzoulias and shrugged.

"No difference the pistol," he said. "You know other." He meant that they had additional evidence. "You not smart like lady. Trick. Good trick. No difference."

"You were sent by your government to . . . 'execute' Ambassador Troyanoskii," said Mrs. Roosevelt. "Weren't you?"

Svischev nodded. "Traitor. Thiefing jewels. We know. *That* one," he said, glancing scornfully at Ignatieff, "must watch him, see what he do. And *sobaka*—"sneering at Goldinin—"must, too."

"Whose jewels were these, and where did they come from?" asked Mrs. Roosevelt.

"Pigs— Czarists. Aristocrats. Capitalists."

"Your government sells confiscated property to obtain western currencies to finance NKVD operations."

Svischev looked at her blankly and shrugged. Nina translated for him, and he shrugged again and nodded.

"This had been going on for a long time," Mrs. Roosevelt continued, "and Ambassador Troyanoskii had carried out many of these operations. What made you think he would handle this one differently?"

Nina translated, and Svischev pointed at Remer and said—"That one. He see that one. Who that one? Why—" He stopped and spoke rapid Russian to Nina.

254

"He says that Boris Vasilievich had always used a small group of brokers in stolen jewels to receive the confiscated property and convert it to cash. When he began to see Herr Remer, who was known to the NKVD as a professional thief, that raised suspicions."

"*And,*" said Svischev, "why New York? Why he go New York? Why he pretend go President Roosevelt with words from Comrade Stalin? Comrade Stalin no. No give message for President Roosevelt."

Svischev lifted his manacled hands from his lap and pointed at the bottle of vodka. Ouzoulias nodded, and Jack Kennedy poured a second glass for Svischev. The man drank thirstily.

"He no come back," said Svischev. "He take all from Paris. All thing he want. Was no come back. Thief jewels. Not give money to Soviet government. Thief money."

"You suspected," said Ouzoulias. "You didn't really know."

"We know," said Svischev firmly. "*That one—*" pointing at Remer—"come on same ship. Thief."

"How did you get a job as a steward on the *Normandie*?" asked Mrs. Roosevelt.

Svischev smirked. "Easy. Good Communists in *CGT.*"

"He means the General Confederation of Labor," Nina explained. "The great French union."

"I'm afraid I have to ask a question I'd perhaps just as soon not ask," said Mrs. Roosevelt. "You said Ambassador Troyanoskii was taking from Paris everything he wanted. He wasn't returning to Paris, so he was taking with him what he most valued. What did that include?"

Svischev paused and let Nina translate. He frowned as he listened to the question, and he glanced back and forth between Nina and Mrs. Roosevelt. "He take . . . *her.*" He nodded toward Nina. "When he buy cabin on *Normandie* for Nina, we know. Very sure then he no come back."

"What do you mean?" Nina whispered.

"The traitor was you father, Nina Nikolaievna," said Svischev solemnly.

When Mrs. Roosevelt returned from Nina's bedroom, she left Moira with her. Nina was still lying face-down on her bed, crying silently when Mrs. Roosevelt gently closed the door and resumed her place in the sitting room.

"He has said a few interesting things while you were with Nina," said Jack. "He paid Flavigny a few francs to exchange assignments with him Thursday night. When Flavigny realized why he had wanted that assignment, realized that Svischev had killed Troyanoskii, he threatened to expose him. Svischev gave him all the money he had to keep him quiet until he could find an opportunity to kill him. And . . . and, of course, the opportunity came."

"We not know him," said Goldinin. "When Ambassador dead, he come to us and want to see the jewel. He identify himself as NKVD."

"You are NKVD agents yourselves," said Mrs. Roosevelt.

"Yes. But we not ordered to kill Ambassador. Only watch him, report. But Svischev come, he say he must see jewel. We say in purser safe. Only . . . Only not in purser safe. Gone. He evil temper."

"He used his fists on you," said Mrs. Roosevelt.

Goldinin nodded.

"What made you think the jewels were in the wine cases?" she asked Svischev.

Svischev shrugged. "Where else? Thief has wine in hold. Then not find. So—"

"So he came to my stateroom and beat the secret out of me," said Remer.

"But by then the cases of wine were under guard," said Ouzoulias.

Svischev tipped back his glass and drank the last of the vodka Jack had poured for him. He waved the glass in front of him, Ouzoulias nodded, and Jack poured him still a third glass.

"Who the jewel?" asked Svischev.

"You mean, who has them?" asked Ouzoulias.

Svischev nodded. "Who has?"

"Officially," said Ouzoulias, "they are now in the custody of *Compagnie Générale de Transatlantique*. They will be handed over to the government of France."

"Property Soviet Union," said Svischev.

"So . . . Pursue the matter in a court of law," said Ouzoulias.

Jack laughed. "Sue us," he said.

"Traitor dead," said Svischev as he gulped vodka. "Important. Traitor dead. Pig aristocrats had much more jewel. Many much to be sell. Ha! Traitor dead. Important."

"Not very important," said Ouzoulias. "Your execution won't be very important."

Svischev shrugged and drank.

"Among the jewels recovered from the wine bottles," said Mrs. Roosevelt, "is a diamond pendant belonging to Nina . . . uh, Nina Troyanoskii. Couldn't you—"

"It will be returned to her," said Ouzoulias. "Dear Eleanor—I have the same sensitivity as you on that point."

Epilogue

*N*ormandie docked as scheduled at the French Line pier on the Hudson River, on Monday, October 3, 1938. Mayor Fiorello La Guardia came aboard from the pilot boat, met with Mrs. Roosevelt in her suite, and escorted her down to the pier in the face of a hundred flashing press cameras.

She did not return to the White House that day but stayed in the Waldorf until Wednesday before catching a train for Washington. On Monday evening the mayor played host to a party for the First Lady. He was amused but pleased to honor some guests she requested—Agent Edouard Ouzoulias, Jack Kennedy, Josephine Baker, and Nina . . . Nina. She had already begun to refer to herself as Nina Troyanoskii.

The invitation went to Jack Benny and Mary Livingstone as well, but they had already left New York on a train for California.

*   *   *

Feodor Josepovich Svischev did not leave the ship in New York. He was confined in a third-class cabin, in handcuffs and leg irons, and returned to France aboard *Normandie*. He was tried in a Paris court for two murders and the shooting of the supercargo.

The French, in 1939, still occasionally executed in public. Early in the morning of Thursday, March 23, 1939, Svischev was taken from his cell, brought out onto a rainy street before his Paris prison, and beheaded on a guillotine set up on the cobblestoned street. French Communists declared him a hero of the proletariat. They were not told that his bowels and bladder had failed in his last minutes and that he had gone to his death fouled and stinking.

Ernst Richter Remer, aka Al Haushofer, was also returned to France in chains. He was sentenced to prison for five years and was confined in an old fort in Strasbourg, lately used as a prison. When the Germans arrived in 1940 he was released, together with all the other prisoners there. He was a German citizen. He traveled to Berlin and established himself as a wine broker, what he had never been able to establish himself as before. In the glory years of the Third Reich, he prospered, dealing chiefly in wines and champagnes confiscated from the great vineyards of France. When the war went against Germany, he was drafted into the *Volkssturm,* the military units of men too young or too old for regular military service. On December 5, 1944, he deserted and was taken captive by Canadian soldiers. Pleading that he was a personal friend of Mrs. Roosevelt and had been compelled against his will to serve in the *Volkssturm*—and of course had never been a Nazi—he secured his release. He went to Speyer, found he was entitled to a small inheritance, married, fathered two children while he was in his fifties, and lived modestly until his death in 1978.

Vladimir Goldinin asked for political asylum, was granted it, and became, eventually, a farmer in Iowa. He was in a crowd that gawked at Nikita Khrushchev many years later, but he did not elect to identify himself.

Grigorii Ignatieff elected to return to the Soviet Union. He was never heard of again; no one knows what happened to him.

Edouard Ouzoulias was aboard *Normandie* when it sailed from Le Havre on its final voyage, in late August 1939. While the ship was docked in New York, the Germans invaded Poland, France declared war, and *Normandie* remained at its pier in the Hudson River for fear of being sunk by German submarines on the return. Ouzoulias returned to France by air, was in Paris when the Germans arrived to occupy the city, became a leading spirit of the Résistance, and was shot by the Gestapo on July 3, 1944.

Ouzoulias did not know when he died that *Normandie* had died two years earlier. The great ship remained at her pier until February 9, 1942. She had sat there in the Hudson since September 1939. Now she was being converted to a troop ship—her luxuries being taken ashore to await refitting on a happier day. That morning—February 9— sparks from a welder's torch accidentally set fire to a huge pile of kapok life jackets. By the time fireboats began pouring water into the stricken *Normandie,* the fire had spread throughout the ship. New York firefighters faced a painful choice—to let the *Normandie* burn or pour so much water into her that she would sink. They poured in the water, and in the afternoon *Normandie* turned over to port and settled in the mud of the river.

She was raised later, but only as a hulk and was cut up for scrap.

Josephine Baker survived the war and became the adoptive mother of many children, orphans of diverse races and nationalities, that she called her "rainbow tribe." She continued to work long after she might have retired, to earn the money she needed to support all these children. When she died in 1975, she was honored in France, barely remembered in America.

Nina Rozanov-Troyanoskii accepted the invitation given her by Mary Livingstone and Jack Benny to come to California, where they would assist her in establishing a career. She was—as her father had understood—not a first-class ballerina. As Nina Troy she became a popular dancer, was nominated twice for an Academy Award, married three times, bore seven children, and still lives comfortably at Lake Tahoe.

Jack Kennedy astounded Mrs. Roosevelt. She lived to see him elected President of the United States. She did not live to know of his assassination.